WANTED

OTHER BOOKS AND AUDIO BOOKS
BY KATHI ORAM PETERSON

The Forgotten Warrior

An Angel on Main Street

The Stone Traveler

River Whispers

Cold Justice

WANTED

a novel

Kathi Oram Peterson

Covenant Communications, Inc.

Cover image: *Silhouette of Person Walking through the Woods* © Casarsa.
courtesy of istockphoto.com. *Jail Indoor* © tierio. courtesy of istockphoto.com

Cover design copyright © 2013 by Covenant Communications, Inc.

Published by Covenant Communications, Inc.
American Fork, Utah

Printed in the United States of America
First Printing: May 2013

19 18 17 16 15 14 13   10 9 8 7 6 5 4 3 2 1

ISBN 978-1-62108-415-0

For my brothers,
Lyle John, William Richard, and Steven Craig Oram,
who are my heroes

ACKNOWLEDGMENTS

I COULD NEVER HAVE WRITTEN this story without the help of many wonderful people.

A huge thank you goes to my sister, Jo. For many years, I have tagged along with her, attending small rodeos most often held in the middle of nowhere. They are not performed in air-conditioned arenas, nor are they like rodeos you see in the movies or on TV. They use weather-beaten, decades-old stands and stalls and showcase cowboys who work hard and get dirty for their sport. And during rodeo time, people travel from miles around to attend, sometimes forming small RV and camp-trailer cities. It takes a lot to put these events together, and some rodeo owners labor their whole lives to make them happen—a true labor of love.

I owe a big thank you to Crystal Brothers Rodeos and especially Joyce Crystal for showing me what a real, down-to-earth, get-your-hands-dirty rodeo is like. Some people have developed misconceptions of how rodeo stock are treated. The people I've met worry and fret over their animals, making sure they are well fed and cared for both day and night. They tend to their animals in good weather or bad, and I developed a great respect for them.

One of the main characters in this novel is convicted of a crime and becomes converted to Christianity while in prison. I need to thank Jerrianne Kolby, who served for several years as a home teacher with her husband at the Utah State Prison. She answered my many questions about prisoners and how some inmates have turned to religion as they've served their time.

I must also thank my writing group, the Wasatch Mountain Fiction Writers, for keeping me on track. A special thank you goes to Brenda Bensch, Dorothy Canada, Ann Chamberlin, Tina Foster, Maureen Mills, Charleen Raddon, Nikki Trionfo, and Roseann Woodward. They are awesome writers whose opinions and comments I highly value. I must especially thank Kathleen Dougherty and Kerri Leroy, my go-to critiquers and mentors who read this entire novel. Their keen insight on logic and attention to detail were an enormous help.

My publisher, Covenant Communications, has been fantastic to work with. Samantha Millburn is an exceptional editor, and her skills and knowledge have helped my writing grow by leaps and bounds. Kelly Schumacher takes great care to see that my novels are promoted. And I'm also very grateful to Jennie Williams and Chelsea Breur, who make such gorgeous cover art for my books.

And of course, I have to thank my family. Sometimes I've taken them with me as I've traveled to remote regions to attend different rodeos, but many times, I've left them home. And they've never complained. Thank you!

CHAPTER ONE

RAIN THREATENED TO FALL AT any moment. With trembling hands, Faulkner wrapped the stolen trench coat more snugly around him. Besides trying to stay warm, he was desperate to hide his prison uniform. The bullet in his left side shot waves of pain through his abdomen and down his leg. When he was first shot, he'd been able to manage the pain, even stop the bleeding with stolen rags, but that was over six hours ago. With each passing second, the pain grew worse . . . and he was bleeding again.

Of the few drivers he'd hitched rides with, only one had grown suspicious. The last one. He was a semi driver who kept fishing for information about who Faulkner was, where he was from, and if he was feeling well. Faulkner had been able to steer the others away from probing questions, but this guy was different. As soon as he could, Faulkner got out of his truck.

However, as he'd jumped from the cab to the ground, the wound tore deeper and started to bleed again. The bullet must have traveled, he thought. He had to find Doc Powers; he was the only man who could help him. A statewide alert had probably already gone out. Faulkner didn't have much time.

A chill breathed over him. His ankles felt heavy, as if he still wore prison shackles. He pressed on, barely able to place one foot in front of the other.

In the distance, Faulkner heard a nasal voice blare through a loudspeaker, followed by the recorded twang of country guitars and fiddles. Walking around the curve of the road, he saw the old familiar sight of Swan Valley's rodeo grounds.

He'd find the doctor there.

* * *

Angry lightning cut through the dark, and heavy clouds banked on the Targhee Mountains. Straddling the wood-splintered rodeo gate to chute number five,

Josephine Powers glanced up at the turbulent sky. A deep rumble of thunder echoed through Swan Valley and reverberated over the ground. Then a strange stillness held the air as if the world waited for the storm to catch its breath. The wet scent of impending rain grew stronger with each second. When Jo was a little girl, her father told her thunder was the devil dancing and lightning was God's warning of bad times to come.

Whatever made her think of her father at a time like this? He'd passed away two years ago. She rarely gave her father's little sayings much thought, brushing them aside as an old doctor's rambling tales. But right now, she missed her father. Missed him a lot. He always knew what to do and say during stressful times.

As the veterinarian for Wymer Rodeos, Jo was more than a little worried about the short-horned Brahma that had been loaded into the chute. Loco was the rankest bull to make Idaho's rodeo circuit in years. He had a large, fatty hump on his shoulders, drooping ears, and huge folds of excess skin under his neck and underline. The bull had become agitated when his hind legs slipped through the sorting pen grate. Jo feared the animal had suffered serious injury. But the cowboys had eased the beast out of his strange predicament and locked him into the chute. Not waiting for Jo to properly assess the animal's physical condition, the rider had mounted the bull and firmly tightened the flat, plaited bull rope around his left hand.

Jo knew Loco was a ticking bomb.

Frightened.

Confused.

And mad.

She was about to voice a warning when an overanxious cowboy reached for the flank strap to tighten it. The temperamental beast turned chute-crazy and rammed into the wood fencing. The cowbell between Loco's legs wildly clanged as the animal kicked against the rail. Panicked, the rider groped for the gate's overhead bar with his free hand.

Lance Wymer, co-owner of Wymer Rodeo and Jo's fiancé, leaped onto the gate beside her. His square jaw clenched, small blood vessels bulging over his temples. His worried gray eyes scanned the anxious crowd perched in the rodeo stands.

Though he balanced on the lowest rung, he still towered over Jo. She had to make Lance listen to her. "This animal can't perform tonight. His hind legs are weak from the grate. With him kicking at this chute, there's no telling what will happen." She grabbed Lance's arm to draw his attention and pointed to the Brahma's hind legs. "Look!" The hide was barely scraped. To the naked eye, the wounds did not appear serious, but Jo knew differently.

"Open the gate!" the rider yelled, his frightened eyes the size of water buckets. Ballistic, Loco pitched his weight to and fro inside the chute. Timbers creaked and cracked, barely able to contain the tormented animal. The rider was in a dangerous situation because he was strapped on and couldn't get off, but Jo knew the bull was in jeopardy too.

Lance shot her a no-time-to-argue glance. He jumped down, flipped the latch, and with the help of Frankie, the sad-faced clown, pulled open the gate.

Jo rode the gate until it neared the corral, and then she quickly leaped onto the wood fence and climbed to the top. Her eyes were glued to the bull as worry for the animal outweighed all else in her mind.

A brilliant flash of lightning streaked overhead. Thunder boomed.

Loco bolted from the chute in a tight spin, hind legs kicking high in the air, horns burrowing the ground. The rider held up his left arm in the bull-riding position as he dug his dull-pointed spurs into the Brahma's loose hide.

The bull's hindquarters rolled as his back legs struck the earth. An unmistakable sound of breaking bones shot through the whoops and hollers of the cheering onlookers. A gut-wrenching bellow resounded through thick, wet air as Loco's full weight dropped to the ground.

Jo knew it! Why did Lance hire her if he wasn't going to listen when she had concerns? She slammed her hand against the wood plank. There was no time for anger, only time to act.

"Get my bag!" she yelled, jumping into the arena. A surge of concerned cowboys had already started over the fence.

Chugger Gibson, Lance's right-hand man—who was as mean and ugly as a blue healer dog—stopped and snagged her medical bag, tossing it to her as he leaped to the ground.

Loco's pitiful groans tore at Jo's heart. She had to help the bull. As she sprinted across the arena, she noticed one of the clowns had helped the bewildered rider off the Brahma. Dazed, he stood staring at his adversary.

Loco spastically attempted to crawl to his feet, hoofing the ground with his front legs as he bawled and snorted. His hind legs, twisted and broken, dragged uselessly behind him. Long dangling lariats of mucus shot out of his nose. Wild fear and tortured confusion filled the animal's widened eyes.

Jo glanced at the stands. Even with the storm upon them, the audience stood frozen in shock. Small children hid behind their parents. Jo knew she should shoot the animal. A bullet in the brain would be the fastest way to ease Loco's suffering. But those little innocent faces peering around their mommies were too pure and terrified to see more violence tonight.

Dropping to her knees, she dug through her bag past the hypodermics, looking for her 60cc syringe with the sixteen-gauge needle. Finally, she pulled it out and loaded the vial with a large dose of phenobarbital sodium—snuff juice.

Watching the liquid fill the syringe, she shouted at the others, "Make a tight circle around us! Get Frankie and his clowns entertaining those people!"

"What do you think you're doing?" Out of the corner of her eye, she saw Lance's boots step beside her.

"I've got to put him down." She pushed the prong until liquid dribbled out of the end of the blunt-nosed needle.

"Let me get my gun." He started away.

"No!" She pulled him back. "Not in front of the children." Before he could argue, she stepped toward the moaning bull. "Lance, I need you to hold his head so I can inject this in his neck."

Lance reluctantly motioned for Chugger and a couple of cowboys to help him. They lashed a rope around Loco's front legs. Lance and Chugger grabbed the Brahma's head. Jo wiped a trembling hand across her face. Biting her lips together, she stole a few fortifying breaths then ran to the bull.

The animal cranked his head, trying to hook her with his horns. Lance and his men struggled to hold the beast. Jo jabbed the needle into Loco's neck, injecting the deadly poison.

More mucus sputtered from his nose. A heartbeat later, he collapsed in one massive heap, his eyes frozen open. The last flicker of life slowly evaporated from his stare.

Jo patted the bull's cinnamon coat. She knew death was no respecter of humans or animals and felt a keen sense of grief at this animal's loss.

Large drops of rain fell, closing the rest of the rodeo's events. Frankie led the other two bedraggled clowns to their waiting van. Lance motioned for the tractor to enter the arena, and Chugger guided it to the carcass.

Jo dropped the syringe into her bag then grabbed an irritating lock of hair and looped it behind her ear. Looking up at the angry sky, she thought once again of her father. He had been right.

Lightning was God's warning of bad times to come.

* * *

Through the pelting rain, a steady stream of cars and trucks left the rodeo grounds. Their headlights beamed in his face. Faulkner flinched from the glare.

What if someone recognized him and stopped? His shaking hand searched the coat's deep pocket until it met the cold, hard steel of the .357 Magnum Colt Python he had stolen from the prison guard. He didn't want to use the weapon, but if someone were to stop him, the gun would frighten them away.

A few straggling rodeo goers trickled out of the stadium. Pickup trucks, campers, and horse trailers were parked in the pasture next to the dilapidated arena and stands. The scent of wet manure brought back memories of his life long ago, a life gone wrong. Because of the scars of his past, he'd developed a strong dislike for animals. They were unpredictable and flighty and bit anyone within reach. He'd trust a good running car over an unstable horse anytime. He walked between the lines of three-quarter-ton trucks hooked to trailers.

Anxious cowboys loaded their prized horses into the safe havens of their trailers. Horses whinnied in shrill protests.

Keeping his head down to avoid making eye contact, Faulkner skirted around everyone he possibly could. Dirt turned to mud on the path leading to the arena. With each sliding footstep, new pain burned fresh in his gut.

Out of his peripheral vision, he saw an old familiar Ford truck with a dented rear fender and rusted joints. A sign painted on the side read *Dr. J. R. Powers*—Jonathan Powers.

Doc's truck. "Thank you, God," he said under his breath.

He tried to stay calm. Acting as if he belonged there, he walked steadily toward the rusty Ford. He checked the area. No one watched. No one cared about anything except moving themselves and their animals out of the rain.

He opened the truck's door and stepped up on the high running board. Pain ate at his side as he climbed into the cab. Sitting on top of a blue plastic tarp and leather work gloves, he doubled over on the seat, fighting the burning ache in his side. His skin prickled with chills, and his lips quivered as he held back a sudden swell of nausea. He sucked in long, deep breaths and swallowed bile as he tried to focus.

Then . . . voices came from outside the truck.

A woman and a man. And neither of them was Doc.

They were coming closer. Easing onto the floor of the passenger's side, Faulkner threw the tarp over himself and drew the gun from his pocket.

* * *

"Jo, listen to me," Lance yelled through the pouring rain. "That animal dying is going to cost us money we don't have. Loco was a big draw. People came from miles around just to see that crazy bull. But the cowboy comes first! I had to get the rider off, and the quickest way to do that was for him to ride."

The timbre of Lance's voice only incensed Jo more. Rain sluiced off her hat, trickled beneath her collar, and ran down her back. Cold, tired, and wet, she didn't give a Fig Newton™ about Lance's justifications. Because of the moronic acts of humans, she had been forced to kill an animal tonight. And Lance could have stopped it if he'd been thinking clearly.

Looking up at Lance's tall, lean form clad in his oilskin Dover coat, Jo became more enraged. Why did she have to be so darned short? She wanted to look him in the eye to tell him what she thought of his barbaric, uncaring attitude toward animals.

Consumed with anger, she balanced on the toes of her mud-caked boots. "That bull should never have been loaded into the chute. You knew that! You saw when his legs caught in the sorting pens."

The injustice of it all burst within her. "Criminey sakes! You hire me to watch out for your animals, and then you don't listen! You cowboys are all alike! You keep going no matter what. Your motto is 'Ride the animal till he drops.' Makes me sick." Tempted to kick him, she made herself turn and vent her anger on the Goodrich tire of her truck. The impact jolted mud and manure from her boot.

Lance grabbed her arm and jerked her around to face him. "That's not fair. I did listen to you, but there was nothing I could do! A rider's life is worth more than a bull's."

Jo's anger tempered a little. Of course, he was right, but the rider should never have mounted the bull until she'd had time to do a proper assessment. Lance should have stopped him.

Lance glared at her, his grip tightening on her arm. "And there's not a cowboy on my rodeo crew who doesn't place the animals *first* when it comes to food or shelter. I've seen Chugger so sick he can hardly stand up, tending to a bull."

The pouring rain mingled with Lance's words dampened Jo's rage further, and she realized she had been lying to herself in her anger. The cowboys did care. But it still didn't change the fact that she had to put down an animal. Wanting to get out of the rain and away from this argument, she tried twisting her arm out of his grip. "Let go of me."

For a moment, they stood almost nose to nose, like a Yorkshire terrier challenging a Great Dane. Even though Lance had made some good points, Jo stood defiant, staring back at him. A mask of command turned his face to rock. His eyes filled with more brooding anger than the storm, an anger she had not seen before. A little shaken, Jo almost backed down, but then determination to make him see her point overrode her alarm.

Finally . . . slowly . . . he loosened his hold on her arm. A lazy smile pulled at his lips. The Lance she knew had returned. "Come on, Jo. What's done is done. Our fighting won't change what's happened."

She hated when he made sense—especially when he was humble or at least appeared to be. No matter what they said now, Loco remained dead. It would serve no purpose to stay angry. But for a moment, her righteous indignation had sure felt good.

Whenever that crooked smile gentled Lance's face, and his gray eyes grew kind and caring, Jo could not stay mad. Lance was cowboy through and through, and when it came to losing one of his animals, he grieved.

"We need to get out of the rain, so stop with the teasing look." She gave him a begrudging smile.

His eyebrows hiked up in mock surprise. "What teasing look?"

"You know." She tried to step away, but he scooped her into his arms before she could stop him. Nothing made Jo angrier than someone who made her feel helpless by picking her up.

"Stop this?" He bent his head to plant a kiss on her.

In that split second, Jo's anger spiked. She was wet and bone tired. A kiss would not make everything all right. As she turned her cheek to him, puddled rain rolled from the brim of his Stetson, splashing onto her face. Jo flinched and wiped away the excess water. Her voice held the edge of her tattered nerves. "Thanks a lot."

Lance set her on her feet, shrugging his broad shoulders as if he'd tried everything to make amends. Then he winked and tipped his hat to her. "Wait until we get out of the rain, babe. I'll make it up to you."

Did he plan to get in the truck with her? She'd had enough. "I'm spent. Let's talk in the morning when you stop by to pick up Champ." Earlier in the day she'd operated on Lance's German shepherd. The dog was recuperating in her clinic. She was in no mood to be a comforting fiancée. Not tonight. She needed space.

"You know it's only a matter of time before I wear you down." He smiled and tweaked her nose, a gesture he must have thought cute.

Jo gripped the door handle tightly.

He leaned over, tilted her hat back on her head, and kissed her wet forehead. "Don't pick up any strangers on your way home." He waved good-bye and headed for his own truck.

Thoroughly chilled, she quickly flung open the door. She grabbed the steering wheel and leaped in, dropping her medical bag on the bench seat beside her as she slammed the door shut. She noticed her tarp on the floor. One of the cowboys must have used it, and instead of folding it up neatly and placing it on the seat, he'd just thrown it in the cab. Exasperated, she reached to pull the blue plastic onto the seat. A hand grabbed hold of her arm. Terror surged through her as the hard steel of a revolver's barrel pressed against her thigh.

CHAPTER TWO

FEAR GRABBED JO AS SHE stared in disbelief at the gun. Her gaze trailed up the arm of the man's coat to wild, scraggly hair, a mustache, and a full beard. He jabbed her with the weapon. Clearly, he meant her harm. She had to get away. Grabbing the door handle to wrench it open, she stopped when he rammed the nose of the revolver into her ribs.

"Don't!" His raspy voice was but a whisper. He gasped and clutched his left side as he crawled onto the bench seat on top of the tarp, so close to her that she couldn't really see him without turning, but she could smell him. Body odor as foul and pungent as a wet dog filled the cab.

She quickly released the handle, not wanting to give him any reason to shoot. What would happen to Rhett if she were to die? Flashes of her six-year-old playing on the tire swing in her yard and feeding the injured animals in her clinic sped through her mind.

Jo tried to face him, but he thrust the gun barrel in her ribs a second time. She could feel him shaking beside her. Was he on drugs or something? "What do you want?"

"Start the truck." Again, his voice was just a raspy whisper. And she could tell by his favoring his side that he was injured.

With the nose of the revolver pressed firmly to her ribs, Jo turned the key. The engine roared to life, and the windshield wipers frantically slapped at the rain as she angled to join the exit line of vehicles.

A steady stream of pickup trucks and horse trailers edged past. Lance's red Dodge pulled in front of her. She stared at his silhouette in his rear window, willing him to turn and look or at least wave. He was busy keeping an eye on traffic and didn't glance at her idling truck. He was probably worrying about the financial strain that would fall on his rodeo with Loco's loss.

If she could somehow signal Lance, this nightmare could end. She stepped on the floorboard switch, flipping the high beams of her headlights from low to high.

"Don't!" Even though his hand trembled, the pressure of the gun against her side became more intense.

Jo took her foot off the light switch.

Lance's truck crawled onto the highway and rumbled down the road. Mile upon mile spread between his truck and hers. Jo watched as his taillights faded into the rain along with her hope.

From behind, an impatient rancher honked. "Go!" The madman's voice nearly broke through the whisper.

Grinding the gears, Jo nervously shifted into first, pulled onto the highway, and tried once again to steal a look at the man beside her. Black sunken eyes met her gaze, and she realized he was seriously ill. This guy was on the verge of passing out or maybe even dying right here in her truck.

"You're sick," she said. Though she was a veterinarian, the doctor within her took over. Life was precious and something she had to fight for. She'd already seen death once today. If she could handle a rank bull, an ill man—who could barely hold a revolver—should be no problem. And yet she couldn't ignore the gun in his shaking hand.

"Gut shot," he whispered. "Take me to Doc Powers?"

"But he's—"

"Just do it!" He leaned heavily to the side he clutched.

Jo pulled the truck onto the road. Maybe she could find help at the Swan Valley Store not too far away. Nearing the building, she saw the closed sign on the door. No one was about. She drove on. As the miles passed, she tried to think of what she could do. She obviously couldn't take him to her father. She could drive him to the Idaho Falls hospital, but that was a good hour or so away. He might not have that much time. Reality claimed her.

I'm his only hope. Jo didn't know if she could handle such a burden. But she had to. Her place was only twenty minutes away. She had medical equipment there. Plus, Denny, her older brother, was tending Rhett. He'd help.

Rhett!

She couldn't place her son in danger.

But the man was barely breathing. Of all the trucks he could have climbed into, he'd gotten into hers, or rather, her father's. Her dad had always said, "God doesn't give you more than you can handle." Staring down at the gun, she questioned that theory. Maybe by the time she reached her place, this guy would be unconscious, and if he wasn't, she'd drive around until he was. He wouldn't be a threat. Rhett would be all right.

The highway curled around the mountain, sneaking along the north bank of the Snake River. The river bridge lay up ahead. The man moaned as Jo slowed and shifted down. He eased the barrel of the revolver away from her, a sign that his pain had grown more intense. He couldn't hang on much longer. Crossing the bridge, she turned down the gravel road that wove along the south bank of the Snake.

After several miles, she took the road up Fall Creek Canyon. A bump jostled the truck as the road changed from gravel to dirt, which was now deep-sucking mud. She pulled to the grassy shoulder.

The man rallied, barely conscious, yet he still seemed aware of movement. "Why are we stopping?"

"I need to shift to four wheel drive." With both hands, she shoved the stick of the transfer case into low range.

Gearing down to first, she started the tedious climb up the canyon. With every bump and slide, Jo worried. In a few hours, the mud-slick road would be impassable.

He moaned and, grabbing his gut, said, "Where are you . . . going?"

"Where I can help you." Jo had to hurry. After an eternity, she saw the yard light from her place shine through long-needled pines, wild oaks, and quaking aspens. If she was lucky, her captor would pass out and Denny could help her get him on an examination table. Once she'd taken care of the man's wound, she'd call the authorities.

She drove onto the concrete pad of her driveway.

Her home/clinic had been built into the mountain, putting the lower two stories on ground level: the garage-stable was on the bottom, her clinic was above that, and the third floor was where she, Denny, and Rhett lived.

The man slouched against the passenger door. Blood had seeped through his coat. He could bleed out right here.

She punched the garage door opener and pulled in. As soon as she parked, she jumped out and raced to the passenger's side, wrenching open the truck's door and catching the man as he slid out. Drawing his arm around her shoulders, she was able to help the barely conscious man stand. He leaned heavily on her, and for a second, she thought he sniffed her hair.

She stared him in the face for the first time.

He stared back. His foreboding eyes grew warm and hopeful, as if he knew her.

And then all at once, with striking clarity, Jo realized she did know who he was. "Faulkner?"

With a great deal of effort, he answered. "Took you long enough."

Jo froze.

Branson Faulkner!

Why hadn't Jo recognized him before? This man was her ex-husband. This man was her son's father. And this man was convicted of killing Lance's brother, Coulton, and was supposed to be in prison. The nightmare of her past breathed fresh life.

Jo shook her head as if she could shake away the images. Seven years ago the tragedy that had befallen her marriage and the Wymer family had been fodder for the newspapers for well over a year.

Son of Legendary NASCAR Driver Accused of Murdering Stepbrother
Tragedy Strikes Three Times with Unexpected Death of Accused's Mother
Son of NASCAR Legend Sentenced to Life in Prison

Now Faulkner stood beside her at death's door. What was she supposed to do? She had to help him. But if she did, what would she tell Lance? Talk about complicated!

Even though Jo loved Lance now, there had been a time when she'd loved Faulkner. And though Faulkner had divorced her after his conviction, a small piece of her heart still cared about the man and had always wanted to believe in his innocence. She'd tried to get his lawyers to appeal the conviction, but Faulkner had let them go. He'd lost the will to fight, released her from their marriage, and had even given up his unborn child.

But he was here now.

Why?

She had to deal with his injury and would worry about what to tell Lance later. Jo guided Faulkner past animal stalls, large feed sacks, and a small stack of hay. She knew only sheer willpower kept him conscious and staggering on his feet as they headed for the stairs. Taking them one at a time, they slowly made their way to the clinic level. Denny came down from the third floor. Jo's linebacker brother was six foot two and towered over her. Their father used to say Denny got all the height in their family and Jo had been shortchanged.

"What the . . . !" Denny grimaced as his eyes took in the heavily bearded, nearly unconscious man Jo propped up.

She motioned for her brother to help her and at the same time asked, "Where's Rhett?"

"He fell asleep watching a movie. And good thing." Denny took Jo's place, pulling Faulkner's arm around him and guiding him toward the largest surgical table Jo had on this level. He helped Faulkner sit on the nearly five-foot table. Jo grabbed the portable examination table near the cages to support Faulkner's feet once they took off his coat and laid him down.

Faulkner moaned, clutching his side. Jo took the revolver from his hand. Denny's eyes grew as large as boulders as he stared at the weapon he hadn't seen until then. Jo didn't take the time to explain and placed the gun on the counter next to the jars of sterile cotton swabs and doggie treats. She tore off her hat and coat and dropped them on the floor. Grabbing her stethoscope from a drawer, she looped it over her neck and flipped on the overhead surgical light.

Denny's jaw dropped as the better light gave him a fresh view of the man who could barely sit up. "Is this who I think it is?"

Jo nodded.

Disgust and anger pinched Denny's leathery face. He had never liked Faulkner. "But didn't he get a life sentence?"

Again, Jo nodded. She scanned the room, looking for something to lay on the cold table so she could ease him down, but she couldn't see anything. Faulkner moaned and leaned against her. Looking at him, she could hardly believe he was the same man she'd married. Images of Faulkner during the trial reeled through her mind. His shoulders were slumped, and his complexion was light gray. The stress had been tough on her as well. She'd nearly lost their baby and had been on strict bed rest, but she'd ignored the doctor and shown up in court, pleading with the judge to not give Faulkner a life sentence.

"Did he get paroled?"

Jo glanced at Faulkner's mustard-colored prison uniform where his coat gapped open. "Doubtful."

Denny straightened his shoulders and went to the counter. His hand reached like he meant to pick up the weapon, but then, as if he thought better of it, he picked up the phone's receiver instead and held it to his ear. "No dial tone, again. This stupid thing goes out whenever there's a storm. I've a good mind to buy a cell phone."

"It would cost a fortune for coverage here." Jo gazed at Faulkner, trying to gain courage to do what she must.

Denny sighed heavily and came to her side, staring at the man. Jo was grateful for Denny's presence, even though he was upset. Her brother knew how much she had loved this man, but he also knew how Faulkner had broken her heart, not only when he'd asked for a divorce but also when he'd given up on being a father. Jo believed Faulkner had reached his limit with being accused of murder, enduring the death of his mother, and then facing his conviction.

But Denny didn't see it that way. To him, Faulkner's giving up confirmed his guilt that he'd killed Coulton. Jo and Denny's differing opinions of Faulkner had become a sore subject for the two of them, and they hardly brought it up.

"He's gut shot," Jo said as she tried to think of a strategy to save Faulkner. "I have to do what I can, and then when the phone is working again, we'll call the authorities and deal with the rest."

Denny nodded. The look in his eyes told her that even though he didn't think this was a good idea, he would do whatever she needed him to because she was his sister and he loved her. Since their father's death, Denny had been as completely devoted to Jo as she was to him.

She peeled Faulkner's bloodstained coat off his left arm. Denny dragged it from his right and dropped it to the floor.

Faulkner's jumpsuit was labeled PRISON in bold black letters across his back. An old, forgotten pain needled Jo's heart. This had been the man she'd thought she would grow old with, the man she'd wanted to share her life with, but that illusion had vanished with a single bullet lodged in Coulton's chest.

So much had changed.

Over time and through her years of struggling to earn an education, raise a child on her own, and endure the knocks and bumps of everyday life, the love she had once felt for Faulkner had transformed. She progressed from anger that he'd thought she'd be better off without him to pity because Faulkner had given up on her love. Jo pushed her feelings aside. She had to concentrate.

Denny slipped off Faulkner's mud-caked shoes while Jo unzipped the prison garb. Faulkner groaned as they jostled him to his feet to pull off the uniform.

"Hold on," Jo told Faulkner as his body shuddered with pain. Finally spying a towel, she grabbed it and laid it on the surgery table. "Lay him back," she said to Denny. "I need a clear view of his injury."

Denny did as she asked while she placed Faulkner's dirty-socked feet on the portable table. Jo quickly went to her patient's side. Beneath fine brush strokes of dark, curly hair were long jagged scars. His body was a map of injuries that hadn't existed when they'd been together. In her quick examination, she found scars from deep cuts that had most certainly been life-threatening. She wondered what terrifying stories he'd lived through during the seven years he'd been locked away.

Jo lifted Faulkner's protective hand away from his bloody wound. Body tissue hung from a gaping hole and puckered around fleshy edges. Blood seeped over his skin.

"What are you going to do?" Denny asked.

"Operate."

Inhaling a lungful of courage, she rolled up her sleeves. Jo grabbed IV tubing and a bag of Ringer's lactate. She stuck the tubing into the small plastic-bag opening and hung it on the IV stand next to the surgical table. Moving as quickly as she could, she filled a syringe with anesthetic and set it aside. She quickly tore open a betadine swab and wiped a spot on Faulkner's arm to stick the IV needle in as she checked his eyes. They were barely open, yet he watched her every move. She sank the needle in his vein. He winced but didn't look away. She taped the needle to secure it then injected the anesthetic she'd prepared into the tubing port.

"Jo, you have to know . . ." He paused and bit his chapped lower lip as his worried eyes searched hers. "I have always loved you." A smile gentled his bearded face, and then Faulkner was out.

* * *

Denny and Jo both put on scrubs, washed, and donned sterile gowns. Though Denny wasn't licensed, he'd assisted her with operations before when she was in a pinch, but that was on animals. She'd never used a scalpel to slice into human flesh.

Surprisingly, Jo found the bullet right away and dug it out. It had missed his intestines, which was good, though it had grazed a bleeder vein. She cauterized it. Once she started stitching the hole, Denny shed the gown and gloves and went upstairs to check on Rhett.

Jo placed a bandage on Faulkner's wound. They'd have a major problem fighting infection. Plus, he had a fever and had lost a lot of blood. She had done the best she could, yet she worried.

Tugging off her surgical mask and cap, Jo's eyes trailed over Faulkner. Damp tendrils of ebony hair plaited his forehead and lay shaggily over his shoulders. Just above his facial hair was the outline of nice, high cheekbones. He had a straight, prominent nose and dark brows. Oh, how she had once loved him. Why was he here? How had he escaped? And why now just a few weeks before her wedding?

This morning she never dreamed Branson Faulkner would land in her life again by nightfall. She thought of their past, the pleasure, and most definitely the pain. She had worked very hard to forgive him for divorcing her. She thought about how he said he'd always loved her just before the anesthetic had put him to sleep.

Of course, Jo didn't believe him. She took a deep breath and rubbed her aching neck as she thought of that horrible night so long ago, the night that had changed their lives forever.

The evening had started out nicely. Jo and Faulkner had settled down on the couch to watch the Coca-Cola 500, an important NASCAR race in the Sprint Cup Series. When Faulkner was a little boy, his father was a NASCAR driver and won enough races in the circuit to earn him the Winston Cup. That was the year before his fatal crash. Faulkner had been only six when his father died. As Jo snuggled with Faulkner, he opened up about the win. He'd been only five and had gone with his mother to victory lane to be with his father in the winner's circle. The smell of gas and burning oil tinged the air. His dad was completely focused on his mother, even though girls dressed in short shorts and midriff-baring blouses tried to give him victory kisses. Dangerous Dan brushed them aside to kiss his wife, and then he boosted Faulkner up on his shoulders for the cameras. His father had been so sweaty after climbing out of his Chevy race car's sweltering cockpit.

The hurt look of remembrance in Faulkner's eyes had nearly broken Jo's heart.

And then their phone had rung.

Cassandra, Faulkner's mother, was hysterical, saying she should have never married Edward Wymer. Faulkner said he could tell she'd been drinking again. Shortly after the death of his father, Cassandra had used alcohol as a crutch. She'd stopped for a while when she and Edward became involved, but since the bloom had fallen off her four-year marriage, she was depending on it again to give her courage and numb her pain. She'd gained a loving husband but also two sons who didn't want or need her. Edward was so wrapped up with his business that he was oblivious to the tension between his grown sons and wife, so when he was gone purchasing new rodeo stock, she drowned her worries with alcohol. When that didn't work, Faulkner was often the one who comforted her. Faulkner had kissed

Jo good-bye as he had headed out the door. He told Jo he'd be right back.

Except . . . he'd never returned.

She stopped the memory from overtaking her. She didn't want to relive what had happened. Not again. The past had dogged her for years. For the next few hours, she would think only of saving Faulkner's life. She was not going to revisit what couldn't be undone.

Jo gently put a pillow under Faulkner's head and pulled the blanket and sheet up to his beard, tucking the covers around him. The time had come to call the authorities. Explaining to Sheriff Padraic about the operation would be tricky, but when she told him the circumstance, he'd understand. And Denny would help her state her case.

She put her surgical garb in the laundry bin, dropped Faulkner's prison uniform in the garbage, and left the night-light on so she could monitor her patient from the next room. Her steps were determined as she neared the desk in her office. She sat on her wobbly swivel chair and flipped on the cracked banker's lamp so she could see to grab the phone.

Still no dial tone. She clicked it several times. Silence. For the second time tonight, she thought of a cell phone, but they were just too unreliable in the mountains and not worth spending the extra money. The storm must have been worse than she'd thought. She hung up, went to the window, and twisted the wand of the Levolor™ blinds. Rain slid down the glass. This summer had been dry, and the forest needed the moisture. But why tonight? The storm made the roads impossible to drive on and messed up her phone.

For now, she'd be safe enough. Faulkner was too weak from fever and blood loss to be a threat, if he ever really was one. And Denny was upstairs. She thought again of all that must have happened to Faulkner while he'd been in prison. It had changed him so much that he'd pulled a gun on her.

The gun!

Jo went back to the counter. She couldn't leave the weapon out where her son could see it. Picking up the revolver, she didn't know where to put it. The lock on her desk was broken. She looked at the lock on her medicine cabinet. Perfect. She pulled her key chain from her pants pocket, unlocked the cabinet door, and gently laid the weapon far in the back behind the morphine. The weapon would be safe there and would be away from Rhett's reach.

Feeling like someone was watching her, Jo whipped around. Faulkner remained asleep. After the evening she'd had, she was jumpy. That's all. Gazing at him, she decided it might be a good idea to restrain Faulkner until Sheriff Padraic arrived.

Jo searched the room for rope. But she found only a short nylon leash. Crossing Faulkner's wrists, she tied the leash in a knot. The task completed, she pulled the sheet and blanket up to his chin and tucked in the covers again. She didn't like leaving him on the surgery table with his feet propped up on the other table, but the only spare bed was upstairs. And she didn't want him in her living quarters. Faulkner'd be okay here because as soon as she could, she planned to hand him over to the authorities. But that didn't sit well with Jo.

When Faulkner had been convicted, Sheriff Padraic, Lance, and Denny had all thought justice was served. Even her father had agreed. But Jo wasn't sure. It was only after Faulkner had turned his back on her that Jo had doubted her judgment. In an attempt to explain away the hurt he'd caused her, she'd begun thinking he was guilty of such a crime. But the longing in his eyes combined with the tender sound of his voice as he'd drifted off had stirred something inside that she'd ignored all these years: she'd never really believed Faulkner was capable of killing someone. And maybe that's why she didn't like the thought of turning him in tonight.

Why would Faulkner risk escaping when it would only make things worse for him when he returned? Obviously he'd attacked a guard to get a gun, and then he'd kidnapped her at gunpoint. All of this would only make his life more miserable. It just didn't make sense. She rubbed her throbbing head and returned to her chair. She had to quit thinking this way.

The first hour after the operation crept slowly by. Jo checked the phone every ten minutes or so. Several times, Faulkner mumbled, "Help, run," and a few good curses. When his face pinched with grief and he said, "Jo, forgive me," she went to his side. He thrashed about mumbling those three words over and over for quite some time.

An old ache in her heart twisted and writhed. She hesitated to touch him. If she did, would it rekindle her feelings? She couldn't ignore his pleas. With a trembling hand, she smoothed his tousled, sweat-dampened hair away from his forehead like she had so many times when they'd been married. Jo leaned over and softly said, "I forgive you."

He calmed a little but still seemed to need further reassurance. Without even thinking, she kissed his forehead as she had years ago. "Everything will be all right."

Immediately, relief softened the furrows of his brow. A peaceful look claimed his face. He had been so foreboding in the truck as he'd aimed the gun at her. But now, even with his wild beard and long hair, he seemed vulnerable. Strangely, an aura of gentleness settled upon him.

Gentleness? What was the matter with her? After everything that had happened, what was she thinking? She had to get away from him.

Jo left Faulkner, went to her desk again, and rolled her swivel chair in front of the rain-slick window. She plopped down. All in all, it had been a horrible night, and she was tired—yet her jangled nerves would not let her relax. Her ex-husband lay on her operating table.

And once again, she'd saved his life.

CHAPTER THREE

FAULKNER SLOWLY OPENED HIS HEAVY eyelids. His vision was blurry, dreamlike, though he knew he wasn't dreaming because every muscle in his body ached, plus he was lying on something hard and uncomfortable. Blinking to focus, he glanced down and saw a blanket and sheet covering him. His gaze trailed to an IV stuck in his arm and a white privacy curtain around his bed. Used to seeing prison bars and grungy cinder-block walls, he was confused. He tried to move his hands but couldn't. Wriggling the covers aside, he found his wrists tied together with what looked like an animal's leash. From behind the curtain, he heard a bird chirp and a cat yowl. What the devil?

Raising his head, he attempted to curl to a sitting position. Sharp pain jabbed his gut. He gasped and lay back. Trying to turn on his side, he was startled to find a young boy dressed in Superman pajamas staring at him. Bright, brown eyes grew large. Auburn hair framed his young face. Faulkner licked his dry, chapped lips, cleared his parched throat, and said, "Who are you?"

At that moment, Jo—the lost love of his life and the woman he'd hurt so badly—hurried around the curtain. He couldn't believe he was actually seeing her. She gave Faulkner a condemning stare as she quickly went to the boy. Her auburn hair hung past her slumped shoulders. Her usually bright eyes, the color of sapphires, were puffy. Scenes of last night came to him: walking in the rain toward the rodeo, finding Jo instead of Doc, and then things grew murky, though he did recall she hadn't recognized him at first and that he'd held her at gunpoint, demanding she take him to her father.

How stupid was that? I needed her help, so what did I do? Scared her to death.

Jo looked at him and then stooped down to smile at the boy. The dimple in her right cheek reminded Faulkner of how much he'd missed her. She said to the child, "Son, you're not supposed to be in here." She hugged him close as though afraid Faulkner might reach out and take the boy away.

Faulkner stared at them. Was this the child he'd never seen? The child he'd walked away from? And the child he'd escaped prison in hopes of saving? Faulkner's eyes misted as he stared at the boy. So many times he'd tried to imagine what his son would be like, and now, here he was before him, all innocent and unafraid. He had Faulkner's father's round cheeks, Jo's auburn hair, and yes, Faulkner's eyes.

The child was close to seven years old. Faulkner had missed so much, years he could never get back. He yearned to hold the boy, tell him he was his father and that he loved him.

But he knew full well he couldn't. He'd given up that privilege long ago. The kid didn't even know him. And if he did . . . if he really knew Faulkner, he'd be afraid—or worse, he'd hate him.

Yet, as much as his child deserved a father, Faulkner knew Lance was not the man for the job. He'd been shocked when he'd read that Lance and Jo were engaged to be married. The paper was several weeks old since it was in the prison library. The article had been about rodeo companies in the state, which, of course, drew Faulkner's attention. The Wymers' success was spotlighted, and it mentioned Lance's upcoming wedding to Jo as a side note. Faulkner had panicked. He'd never trusted Lance. For some reason, Lance had lied under oath. And Faulkner certainly didn't believe Lance would take care of Faulkner's child. No, Lance hated Faulkner and always had. Marrying Jo was probably Lance's way of getting even with Faulkner for Coulton's death. He knew Faulkner would hear about the wedding and that being stuck in jail, unable to do anything, would nearly kill him. The only way Faulkner could stop the marriage was to somehow prove his innocence, which wouldn't be easy. That's why he needed Doc. He'd help him.

"Denny will be looking for you," Jo told the boy.

Faulkner had glimpsed Denny the night before. If her brother was here, her father probably was as well. Surely Doc was the one who had seen to his wound.

"Denny sent me and Jacob to tell you the mush is ready." The boy cautiously looked from Jo to Faulkner and back again.

Who was Jacob? Faulkner heard claws click on floor tiles as a three-legged timber wolf hobbled up to the child and licked his cheek. The boy slung his arm around the animal's furry neck.

The wolf looked up at Faulkner with yellow, penetrating eyes. A chill passed through him. He knew that with one wrong move, the animal would tear him apart. Faulkner'd dealt with shady characters in prison, but he didn't know how to deal with a beast like this or any animal for that matter.

"Take Jacob with you, and tell Denny our visitor is awake." Jo elbowed past the curtain, making a clear path for the child to leave.

The boy didn't say a word and left with the wolf following him. So Jacob was the wolf. Odd name for such a beast.

Jo returned to stand beside Faulkner's bed. "I don't know why you escaped prison, and I know you're recovering from surgery and weak, but I'm warning you: I don't want you anywhere near my son. You got that?"

Faulkner nodded. He couldn't blame her for feeling like she did. In many ways, he deserved it, but in many more, he didn't.

"Good." Jo straightened her shirt. Putting on her professional mask, she said, "How did you get shot?"

"Was on a work detail, cleaning the barrow pits along the freeway. The guard took exception to me walking off." Faulkner really didn't want to talk about it.

"Did you kill him?" Jo seemed to hold her breath.

"Nooo." Faulkner could see why she might think that. Still, he was disappointed that she'd lost all faith in him. "Took his gun away, though, and left him with a bruise on his head; after all, he did shoot me. Where is the gun?" He glanced at the medicine counter close to the surgical table. If things didn't work out the way he hoped or if he had to leave quickly, he was going to need the weapon.

She seemed relieved that Faulkner hadn't shot the guard in return, but her right eyebrow rose when he asked about the gun. "Like I'm going to tell you where I hid it. How do you feel?"

There couldn't be many places to hide the weapon. He'd find it later. "Been worse. What's our son's—" Faulkner stopped as soon as he saw the flash of anger appear on her face. "Your son's name?" Faulkner had given up any claim to the child. Jo had sole responsibility of him. The child was hers.

Jo yanked the stethoscope from around her neck. By the familiar way she handled the medical instrument, he knew she must have become a nurse and now assisted her father. She pulled her hair away from her face and put the stethoscope's ear tips in her ears.

"Rhett Powers," she replied.

So Jo was letting Faulkner know her son used her maiden name. Under the circumstances, that was understandable.

Pulling down the covers, Jo probed Faulkner's chest. She leaned over to listen. Her long, auburn hair brushed his skin and sent a tingling awakening through him that he hadn't felt in years. He wanted to take her in his arms as he had when they were married and happy, wanted to tell her how much he'd missed her, that he loved her, and he'd do anything to win her back. Instead, he bit his lower lip and kept his mouth shut. He had to.

She straightened and looped the stethoscope behind her neck once again.

Faulkner attempted to curl into a sitting position, but knifelike pain cut through him, sucking strength from his limbs. He sank back on the pillow. Catching his breath, he said, "Please thank your father for saving my life."

Jo shook her head. "Can't. He died a couple of years ago."

Doc's dead? Has been for a while?

Faulkner felt like his cell door had slammed shut in his face. He could hardly believe it. All those times he'd worried that something bad had happened to Doc . . . and he'd been right. Faulkner felt an earthquake had rattled his soul. Fear rippled through him. Somehow, he had to remain calm and think.

Two years ago, Doc had paid Faulkner an unexpected visit. He'd apologized for not believing in Faulkner's innocence. Doc explained that Edward had been his friend for years. When it looked as though Faulkner had gunned down Edward's son, Doc couldn't turn his back on his friend, even though, or maybe especially because, Faulkner was his new son-in-law. But over the years, his conscience ate away at him. Doc said the more he thought about it, the more things didn't add up. He was following a hunch that might set Faulkner free, but he didn't want to tell him what it was in case it didn't pan out. Many people could get hurt, people close to Doc, and he couldn't take the chance. Doc never returned to say what he'd found. Faulkner's calls and letters went unanswered. What had Doc's hunch been? Faulkner needed more information. "I'm so sorry. I know you and Doc were close. What did he die of?" Faulkner looked into Jo's eyes and saw that she still grieved her father's death.

For a moment, she stared off, deep in thought. Then she sighed heavily. "You know how Dad loved hiking Table Rock Mountain. He must have misstepped and fallen. When he didn't come home, Denny went looking for him. Found him at the base of the cliff." Jo's bottom lip trembled slightly.

Falling off a cliff was not like dying of a heart attack or a stroke. Falling from a cliff could have been murder. Before Faulkner could make such an accusation, he needed to know more. He reached to take Jo's hand, but because of his tied wrists, he only managed to knock the blanket and sheet that covered him onto the floor, revealing that he only wore briefs and socks.

A red flush streaked across Jo's face. She was embarrassed. Instead of dwelling on her discomfort, Faulkner decided to draw her attention to his wrists. "You really think tying me up is necessary?"

Jo retrieved the blanket and covered him. Scrubbing her face with her palm, she stepped away. "You held a gun on me."

"I'm sorry. At the time, you didn't know who I was, and for a while, I thought it best you didn't know. Besides, I couldn't think of another way to make you take me to your father."

"And knowing my father, he would have helped you," she said begrudgingly. Jo folded her arms.

Faulkner nodded. Doc would have helped him in so many ways. But now Faulkner was back to square one . . . unless he could somehow cut through the mistrust and enlist Jo's help. "So, have you called the authorities?"

"What do you think?" she huffed as she wiped her brow with the back of her hand. At the top of her worried forehead was a widow's peak. Dark thick lashes framed her eyes. The blue denim of her shirt enhanced their mesmerizing color.

He cleared his throat. "Then we don't have much time, do we?"

She appeared puzzled.

"You have to listen to me. I know it was tough on you when Coulton died. He was your first love until I came along and stole you away. And maybe my being convicted of his murder makes you feel guilty or beholding to the Wymers, but you can't erase what happened by marrying Lance. Something is very wrong at the Wymer ranch."

"Excuse me? Whom I marry is none of your business." Her brows bunched together as her eyes cast condemning darts his way.

"You're right, but . . ." Somehow Faulkner had to reason with Jo. And to do that, he'd have to rely on God's help once again. He'd led Faulkner to Jo; surely He'd help him know what to say. "Your father came to visit me a couple of years ago."

"I'm surprised you didn't refuse his visit." She turned her back to Faulkner and walked to the counter. The sting of her words was nearly as painful as the bullet had been. After she'd testified on Faulkner's behalf and saved him from the death penalty, and before his attorney could deliver the divorce papers, he'd refused to see Jo. She'd tried several times. Sending her away—without seeing her, without holding her one last time—had nearly killed Faulkner.

And it had obviously hurt Jo deeply. But he'd always told himself he had done it because he loved her.

"Josephine . . ." He'd never called her that before. Even when they'd taken their wedding vows, he'd called her only Jo. She slowly faced him. He continued. "I'm so sorry I screwed up our lives."

Disbelief showed in her gaze. Mistrust soon followed. However, she still seemed willing to listen.

"I need to tell you something." Faulkner hoped the words would come to him.

She stood stone still.

He didn't know exactly how to say it other than to start at the beginning, at the time he had learned to hope again. "Several years ago, I met this couple, LeVar and June Kimble, who visited the prison every Monday night. They were Christians. I'd never given religion much thought until my life was derailed. Never thought it was something for me. I wanted to race cars, not think about God. But sitting in on their visits, I gradually realized I wanted to believe in God."

Jo slowly walked to the side of his bed.

"I started reading the Bible. I can't explain the feeling that came over me except a warm comforting peace wrapped around me, and for the first time in years, my life had purpose. I knew I wouldn't always be in prison. Not long after, your father visited me."

Jo's eyebrows raised.

Faulkner choked up for a moment. He wished he could tell her what was in his heart, but those feelings were beyond words. Quickly regaining his composure, he continued. "He visited me only once and said he had a hunch that Mom's death was not suicide or an accidental overdose like the county coroner believed. He was researching something but wouldn't tell me what. Said if word leaked out he was looking into Cassandra's death, people close to him could get hurt. Because Doc was suspicious about Mom's death, he came to believe I was innocent. He said he'd do everything he could to get me out of jail. That was the last I saw him."

"Why didn't he tell me about this?" Jo stared skeptically at Faulkner, watching for a sign that he was lying.

"Perhaps it was like he'd told me—he didn't want word to leak out. He was probably protecting you." Faulkner wished Doc had told her. It would have made convincing her so much easier.

"When my father didn't return, why didn't you try to get ahold of him? Or me?"

"I did," Faulkner said. "You disconnected our phone."

"It's been a long time since I've had that number. I went to school and have moved several times over the years." Jo smoothed her hair behind her ears.

"When your father didn't come back, I tried to call him, but there was no answer. So I wrote to him. And when he didn't reply, I took a chance and wrote to you. Those letters went to your father's address, but they came back 'Return to Sender.'" At the time, Faulkner had thought Jo was sending him a message to leave her alone. It hadn't dawned on him that her father was dead and she had moved with no forwarding address.

"I sold Dad's place . . . Well, Denny lived in his house for a little while until the deal was finalized, but he would have given the letters to me." She rubbed her chin.

She was warming up to him. Faulkner felt a sliver of hope. He had to make the most of it. Right now, rehashing the past would not help. "It's all right. The thing is, when I read in the paper that you were marrying Lance in a few weeks, I panicked. I don't know who killed Coulton, but I know I didn't. I don't know if my mother killed herself or not, but your father didn't think so. And don't you think your father's accidental death was a bit too convenient?"

"Convenient?" Jo scowled.

"Look at the whole picture, Jo. First, Coulton was shot. Two days later, my mother died of a supposed suicide or accidental overdose. And five years later, after your father—who was a good friend of the Wymers—visited me, he fell from a cliff, hiking a trail he knew like the back of his hand. Seems mighty suspicious."

Jo shook her head. "Dad's death was an accident. Sheriff Padraic believed that for some reason he'd walked off the path. And Denny agreed."

Faulkner knew Denny was an experienced hiker as well. Father and son had hiked most of the Teton Mountain Range. Still, there could have been something the sheriff and Denny had missed. "But were they certain how he fell? I mean, did the sheriff do a full investigation? Check the trail? Look for anything out of the ordinary?"

Jo didn't answer at first, merely stared at Faulkner like he was speaking in a foreign language. She cast her gaze to the floor. "We were all in shock at the time. I didn't drill the sheriff about the investigation. I was too shaken up. My father had just died." She paused for a moment, deep in thought. As she looked up, Faulkner saw that the grief reflected in her eyes before was now replaced with something else . . . something akin to conviction to learn more. "Denny is upstairs. He should be able to answer your questions. I'll go get your breakfast and find out." Jo left.

As Faulkner watched her go, he wondered if he'd done the right thing. He hated making Jo relive such a horrible time in her life. But if Faulkner's guess was anywhere close to the truth, it was better to find out now before another person was killed. He didn't know for sure what was going on, but he believed pretty strongly that the people closest to this mystery were slowly being picked off one by one.

And Faulkner feared that Jo and Rhett were next.

CHAPTER FOUR

As Jo HEADED UP THE stairs, she didn't know what to think. Faulkner being here was messing with her mind, making her doubt everything. Hadn't she sacrificed enough for that man? It had taken her years to get over the hurt and pain of his murder trial and their divorce. And now her license as a vet was in jeopardy for operating on him. But that wasn't enough, no; now he had her doubting her upcoming wedding to Lance and even how her father had died.

Jo thought about Lance. Her love for him hadn't developed because of some misplaced guilt she felt over his brother, Coulton, had it? True, when she'd been young, she'd had a crush on Coulton. And yes, she'd always felt badly that she'd broken up with him to be with Faulkner. But what she'd felt for Faulkner had been true love. They'd been married only two years and were going to have a child when the tragedy happened. And though she knew the whispers behind her back during Faulkner's trial had been vicious and had gone so far as to say that maybe Faulkner had killed Coulton because Jo was actually having Coulton's baby, she knew they were just wicked, horrible rumors that didn't have a grain of truth in them.

But Lance . . . he was different from Coulton. And she hadn't started seeing him until after her father had died. Lance had helped her with her father's estate, had helped her clean out his office, and had been there on nights when she'd felt so utterly alone. No, she loved Lance. But he was going to be really upset with her when he found out she'd helped Faulkner. She knew she'd have to tell him because she couldn't start their marriage out by keeping secrets. However, telling Lance could wait. Right now, getting answers about the day her father died took priority.

Entering the kitchen, Jo found Denny cooking scrambled eggs. He glanced up. "Thought Faulkner could use some protein after his operation.

Don't worry, your mush is on the back burner." He pointed with the spatula to a kettle with a lid on it. Denny made the creamiest brown-sugar-laced oatmeal she'd ever tasted. The eggs he'd been fussing over were done, so he carried the frying pan over to a stoneware plate on a breakfast tray and scooped the fluffy yellowness onto it.

Jo didn't know how she was going to subtly bring up the subject of what happened on the day their father died, but she had to. She opened the fridge, grabbed the ketchup bottle, and proceeded to squirt some on Faulkner's eggs. Years ago he'd liked ketchup on his eggs. She supposed that hadn't changed. She returned the bottle to the fridge. "I need to ask you something, but I don't know how."

Denny put the pan in the sudsy sink water. It sizzled. Steam rose. And then the room fell quiet.

"Where's Rhett?" Jo scanned the open kitchen, small dining area, and living room but didn't see him.

"Getting ready to go with me. Yesterday I promised him we'd hike down to the pirate cave behind Fall Creek Falls. So I thought I might as well take him. That way he'll be gone while you call the police and have them collect Faulkner. With Rhett being his son and all, there might be a scene. I should have tried to drive down the mountain last night to call Sheriff Padraic from the Swan Valley Store."

"It was closed. Besides, the road was in bad shape," Jo said.

"Well, I could take Rhett with me and go call for help now." Denny looked willing and worried.

Jo knew that was what they should do—that's what she'd do if it were anyone else—but Faulkner's story about her father visiting him had her wondering. Plus, she had unfinished business with Faulkner. "No. I don't want Rhett alarmed or scared. I'll call when you leave."

"If you're sure you'll be all right." Denny studied her face.

"Yep. Besides, you can pick some fresh watercress for lunch. Fall Creek has the best." She smiled and reached for the phone to check the dial tone. Still nothing. "It's bound to get fixed in an hour or so." She grabbed a bowl and nestled it over the eggs to keep them warm.

"I won't leave if you feel you're in danger." Denny stared at her. No doubt he was thinking of the gun Faulkner had had with him when he'd arrived.

"I'll be fine. Faulkner's too doped up on meds, plus I tied him up and hid the gun. I'd appreciated it if you took Rhett on an adventure. I don't know what to tell him about his father. I don't even know if I want him to know that Faulkner is his dad." Jo hadn't thought this through. With Faulkner serving a life prison sentence, she'd thought he was forever out of her son's life. So when Rhett had asked about his dad, Jo had told him that even though his father loved him, he was never coming back. She really didn't know what else to say. How did a mother tell her son that his father was convicted of murder? Jo had wanted Rhett to know the part of Faulkner she knew, the good part. And some day she would tell her son the truth, when he was older and would understand. But now was not the time.

"If you're certain." Denny tilted his head, a sign that he wasn't sure at all.

"Yes." Jo didn't want him to doubt.

"So did he tell you how he got shot and why he came here of all places? I mean, this is the first place the police will look." Denny waited for her answer.

She was about to tell him what Faulkner had told her about their father visiting him in jail, but for some reason she felt she shouldn't, which was total nonsense. She needed Denny to confirm that their father really did go see Faulkner in jail.

But . . . if her father hadn't told her, why would he have told her brother? Besides, Denny would have told her already. He wouldn't have kept that a secret. No, Denny didn't know about their father's visit to Faulkner or about whatever their father was looking into in regard to Cassandra's death.

If her father hadn't told Denny, then Jo needed to choose her words wisely. But how was she going to find out what Denny remembered about the investigation of their father's death? An idea came to her. Referring back to Denny's question about how Faulkner got shot and why he'd come here, she said, "A guard shot him. And I'm trying to find out why he came here. That pirate cave behind Fall Creek Falls . . ."

Denny had washed and rinsed the pan before setting it in the drainer. "Yeah. We've been there hundreds of times."

"I know, but I always worry. The river is right there. One slip and Rhett would be washed downstream. I mean, when Dad died . . . well, accidents happen."

Denny pulled the plug in the sink, wiped his hands on a dishcloth, and put his arm around Jo's shoulders. "Faulkner being here has brought all your unpleasant memories to the surface. Don't worry."

She paused a moment, regretting she'd gone down this path, but she had. She was so close to finding out what she needed to know that she forged ahead. "That day when Dad died, did you notice anything unusual? Did the sheriff poke around and investigate?"

Denny's arm dropped from around her. With his big, pawlike hand, he took hers. "Dad was as sure-footed as a mountain goat, but even the most experienced hiker has accidents. After the search-and-rescue team left, Sheriff Padraic spent a whole lot of time on that mountain, checking it over. If you want details, you'll have to talk with him. All I know is after finding Dad . . ." His voice drifted off, and Jo knew he was probably reliving the ordeal. She remained quiet, waiting for her brother to go on. Denny took a deep breath, and his solemn concern lightened. "Don't worry. Rhett will be safe. I'll hold his hand."

She had the answer, but it didn't make her feel better. Not by a long shot.

At that moment, Rhett rushed in. "Did Uncle Denny tell you we're going to see if we can find Captain Hook?"

"Yes, he did. Where's your lucky hat?" Jo always tried to make him wear one in the sun. He wore his jeans with a hole in the right knee and his wrinkly, long-sleeved T-shirt where the faint words *Lost Boys* was sprawled on the chest—his adventure shirt. She'd bought it for him a year ago when they'd gone to Disneyland. The sleeves were now an inch too short, but that was all right. He loved it.

Rhett turned around and nearly ran into Jacob, who always tailed him. Many times, Jo felt the wolf had adopted Rhett as a cub. Rhett skirted around the wolf, anxious to fetch the cowboy hat Lance had given him, and disappeared down the hallway.

Jo turned to Denny. "Captain Hook?"

"What does it hurt?"

Jo chuckled. "Nothing. Just be careful."

"We will. And when I return, we'll have watercress with our sandwiches. I'd better check and make sure we have the other ingredients." Staring in the fridge, he said, "Sure you'll be all right here alone with Faulkner?"

"He's pretty weak. And speaking of Faulkner, I'd better take his breakfast down to him." She picked up the tray.

"And call the sheriff," Denny added.

"As soon as the phone is fixed, that will be my first call." Jo started for the stairs to her clinic below, but all at once, an odd feeling overcame her. She looked at Denny. He stood with the fridge door wide open, staring into it, deep in thought. A trace of guilt and doubt tugged at the corners of his eyes.

Jo knew her brother was probably blaming himself for their father's death. Not wanting him to know she'd seen him during a private moment of contemplation, she hurried downstairs.

* * *

When Jo returned with his breakfast, Faulkner was feeling a little nauseated. "Not sure if I can eat."

"That's understandable." Jo set his breakfast tray on the counter near him then turned her back toward him. Finally, she turned around but avoided making eye contact. Faulkner wanted her to be the one to bring up the subject of her father again, but he knew she was upset.

Jo took a deep breath. "I need to look at your incision." She came to his side.

"So you're the one who operated on me?"

She nodded.

He should have known she'd follow in her father's footsteps. When they'd married, she'd just earned her college degree, and if he remembered correctly, she'd taken a lot of chemistry classes because she was thinking of a degree in medicine. But once she'd become pregnant, she'd decided to put her education on hold for a while.

And then their world had fallen apart. While he'd been in prison, she'd had more than enough time to earn her doctorate.

With small, delicate hands, Jo folded the sheet and blanket away from the bandage. Her eyes widened then squinted as she gently peeled it back.

"Am I going to make it?" Though his stomach was upset and he felt flushed and weak, he knew he'd be all right, but he wanted to hear her say it.

She glanced at him. Her brows bunched together. "Probably."

Her fingers lightly pressed the bandage back in place, stroking his skin at the edge of the tape. Her touch ignited electric sparks that shot through his gut and spun to his vitals.

"You should really try to eat. Instead of mush, Denny cooked scrambled eggs for you. You need the protein." She pulled the sheet over his bandage.

Faulkner couldn't stand waiting to hear what she'd learned. Before she moved, he awkwardly managed to grab her arm even though his wrists were still tied. "Did Denny tell you what happened?" He didn't know what to hope for, but if Denny remembered anything, it could help.

She stared at him long and hard. "Nothing new. But Dad was alone when it happened, and Sheriff Padraic spent a great deal of time searching the mountain."

Disappointed, Faulkner knew the sheriff had missed something. "Still, he was alone. And he'd hiked that trail many times. It doesn't add up."

Jo pulled away from him. "I don't know what to think." She stared at Faulkner. "But I do know that you held me at gunpoint! Why I'm listening to you is beyond me."

"I'd never hurt you." Regret washed over him.

She took the stethoscope from around her neck and fidgeted with it. "Look, Faulkner. I'll take care of you like I do all of my patients until I decide what to do."

"Decide what to do? I thought you had already called the police."

"Couldn't reach them."

Faulkner had that glimmer of hope he'd prayed for, but he had to warn her. "Someone else killed Coulton. If that someone else killed my mother, then killed your father after he visited me, that means *someone* very close to you is a murderer. For your safety and Rhett's, don't tell anyone what I've told you."

She drove her fingers through her long, auburn hair. "Honestly, I don't know who or what to believe. Deep down, underneath the hurt your filing for divorce and turning your back on me and our child caused—and despite the facts presented in court—I've always felt you were innocent. And I would have done everything I could to prove it, but you shut me out. I had to think of our child and how I would provide for us, so I let you go. See, Faulkner, I believed in you even when you stopped believing in us, but I couldn't hang on forever. I thought I knew you . . . but I didn't then, and I don't now."

To hear Jo actually say she thought he was innocent was encouraging. Still, he was confused. "How could you believe I'm innocent and at the same time turn to Lance, who testified against me?"

Jo stared at him, anger building on her face.

Unable to stop himself, Faulkner went on. "How could you turn around and fall for Coulton's little brother?"

Jo's face pinched with surprise like she'd been slapped across the face. "You don't know what you're talking about. And Lance only reported what he saw. In your trial, you admitted that you held the gun and stood over Coulton."

She was right. The prosecutor had tricked him. But Lance had testified as though he'd seen Faulkner pull the trigger. During the trial, Faulkner had been grieving his mother's death and struggling within himself over who he really thought could have killed his stepbrother.

But that was then.

And over the years and especially after Doc had visited him, Faulkner had realized Lance must have been hiding something. Could it be he was covering up for someone else, like Chugger or one of the other ranch hands? But why would he? His own brother had been killed. Yet he had to know more about what happened that night than what he'd told in court. Faulkner didn't trust the man. Never had really, and now after learning about Doc's death, Faulkner was even more worried for Jo and Rhett's safety.

Obviously, Jo felt differently. Faulkner might still have a chance to set things right. But he'd have to choose his words wisely. If he said the wrong thing, any progress he'd made would evaporate. And the problem was he didn't have a whole lot of time. "Jo, let me just say I was pretty messed up back then, but after your father visited me a few years ago, I started rethinking everything about that night and who could have done it and why people said what they did at my trial. You might want to think it over as well."

She stared at him for a moment.

Faulkner figured the best thing he could do was change the subject so she'd mull over what he'd said on her own. "You're a doctor now?"

Jo shrugged and nodded. Looking at the drape around the table where he lay, she said, "I'll move the privacy curtain so you can look out the windows." She tugged them open.

For one elongated minute, Faulkner's gaze darted around the room from one caged animal to another: a tabby cat with bandages around its paws, a pinched-faced raccoon with a wrapped tail, a hawk with a splint on its wing, and a German shepherd with a wrapping around his middle and upper hind leg.

"You're a . . . a . . ."

"Veterinarian." She filled in the word and smiled.

Faulkner was speechless. He couldn't remember her ever saying that she wanted to become a vet. Sure, he knew she had a soft spot when it came to animals, but he'd thought it was her way of balancing out his dislike for them. He never dreamed she had a desire to care for and nurture the creatures.

She pulled keys from her pocket, unlocked a medicine cabinet, took down a small bottle, and closed the door. Filling a syringe with liquid from the bottle, she crossed to the German shepherd's cage and opened it. Jo stroked the dog's head. With tender care, she gave the animal a shot. The dog didn't yelp or whine. After pulling out the needle, she gave the mutt a loving pat. Jo looked like she knew what she was doing, but Faulkner had his concerns.

"Are vets allowed to operate on humans?" He really didn't think so.

"Maybe I should have let you bleed to death." She came to stand beside him, a little smirk on her face.

"You were tempted, weren't you?" He smiled up at her, gauging her reaction.

She tilted her head. "Of course not."

"Well, my death would have made many people happy. Why did you save me, Jo?" He'd put the joking aside for a moment. He wanted to know, needed to know.

She stared at him with no discernible expression on her sculptured face. Finally, she said, "I can't stand to see any animal . . . or person in pain. Even you."

Faulkner raised his head and looked at the other critters. "Too bad your patients can't appreciate your bedside manner the way I do."

She nodded to the German shepherd. "As a matter of fact, I have a very good bedside manner. Just ask Champ. By the way, he's Lance's dog." She glanced at Faulkner. He could see in her eyes that she was gauging his reaction.

Lance's very name rankled him. The moment of light humor threatened to disappear, but he held his tongue and looked up at the ceiling.

"Yesterday, before the rodeo, I removed a tumor from Champ's thigh and neutered him. He's past his prime. Old age is his main problem. Do you still want your breakfast? It's probably cold." She went to the counter where the tray waited.

Clearing his throat and faking concern, Faulkner glanced down at his sheets. "Neutering . . . isn't standard procedure, is it?" A smile tugged at the corners of his mouth. He so wanted to see her smile, needed to see her smile. Their previous conversation had been too intense.

Her brow arched. "Actually, with humans who hold me at gunpoint"— her eyes lit up—"I operate on them for free. They're beholden to me forever." She innocently blinked.

As usual, Jo had been able to switch from a topic of high emotion to nearly a smile. He'd missed her so much. He was encouraged because this meant that underneath the bluster, she still had feelings for him. It meant she was comfortable being with him again.

And it meant that he might be able to repair the damage of the past.

CHAPTER FIVE

BEFORE TENDING TO THE ANIMALS in the stable, Jo tried the phone once again. Still no dial tone. To take her mind off of Faulkner and his crazy claim that her father may have been murdered, she quickly set to work taking off the old dressing on a pregnant Hereford's barbed-wire wounds. The cuts were deep on the animal's legs. Jo was hopeful the medicated ointment she'd applied to the sterile dressing would stop infection from setting in. But just in case, she wanted to keep the animal under her care for a while. The Beasley ranch was struggling, and they needed every cow of their herd.

Leaving the Hereford, Jo turned her attention to the fawn in the next stall. Grabbing a new fly trap from her workbench, Jo pushed open the gate. This pen was reinforced with chicken-coop wire to keep the little fawn safe. Too bad she couldn't put Faulkner in a pen like this until . . . until what? He'd already been in jail for seven years, and nothing had been solved. During those years, Jo'd had no idea that Cassandra, Faulkner's mother, could have been murdered. And she'd never suspected foul play in her own father's death.

Jo would go crazy trying to figure this out. She listened to see if she could hear Faulkner stirring. No sounds from the clinic above. She hoped he was asleep. She unhooked the old fly trap hanging from a tall stall post and tossed it in the garbage on the other side, then she hooked up the new one. The fawn walked over to her. "You're such a pretty girl, Argi." Flies seemed especially fond of the deer, as if they were picking on the little thing for being alone in the world.

Faulkner came to mind again. He was alone in the world. *Except for me . . . and his son.* She couldn't think like that. Trying to stay focused on the job at hand, she rubbed the fawn's soft coat. This little one was Rhett's favorite animal. Rhett had inherited her love of animals, but she realized now that she'd had a blind eye to traits he may have inherited from Faulkner. What would Rhett think if she told him the strange man he'd seen on her surgery table was his father? Her son's life would change forever. Could he handle knowing that his father was an escaped prisoner? And that he'd been convicted of killing Lance's brother?

She knew the answer. She couldn't put her son through that. The best thing for Rhett was for Jo to call the sheriff and have Faulkner picked up and taken out of their lives. That was the only answer. Jo would further investigate her father's death on her own, and she'd see what she could find out about Cassandra's death as well, but Faulkner had to leave. Jo'd already done enough for him.

The fawn nuzzled her hand. Jo looked down. When the little doe had come under her care, Jo had stayed up many nights giving the animal extra feedings of milk laced with Karo syrup and pabulum in an empty brandy bottle topped with a lamb's nipple. Now energy beamed from the fawn's dark brown, soulful eyes. She was getting better but would need sunshine and exercise soon. Yes, sunshine would be good for Argi.

Jo wondered if Faulkner had been able to enjoy much sunshine in the last seven years. She really didn't want to think about his life in prison. Instead, she peered out the stable doors. She would ask Denny to build a pen around that old, craggy willow tree in the meadow not far from the house. The fawn could nibble at the dragging branches and prune them.

Argi nuzzled Jo's hip pocket for the treat hidden there. "Pushy today, are we?" She dug out the sandwich bag she had filled with bite-size chunks of carrots and miniature marshmallows. Rhett usually gave them to the fawn, but he wasn't here. After emptying the plastic bag into her hand, Jo let Argi lip up the tasty treat.

Giving the fawn a pat on the forehead, Jo slid through the gate, closing it behind her. Argi blinked up at her, standing on spindly legs that were growing stronger each day. Jo had prepared a pan of formula before coming down and had let it cool while she worked on the Hereford and pampered the fawn. It should be ready now.

She scooted the pan under the stall door where Argi could get to it. Jo had taught the animal how to drink by pouring milk over a slice of whole wheat bread. Argi had sucked the bread and soon learned that it was an easy and quick way to drink. She now hungrily drank without the bread.

Like a river fly drawn to a porch light, Jo's thoughts returned to the man upstairs in her clinic. She hoped Faulkner was still asleep. He'd heal faster with rest.

She chuckled as she thought of the look on his face when she'd pulled the privacy curtain from around his table. He really hated being stuck in there with the animals. This morning, weak from the operation, he had appeared vulnerable. She much preferred the vulnerable Faulkner. When he'd smiled at her and asked if neutering was standard procedure, the years of being apart had melted away.

Such a mirage.

But nice while it had lasted.

She heard Apollo whiny. He wasn't in his stall. Jo craned her head to peer outside. The pampered horse had gone to the outside part of his corral. Apollo had paid his dues living his prime on the rodeo circuit. When the animal had broken his right front leg, Lance had told her to put the horse down, but she was able to convince him she could save the animal. Lance told her that if she did, she could keep him because the horse would no longer be fit to perform for a rodeo. That was over a year ago. Apollo got better and, despite his weakened leg, had become a fine trail horse.

The distant sound of a truck chugging up the road drew Jo's attention. Lance's four-wheel-drive Dodge rounded the bend. Dang! She'd forgotten that he'd said he would stop by to check on Champ. She should have called him. But with the phone out of order, she couldn't have. What was she going to do? With Faulkner feeling the way he did about Lance, things could get out of control real fast.

Plus, if Lance saw that she'd helped Faulkner, he'd never understand. Somehow, she was going to have to keep the two of them separated.

* * *

Faulkner heard a car pull up outside. Had Jo called the sheriff? But she'd said the phones weren't working, so that meant she had company. If someone found him and learned that she'd helped him, she'd be in a world of trouble. He had to get out of there.

He frantically tugged at the leash tied around his wrists. Jerking at the nylon, he tried to reach the knots, but his fingertips barely touched them. He twisted the leash this way and that. It felt a little loose, but the knots held true. Jo's medical training had taught her well how to tie good knots. He needed something to cut it off.

He rolled onto his side, threw his legs over the edge, and used sheer willpower to ignore the pain in his gut and force himself to sit upright. The room swirled like a blur of speeding race cars.

Easing his bare feet onto the cold tiles, he stood. His covers fell in a pile below him on the floor. Dressed in only his briefs, he shivered as gooseflesh rippled his skin. Idaho seemed to always be cold, even in August. He grabbed the IV cart and started to cross the room. Dizziness made him feel like he was spinning out of control, but he managed to reach the counter and grabbed hold until the motion stopped.

He stared at the leash binding his wrists. He had to get rid of it. Faulkner jerked open the top drawer. All he could see were rolls of paper towels, wipe-ups, and cotton swabs. He rifled through them and found scissors at the bottom. Taking the handle in one hand, he was able to use his fingers to open the blades but couldn't quite reach the leash.

As he worked, Faulkner kept listening, afraid that at any moment someone would come up the stairs. He had to hurry. Knuckling the handles until the blades were wide open, he turned them to leverage one sharp side to the nylon. He sawed the scissors back and forth, sometimes jabbing himself; still, he continued until he finally broke free. The leash dropped to the floor.

Faulkner yanked on the IV tubing, pulling the needle out of his arm. Again without warning, the room swirled.

He wasn't going to get very far in this condition. Maybe Jo kept something in the cupboard that could help him. She had unlocked the medicine chest to get drugs for the dog. Had she locked it when she'd finished? Grabbing the handle, he wrenched the cupboard door open. Luck had finally smiled down on him.

He pilfered through the bottles: amoxicillin, rimadyl, and something else he couldn't read. He didn't think any of these would help his dizziness. He reached far into the back and touched a gun.

His gun!

He had leverage now. If someone found him, he could at least make it look like Jo hadn't had a choice in helping him. Now he needed clothes.

He blinked and blinked again until his vision cleared. He noticed a closet just past the wall of animal cages and thought he might find clothes in there. With his vision somewhat cleared, he cautiously walked past the animal cages. Lance's dog was sleeping. The other critters quietly watched Faulkner's progress. They knew a shifty-eyed bandit when they saw one.

Reaching the closet, Faulkner tried to turn the knob. Locked. Of course, this she locked. Glancing down at his bandage, he saw a small spot of blood that hadn't been there before.

Great! Please, God. You know this is a worthy cause. I'm trying the best I can, but I need help.

* * *

"Did you know your phone isn't working?" Lance asked Jo as soon as the soles of his Tony Lamas hit the concrete on her driveway.

She should tell Lance she had Faulkner upstairs. Despite what Faulkner thought, Lance was a reasonable person. Yet she hesitated. Faulkner had looked so betrayed awhile ago when he'd asked her how she could turn to Lance after his testimony had convicted him. She'd defended herself, but she knew her words hurt him. Deep in her soul she believed that Faulkner and Lance could not be in the same room or something very bad would happen. Too much history, too much turmoil lay between the two men. And with Lance's hot temper, anything could happen.

He had many redeeming qualities, but expecting him to keep his cool when he found out that she'd helped the man he believed killed his brother was asking too much. It would be best for everyone if she could somehow get Lance to leave without finding Faulkner. Then, when her phone was working, Jo would call the sheriff to let him deal with the law and order of things.

Not knowing what to say and steeling herself for the lecture that would surely follow, Jo grabbed a pitchfork and speared a clump of hay, tossing it over the wood fence for Apollo. The horse saw what she was doing and moseyed into the stable from the outside corral, shaking his long black mane.

If Jo told Lance his dog was doing well, he may leave. "Yeah, I know about my phone. By the way, Champ is doing fine."

"Good. But I also drove over to tell you some bad news." Lance came to stand in front of her.

His sad cowboy eyes stared down on her, and for a moment, Jo worried that something really awful had happened. "What is it?"

"Yesterday, I was so busy getting the stock ready for the rodeo that I didn't see Dad come home from town. Before I left, I went in to get him so we could leave. He was drunk and could hardly walk. I left him to sleep it off in the den."

"I wondered where he was. Is he all right?"

"Well, this morning he sobered up. At breakfast he told me that while he had been in town, he heard that Branson Faulkner had escaped prison." Lance pushed his cowboy hat to the back of his head. "So much for maximum security. You'd think Sheriff Padraic would have called or driven out to tell us. Anyway, I told Dad Faulkner was probably halfway to Canada by now. He's still worried that he might come here."

"Is that why he got drunk?" Jo wanted Lance to remain focused on his father, then maybe he wouldn't dwell on Faulkner.

"What can I say? Since Coulton and Cassandra died, it's like he picked up drinking where Cassandra left off. Budweiser™ has become his best friend." Lance gave a deep sigh. "Since you rarely turn on your TV, I wanted you to know about Faulkner so you would be careful. If he comes around . . ." Lance didn't finish and grew quiet, his eyes fixed as if bad memories flickered before him.

Regaining his composure, Lance continued. "I didn't want to worry Dad, but Faulkner could very well be on his way here." He looked around the stable/garage, obviously searching for the fugitive behind her rusted Ford, the snow blower, or the small stack of hay near the stalls.

"Well, I've moved around a lot going to college and establishing my clinic. He'd have no idea where to find me." Jo drew Lance's attention back to her. "And since he divorced me, I really don't think we need to worry."

"Just because he divorced you doesn't mean he quit loving you." Lance drew her into his arms, pitchfork and all. "I'd love you no matter what." He leaned over and kissed her lips. The kiss grew hard, demanding. Feeling guilty for her secrets, she wanted to pull away but couldn't.

A noise came from overhead.

Faulkner?

Jo stepped back from Lance's embrace and, hiding her fear behind a teasing smile, said, "Rhett could walk in." She tried to act coy to lighten the mood. Her ears were tuned to any sound from overhead.

"I know you don't want Rhett to see us kissing, but, babe—" He stepped closer. "When we're married, things are gonna change. He's going to see it 'cause I plan to plant a hundred kisses on you a day."

Jo smiled, knowing that's what Lance expected, but she also held her breath, worried that at any moment her world could erupt into total chaos. She glanced up and saw desire in Lance's eyes. Standing there, staring at him, knowing Faulkner was in her clinic, she felt conflicted, confused, and bewildered. She was walking a tightrope between right and wrong, old feelings and loyalties verses new feelings and loyalties. At the moment, she couldn't separate them. Neither made sense.

But the time to contemplate such emotions was not now. She had to get Lance in his truck and down the road. She could deal with these issues later when the two men in her life—the two enemies that would gladly beat each other to a pulp—were miles apart. Wanting to act nonchalant, Jo speared the last of the hay bale and dropped it over the stall of the injured Hereford.

Lance quickly fetched another bale from the stack nearby. "If Branson Faulkner so much as shows his face in Swan Valley, I'll . . ." He stared at Jo as though rethinking what he was about to say. "Well, I'll make him sorry he was ever born. If he turns up here, call me."

Jo's blood ran cold. She had the distinct feeling he was about to say he'd kill Faulkner . . . and that it wasn't just talk.

All at once, she was very grateful she hadn't told Lance that Faulkner was upstairs. The urgency to get Lance on his way became dire. Trying to appear normal and not at all upset, Jo said, "Until my phone is working again, I can't call anyone. But when it's fixed, and if I see Faulkner, shouldn't I call Sheriff Padraic?"

"Well, of course, but call me right after. I'd give anything to get my hands on him." Lance pulled out his pocketknife and cut the twine holding the bale together. "By the way, Seth Dutson called, said he had a bull he thought could replace Loco, so all is well, and you don't need to worry."

"That's good news." Jo was glad the topic had changed. Lance went on. "If it's the one I've heard about, this bull's going to be an even bigger draw than that old cantankerous Brahma."

About to tell him that was great and that she'd see him later in the day because she needed to get going, Jo again thought of what Faulkner had said about rethinking things. She couldn't help but wonder where Lance had found the money to buy the bull. "The way you talked last night, the rodeo was broke. Did you win the lottery or something?"

Lance pulled the twine from beneath the bale, rolled it into a ball, and threw it in the garbage barrel next to the stall. "Well, Dad had a little savings. I put his money with mine for the bull. We might not be able to have as nice a honeymoon as I'd hoped, but we're fine."

Jo smiled and felt guilty for her moment of doubt. She tossed more hay into the cow's stall. The critter looked like she knew Jo's secret and was waiting to see what would happen next."

Lance stopped a moment. "But something else is eating at Dad. He'll tell me sooner or later. I hate it when he drinks. Happens every time something reminds him of what he's lost. Wish he could remember he still has one son."

Jo patted Lance's arm. When he talked like that, he reminded her of a little boy wanting to be loved. Her doubts about him nearly vanished. She wanted to give Lance the love he craved, but she couldn't right now. She had to get him on his way. If she timed this right and the phone was working, she could call the sheriff a little while after Lance left and then call

Lance after the sheriff collected Faulkner. This could still work out without anyone getting upset or hurt.

"You said Champ was fine. I wanted to take him home." Lance's forehead crinkled with worry.

"I'd like to keep him another day. While I was operating on his leg, I neutered him."

Right away, anger flatlined the crease of concern on Lance's brow.

Defending her medical decision, Jo said, "That tumor was too close to his reproductive organs. Champ is too old for breeding anyway. I knew you wouldn't want to take any chances with his life."

"You have a way with your patients." He reached for her.

Jo dodged his embrace and, with a teasing smile, headed for the stable doors, hoping Lance would follow her to his truck.

He turned in the opposite direction. "I want to see the old mutt before I go."

"I don't think—"

Lance was already bounding up the stairs.

CHAPTER SIX

LANCE REACHED THE TOP STEP, opened the door, and entered the clinic before Jo could stop him. She braced herself for an explosion, certain he would see Faulkner on the surgery table. But instead, Lance walked in as calm as could be. Jo followed and was surprised to find that the privacy curtain had been pulled around the table, hiding everything in that section of the clinic.

That meant Faulkner had somehow gotten up. Was he still behind the curtain or somewhere else? Jo stared toward her office, expecting to see Faulkner, but saw only her desk and chair. She quickly glanced about and couldn't see him anywhere. The animals in their cages were oddly quiet.

"What's the curtain pulled for?" Lance asked on his way to the cage where Champ was waiting.

"I have a project I didn't want Rhett to see." Jo kept her fingers crossed that Lance wouldn't want to look.

"Dissecting a frog or something?" He stopped in front of Champ's cage. The dog struggled to stand but gave up and laid down, slowly wagging his tail.

"Something like that." Jo opened the cage. "Champ's happy to see you."

Lance grinned and reached inside to pet his dog.

"He's pretty weak." Jo's eyes darted to the white drape. At this angle, she saw Faulkner's dirty-socked feet and hairy legs beneath the curtain. He was near the counter, away from the drape's edge. Her gaze slid up to the mesh, see-through material at the top, and she noticed the medicine cabinet was open. That's where she'd stashed Faulkner's gun. She'd forgotten to lock it after getting Champ's medicine. Fear squeezed her throat, nearly choking her. She forced herself to turn her attention to Lance, all the while knowing that Faulkner could step out from behind the curtain at any moment.

"Champ'll get stronger at the ranch than he will in this cage." Lance smiled at her and opened the wire door, oblivious to the drama going on behind him. "Besides, and I know this sounds strange, but I think Dad needs Champ. The dog will help him not think of Faulkner and where he could and couldn't be."

Had Faulkner heard him? Of course he had. Stupid question. So now he knew that Lance and his father were aware of his escape. Hot panic washed through Jo, filling her from the inside out like a river bursting its banks. What could she do or say? She stared at Lance, trying to give him her full attention.

He scooped the German shepherd into his arms. "Come on, boy. I'm taking you home." Lance glanced at Jo. "Remember, if you see Faulkner, call me—I mean, call the sheriff and then call me."

She nodded.

Carrying the large dog in his arms, Lance started for the stairs, stopped, and swung around to face Jo and the curtain. "But your phone isn't working. Take my cell phone out of my pocket."

Horrified that he'd stopped and worried that he might see Faulkner's feet, she rushed to Lance, blocking his view. "Cells don't work here."

"I use a cell company that has awesome coverage. It should work anywhere." Lance waited patiently.

Jo guided him around so he wasn't facing the curtain and tried to ease the phone from his back pocket. Her stiff fingers slipped on the small phone, making it difficult for her to grasp.

"Need some help?" Lance asked.

Panicked, she shoved her hand inside and grabbed the phone and his bottom at the same time.

Lance chuckled as Jo pulled the phone out. "Now you come onto me, while my arms are full with Champ."

"I like to keep you on your toes." Jo forced a smile. "Besides, it was deep in your pocket."

The German shepherd whimpered, reminding Jo that she needed to send meds home with Lance. However, the medicine was behind the curtain, where Faulkner was.

Still, she had to risk it. She couldn't let the animal suffer. "Go ahead downstairs. I'm going to grab some pain meds for Champ."

"I'll wait." Lance gave her a playful grin. "I like to watch you walk."

Not knowing what to say, she headed for the curtain.

* * *

Heat surged through Faulkner as he fought off the pain. Sweat soaked him. He wrapped his fingers around the hard handle of the gun. He didn't know how much longer he could stand without toppling over. Using sheer willpower, he forced himself to focus on the curtain and who would step around it. It seemed to take forever, just like Jo and Lance's entire conversation.

When he'd heard them coming up the stairs, Faulkner knew someone was with Jo. Pure adrenaline had raced through him as he managed to hide behind the curtain. If he'd been stronger, Faulkner would have stepped out in the open and faced the man who had destroyed his life.

Jo and Lance's voices had muted to muffled sounds as old emotions surged through Faulkner. Lance's testimony in court had stolen Faulkner's life and now even the woman he loved.

The time to act was now.

Faulkner stepped toward the curtain, but pain hit him head on, nearly spinning him out of control. He stared at the bandage on his side. More blood oozed from it. His gaze moved to his briefs and naked legs. Lance would see him weak and bleeding. Even though Faulkner had a gun, too much could go wrong.

He heard footfalls headed toward him.

Was it Lance or Jo?

His hand that held the gun threatened to shake, yet he held the trembling in check. Gaining control of his labored breathing, he watched the hem of the curtain move slightly.

A shadow drifted across the drape. He tightened his grip on the gun handle. And then Jo walked around the curtain instead of pushing it aside. She gasped and stared at the weapon in his hand.

"You all right?" Lance was coming.

Jo glowered at Faulkner then poked her head around the drape. "Fine. I left something out is all."

"Just what do you have back there?" By the sound of his voice, Lance was moving even closer.

"Well, maybe the project I'm working on is a wedding present for you. Did you ever think of that?" Jo teased.

"I see. A top-secret gift for me, huh?" Lance stopped.

"Yes, top secret," Jo agreed. "I think you'd better get Champ to the truck. Go ahead. I'll meet you there."

"I can wait, but hurry. This dog's heavier than he looks."

Jo pulled the drape closed and scooted past Faulkner to the cabinet. He eased the gun down, pointing it to the floor.

"I gave Champ a shot this morning," she said loudly to Lance. "But by tonight, he's going to be hurting." She grabbed a bottle of pills, glared a warning at Faulkner to stay put, and left him staring after her as she walked around the curtain again.

"He won't take a pill," Lance said.

Feeling woozy, Faulkner leaned against the counter. His vision swirled like he'd been rolled end over end. He stared at the surgical table that quickly became two, then three, then blurred with too many to count. At any moment, he was going to collapse. But he couldn't, not with Lance standing so close.

"Wrap the pill with bacon. He'll eat it." Jo's voice drifted away. They must have been going downstairs. Faulkner prayed he could hold on long enough to tell Jo he had to leave. His being here was putting her and his son in danger.

* * *

Jo waited until she saw Lance's truck disappear around the bend before she hightailed it back up the stairs. She took the steps two at a time and rushed to the curtain, flinging it back.

Faulkner stood beside the examination table. His broad shoulders slumped, his head hung until his straggly beard touched his chest. Though his body was one lean, hard muscle, at the moment, he looked weaker than a newborn calf. His left hand covered his wound. She could see between his fingers that the dressing was bloody. She must have missed something in surgery, either that or he'd pulled out his stitches.

Slowly, he looked up and raised the gun, pointing it at her. A startled nerve prickled her upper lip. Faulkner looked like a crazy person with his wild hair, beard, and mustache. He was clearly distraught. She knew he'd never shoot her. Trying to comfort him as she would a cornered bear, she said, "He's gone. Put the gun down."

Faulkner's arm quivered. Still, he kept his aim on her. "Can't. After I'm gone you need to truthfully say I held a gun on you."

His cheeks were flushed. His eyes red-rimmed. Jo was amazed he could stand.

"My being here is putting you and Rhett in danger. Get my clothes." He shakily motioned with the weapon, demanding she take action.

Jo willed herself to ignore the revolver and stared at him. "Faulkner, you need to stop this foolishness and lie down."

"Get my clothes!" He took a couple of steps then swayed against the table, pushing his pillow to the floor. He was growing weaker by the second. If she kept him talking, he might abandon this notion of leaving.

She picked up the pillow. "Let me look at the wound. You're bleeding. You might have torn your stitches."

Faulkner sucked in a long breath. "If Lance had found me here . . ." He didn't finish his statement. With determination on his face, he stared straight into her eyes. "After everything that has happened, how could you get involved with him, of all people?"

Jo racked her mind, trying to find the right explanation—something that would make sense—but couldn't. "It isn't what you think. We actually didn't start dating until after Dad died. Lance helped Denny and me so much with Dad's funeral and settling his estate. And Rhett, well you should see Lance with . . ."

Pain reflected in Faulkner's eyes, and Jo knew it wasn't from his wound. This pain was much more than that. For the first time, Jo realized that Faulkner deeply cared for his child. It was probably tearing him up inside knowing Lance was going to be the father he couldn't be. She strangely felt ashamed, even disloyal. But there were all of those nights she'd cried herself to sleep, all of those nights she'd stayed up with a fussy baby, and all the times she'd yearned for help parenting her child—the child Faulkner had given up without even a fight.

How dare he turn this around on her. How dare he aim a gun at her even if he was only trying to give her an alibi with the police. "Criminey sakes, Faulkner. You were the one who pushed us away. Rhett needs a father, and I need a husband."

Faulkner grimaced and clung to the table with one hand. The hand holding the gun fell to his side. "Is your bed lonely?"

"Excuse me! Whether my bed is lonely or not is none of your business."

"You're right." He hung his head. "It isn't my business. Just hearing you talking with Lance . . . well, it made me jealous. Add that to the pain . . ."

The contrite expression on Faulkner's face dissipated her anger. She might as well tell him the truth. "Since our divorce, I haven't been with another man. I couldn't open myself up to the hurt that might follow."

His caring eyes fixed her in his gaze.

"You broke my heart, and even though I love someone else now, I still care for you and believe you're innocent." Telling Faulkner her deepest thoughts was hard, but Jo felt she had to.

"You said that before. If you truly believe I'm innocent, who do you think shot Coulton? A stranger?" His breathing grew more labored.

"Yes. Do you read the papers? It happens. Some creep sees a big ranch and decides to rob it." Rubbing her temple, Jo chuckled. "Of course you read the paper. That's how you found out about my engagement."

Faulkner teetered a little but still stared at her like she was an anomaly.

"Please, Faulkner, let me see to your wound." She reached out to him.

But he drew the gun between them. Backing off, she glanced at the clock on the wall. Denny and Rhett would be returning soon. And though Rhett didn't know Faulkner was his father, some day he would. She didn't want Rhett's only memory of his father to be of Faulkner holding a gun on her. If she gave Faulkner what he wanted, he wouldn't get far in the shape he was in. She'd thrown away his bloody prison uniform, and Denny's clothes would never fit him; they'd be too big. But she did have clothes that might work. "I kept some of Dad's things in his old travel trunk downstairs in the garage."

Faulkner motioned for her to lead the way. "I'll follow." He staggered as he stepped away from the support of the table. Righting himself, he kept the gun's barrel aimed at her. "Get moving."

Jo did what she was told but talked over her shoulder. "Faulkner, you heard Lance. They're looking for you. Why don't we call the authorities? You could turn yourself in." She stopped at the head of the stairs, hoping he'd get close enough that she could knock the gun out of his hand, but he didn't.

He stopped a good five feet behind her. "Time's running out. Move it."

She started down the stairs, still talking. "You can't confront Lance and his father as weak as you are." She glanced back to find Faulkner still following, gripping the handrail tightly. "You can barely walk. Lance will kill you."

He motioned with the gun. "This will make him listen."

Jo didn't know what to say. She hoped to find something at the bottom of the stairs that she could use to stop him. A broom? A shovel? Anything to knock the gun out of his hand. Her truck blocked her view, but she could see that the back door was open. The garage doors were open as well. In her hurry to return upstairs, she'd forgotten to close them. She spied the pitchfork leaning against Apollo's stall, a good twenty feet away. She'd have to be quick.

"Wait up." Faulkner gasped as he reached the last stair.

Again her thoughts returned to giving in to his demands because he wasn't going to get far in his condition. Resolved that she would have to get the clothes, she went beneath the stairs to the alcove where she'd stored her father's trunk.

A pile of dirty gunnysacks sat on top of the trunk. Jo shoved the sacks off. Dust billowed in the air, making her cough. Once the air cleared, she fumbled with the latch. It had rusted and didn't budge.

"Come on. What's taking so long?"

She grabbed hold of the latch, gave it a hard shove, and the hitch popped open. Ornate hinges creaked as Jo pushed the wooden lid up. The musty smell of old clothes and mothballs breathed out. She hadn't been in here since she'd packed away her father's belongings two years ago. She found fond memories closed within: her father's sailor uniform, sepia photos of her father and mother when they were young, yellowed love letters, and even papers from his desk. Jo had been unable to part with things his hands had touched.

Finally, she found a pair of button-fly jeans and a flannel shirt she'd loved seeing her father wear. She dug farther down and came across a pair of black socks and her father's old, scarred work boots. She bundled the clothes to her, stepped over the gunnysacks, and made her way to Faulkner. "They smell musty, but maybe after you wear them for a while, they'll air out."

Faulkner motioned with the gun to a sack of grain. "Just set them on top and move away slowly."

Jo did what she was told.

He carefully laid the gun on another nearby grain sack. She wondered if she could snatch it away.

"Don't!" He had been watching her. He grabbed the faded jeans and, leaning against the wall, jerked them on. His eyes pleaded with her to just let him go and not cause a scene. Next, he tugged on the shirt. The red and brown plaid flannel she'd seen her father wear so often brought a catch to her throat. Faulkner struggled with the socks, but once he got them on, he stepped into the boots. Strands of black hair stuck to his sweat-dampened forehead. His breathing was labored, his cheeks flushed. Finished dressing, he grabbed the gun again. "As soon as I'm gone, use Lance's cell and call the police. That will exonerate you from any of this."

"Faulkner, please stay."

"Sorry, but I have to leave, for you and for Rhett."

Jo moved closer, blocking his path. "Don't do something stupid. Let me talk to the sheriff. Once he hears that my father thought your mother was murdered, it will catch his attention. But we'll never find out the truth if you leave. It will only make matters worse."

"You've forgotten that Sheriff Padraic helped convict me." Faulkner motioned with the revolver for her to step back.

For one mindless moment, bravery propelled her to trust her instincts. Jo reached out and took hold of Faulkner's gun hand. She stared at him, praying that she'd done the right thing. "I won't let you go."

Astonishment distorted his sad eyes.

"I worked hard patching you up last night. You owe me. And you owe your son." She stared intently at him.

His breath grew raspy. His dark pupils dilated with confusion and then need. Suddenly, his arm encircled her and pulled her against him. His long beard and mustache brushed her face as his lips claimed hers. The kiss became urgent, demanding, hungry for affection. A flurry of forgotten love fluttered through her limbs, weakening her knees. The pressure of the kiss gentled as his hand rubbed up her back.

In the distance came voices.

Rhett's childish laughter.

Denny's patient reply.

Faulkner pulled back. "I owe my son the truth. The Wymers know more than they're saying. And if it kills me to find out what it is, so be it." He stepped away and started to leave.

Jo had to stop him. Out of the corner of her eye, she saw his gun hand again. Without a second thought, she hit his arm, trying to knock the weapon out of his hold.

He jerked her around, pinning her in a headlock. Her back pressed against his flat stomach. His ragged breath fanned the side of her face.

His lips brushed her ear as he said, "Jo, you're a lot of trouble."

"So are you," she replied, defiant to the end.

He kissed her ear, softly, gently. Like a ghostly whisper, he said, "Have a good life."

Before she realized what had happened, he had set her free and disappeared through the back door.

CHAPTER SEVEN

Jo's lips throbbed, still moist from Faulkner's kiss. Her skin felt flushed from unexpected emotions, but frustration soon chased it all away. Faulkner was going to get himself killed. Or worse, if he happened to have strength enough to reach the Wymers' place, he was going to kill Lance or Edward. She had to do something.

"I'm going to show Mom!" Rhett dashed into the stable, making a beeline for the stairs. He didn't see her in the shadows.

"Show me what?" Jo stepped out and tried to sound excited and enthusiastic, while behind her words she was tortured with worry.

Rhett held out his little-boy hand, showing her a small brown garter snake that curled around his index finger. Its head bobbed here and there, its tongue flicking in and out.

Startled, Jo reared back. She wasn't afraid of snakes, but if she had to pick one critter she didn't like, snakes would be the one. Putting on her "good mother" mask, she said, "Wow! Where did you find that?" She smiled down on her son, who beamed with pride.

"On the road out there." The snake slithered up Rhett's arm to his elbow. He caught it with his other hand.

"You better put him back. He's a baby. His momma will be looking for him."

"Can't I keep him? I could put him in Grandpa's old aquarium. The one you never use."

Jo squatted down to eye level. "If you were a snake, would you want to be with your family enjoying the forest or placed in a stinky old aquarium?" The thought of Faulkner in prison flashed through her mind.

Denny walked in. His boots and pants were wet from gathering watercress, but his bag was full of the spicy green leafy plants. "I told him to leave the snake alone, but he insisted that you would want to see it."

"Well, I'm glad I did, but Rhett, you have to let it go. It would be torture for the snake to keep him inside with us."

Denny gave her a skeptical look, and she knew he was wondering if it would be torture for the snake or for her. He winked at Jo. "Come on, squirt. Go put the snake back, then you can help me rustle up some lunch."

With slumped shoulders, the boy walked out to the driveway. Denny trailed after him, ever the devoted uncle.

Jo numbly stumbled upstairs to the clinic, Faulkner's bearded face still fresh on her mind. Was she crazy? Had she lost all common sense? She must have. That was the only explanation for why she'd taken such a risk by grabbing his hand. And then Faulkner's warm, demanding embrace and the taste of his kiss . . .

Oh, how she'd missed him. Guilt bubbled up. What was wrong with her? *Faulkner is my ex-husband. I'm going to marry Lance.* Yet, she couldn't forget Faulkner's breath on her cheek.

She moved toward the phone on her desk. Surely it was connected by now. If not, she had Lance's phone. She had to call Sheriff Padraic.

But deep down she knew she couldn't.

Besides, Faulkner would never make it to the Wymers'. Even though his stamina was extraordinary, he couldn't walk fifteen miles. No man in his condition could walk that far. And he wouldn't risk hitchhiking.

She glanced at the empty surgery table, the covers rumpled on the floor and the pillow lying where his head had been. Faulkner'd had bloodhound determination in his gaze as he'd stood there. Selfish determination couldn't propel him to get up and leave. But the need to protect his family, to clear his name, and to find the true murderer had. Pain must remind him of all he'd lost and all that he stood to gain.

Again, Jo thought of calling the sheriff. She imagined Faulkner's eyes shining black as flint, pleading with her to understand and asking her for help. If she spoke with him again, she was going to do all she could to convince him to turn himself in. That would be the best thing to do in this case. But in the meantime . . . she had to do all she could to help him.

She couldn't let him down, not again. Jo couldn't turn her back on him any more than she could an injured badger—he might snarl and growl, but he needed her.

* * *

Pushing beyond his limit, Faulkner ran on. His flannel shirt grew moist with sweat. His pants were soaked from the wet foliage after last night's downpour.

His vision swirled. Out of nowhere, trees appeared in front of him. Ruts and rocks tripped him. The jarring tugged at his wound.

He pressed on.

All he could think about was putting distance between Jo and him. Before facing off with the Wymers, he intended to find a place to hole up and regain his strength.

Desperate for a drink, he followed a deer trail to a creek, but a strong sulfur smell hung in the air. He crawled on all fours to the edge, where he noticed that the streambed appeared white, which he thought was odd. And when he cupped the water into his hand, it felt warm. No matter how thirsty he was, he couldn't drink it. It was a hot spring. The white coloring under the water was calcium carbonate coating the vegetation and rocks.

The rumble of an automobile trying to drive up the muddy road drew his attention. He didn't realize he'd come so close to the road that led up to Jo's place. Rolling into the cover of chokecherry bushes, he positioned himself so he could watch. The sheriff's SUV stopped by a Dodge truck. Faulkner could barely hear the voices. But he knew immediately that one of them was Lance's.

"Not there . . ." Faulkner managed to hear.

The sheriff said something else Faulkner couldn't make out. And then the SUV and truck parted ways. Sheriff Padraic was headed toward Jo's. Had she called him already? Faulkner'd told her to call. He had hoped she wouldn't, or rather couldn't. Deep in his heart, he wanted to believe that Jo still cared about him. Disappointment sped through him. She'd probably told the sheriff everything Faulkner had told her. What did he expect? The right thing to do would be to call the sheriff. Jo was made of strong moral fiber. Even at the threat of her own life, she would never back down.

But the kiss? Had it scrambled her thoughts and churned her emotions as much as it had his? He raised his fingers to his chapped lips to recapture the moment. It had been so long since he'd kissed her. He licked his lips. The sweet yet slightly salty flavor of her lingered, along with the airy fragrance of lilies of the valley.

He inhaled a deep, mournful breath then exhaled. Life was up to its usual dirty tricks. *Give me a little joy then knock me off balance so I can't see the next challenge coming.*

But those were old thoughts taunting him. He'd changed. His new understanding of God had taught him that he wasn't alone in his trials. He had to remember that.

God had guided him to Jo. She'd patched him up, and Faulkner had even been able to see his son. He marveled at how blessed he'd been. Would God continue to guide his footsteps and lead him to a place where he could mend and recuperate before facing Lance and Edward?

He tried to rise, tried to force his legs to push him up, but they refused to do his bidding. His muscles burned and ached; his head pounded. He decided to lie still for a few minutes, close his eyes, and rest.

* * *

Jo helped Denny make sandwiches while Rhett went to the bathroom to wash up. While he was gone, she quickly told Denny that Lance had been there and that Faulkner had left.

"I thought I saw Lance's truck from the trail overlooking the road. And as far as Faulkner's concerned, I say good riddance to bad rubbish." Denny had never liked Faulkner. But his friendship with Lance influenced his view.

Rhett returned with the wolf trailing after him. "What's rubbish?" He tossed Jacob a potato chip from his plate once he sat down. The wolf let it drop to the floor before he ate it. Rhett chomped down on his own.

Jo hoped he hadn't heard all of their conversation. "*Rubbish* is another word for *garbage*."

"Did Faulkner take the garbage out when he left, 'cause then I won't have to do it?" Rhett tossed another chip to Jacob. The wolf caught it midair.

She hadn't told Rhett Faulkner's name. Maybe he'd overheard her talking with Denny, or maybe Denny told him. Jo glared at her brother.

He shrugged. "Rhett asked me the name of the guy in the clinic, that's all."

Hoping that was truly all her brother had told her son and grateful that Rhett didn't know Denny meant Faulkner was rubbish, she said, "Since that's your and Denny's job, that would have been nice, but he left in a hurry. I don't think he had time."

Rhett grabbed his glass of milk and took several swallows. Jo set her son's sandwich on his plate. He put down the glass and wiped away a milk mustache with the back of his hand. "He probably wasn't feeling good."

"No, he wasn't." Jo picked up her plate with her lunch on it and came around the counter to sit on the stool next to Rhett. Denny took his and started down the hallway to his room. "Come join us." Jo was not going to let him drop a bomb and leave, and though she'd definitely have an easier time explaining Faulkner without her brother there, she wanted Denny to hear what she was going to say.

Denny shrugged like it was no big deal, came back, and sat on the other side of Rhett. He stole one of Rhett's chips, and Jo rolled her eyes at her brother. He was four years older than she was, yet he acted like a kid at times.

Rhett took a bite of his sandwich and started talking. "What's Faulkner got?"

Jo motioned for Rhett to cover his mouth when he talked with food in it. Rhett put his hand over his lips.

"You mean, what does Faulkner have?" She corrected him.

Rhett shrugged and nodded, used to his mother correcting him.

"I found Faulkner in the truck last night. He was very sick, so when he saw Grandpa's sign on the door, he assumed Grandpa was at the rodeo." Jo wanted to be as truthful as she could with her son. And though omitting some of the story could be considered a lie, she thought in this case she was well within her right. After all, she was protecting Rhett. And that was her main priority. "Since it was raining so badly and my clinic was close, I offered to help him."

Rhett nodded. "Mom, can I go to my room and play my new game on the DS? I promise not to spill or leave crumbs."

So her son's curiosity over their visitor had been satisfied, and he was on to something else. Since she needed to talk with Denny alone, she decided to let Rhett go. "Sure. Please be careful."

"Ah, Ma, I'm always careful." He climbed down from the stool, grabbed his plate and his glass of milk, and hurried down the hallway with the wolf hot in pursuit, the animal's eyes on the sandwich. Jo wondered how much Rhett would eat and how much he would give to Jacob.

"You must need to tell me something really bad to let him eat in his room." Denny had finished his lunch. Did her brother chew or merely swallow his food whole?

She proceeded to tell him that their father had visited Faulkner in jail, which made Denny's brows bunch together. She told him their father believed Cassandra may have been murdered, which made his brows rise high on his forehead. But when she told him their father may also have been murdered because of what he knew, Denny's jaw dropped open.

"Wow . . ." He folded his arms. "Is this why you were asking me this morning about the day Dad died?"

Jo nodded. She probably should have told him all of this then, but she wasn't quite sure what to believe at the time, and besides, she didn't want to get Denny even more upset unless she had to. With Faulkner on the loose and needing her brother's help now, she felt she had no other choice.

"You know Faulkner is probably blowing smoke up your shirt so you'll feel sorry and hide him from the sheriff." Denny straddled his stool.

"If that were the case, why did he leave?"

Her brother rubbed his chin. "That's simple. Because Lance came."

Jo shook her head. "Faulkner was hiding behind the curtain while Lance was here."

Denny stood and took his plate to the sink. "That had to be intense. Can't believe Lance didn't see him."

"He was worried about his dog. Here's the deal. What if Faulkner is right?" She was so hopeful her brother would have some insight.

"Don't you see what he's doing?" Denny leaned over the countertop, staring at her.

Jo had no idea what he was talking about.

"He's trying to make you doubt Lance so he can worm his way back into your heart. I know you've always believed in Faulkner's innocence, which, for the life of me, I've never understood. Faulkner was found standing over Coulton with the murder weapon. Facts are facts, sweetheart. It's been seven years. You're about to marry a wonderful man. Granted, he's my best friend, but I know Lance. Don't let Faulkner screw this up for you. You have a chance at real happiness. Don't go chasing after some imaginary villain when the real one has already been convicted. You're setting yourself up for even more heartache."

Jo knew logically that her brother was right. She stared at him. "I know you don't believe that Dad visited Faulkner. But the least we can do is look into his claim. Plus, don't you think we owe it to Dad to see if Faulkner's theory could be true? I mean, what if someone did kill him? I, for one, want to know."

Denny bit his lips and folded his arms. He and their dad had been at odds most of the time. Denny had worked hard, trying to prove himself in a lot of areas, but when he was getting ready to start college, it came out that he had used his funds to invest in every get-rich scheme that had come his way.

And not only had Denny spent all of his money, but when Jonathan finally learned of his son's deception, Denny was also indebted to Lance. But being a loving and forgiving parent, Jonathan found Denny odd jobs so he could pay the Wymers back. Denny had finally succeeded in zeroing out his balance, and what did he do? He turned around and invested money he didn't have in a gold mine. Jo didn't learn about this venture until after their father died and Denny used his inheritance to pay it off. She didn't want to remind Denny that he owed her big-time for taking him in. He knew it without her saying it aloud. She and Rhett were the only family he had left, and she knew Denny would do what she was about to ask him because he loved her.

Finally, reluctantly, he nodded, agreeing with her that the theory could be true.

"Okay then." Relief settled on Jo's frayed nerves. "You have to go look for Faulkner."

"What?"

Jo knew her brother wasn't going to be excited about the task, but she had to stick around the clinic and watch Rhett. "Saddle up Apollo and search the mountain for him. He was really weak when he left. I don't think he could have gone very far."

"Can't we look into Dad's death without Faulkner?" Denny huffed. "He's an escaped prisoner. Authorities are looking for him. We can't harbor a fugitive."

"Dad believed he wasn't a murderer, and he would want us to help him." She hated playing the Dad card, but she knew what she said was true.

Denny rolled his eyes. "All right. I can't believe I'm going along with this. I'm only doing it for you and Dad. But if Faulkner so much as sneezes wrong, I'm calling the sheriff." Denny grumbled as he headed for the stairs to saddle up Apollo.

"I'll check on Rhett and join you in the stable in a second." Jo walked down the hall and poked her head in her son's room. Rhett had fallen asleep on the floor with his DS in one hand and his other arm wrapped around the dozing wolf. The trek to the cave had tuckered them both out. She tiptoed away.

By the time she got down to the stalls, Denny had lassoed Apollo and brought him into the stable. Before he could heft the saddle on the horse, they heard a vehicle climbing up the hill.

Peering through the aspens and pines that lined the road, Jo saw Sheriff Padraic's SUV.

Jo glared at Denny. "Did you call him?"

Denny tilted his head and gave her the think-about-it look. "The phone doesn't work, remember?"

And she hadn't given him Lance's cell. "Please don't say anything about Faulkner. Let me do all the talking." Jo couldn't believe she was asking her brother to hide the truth from the law.

The sheriff pulled up, got out of his vehicle, and closed the door. While Denny continued to saddle the horse, Jo went out to greet Sheriff Padraic. "Hey there. What brings you up to my neck of the woods?"

He tipped his Stetson to her. The man was average height but stocky. "Just stopping to see if you're all right. Passed Lance on my way. He said he told you about Faulkner."

Jo wished he'd take off his sunglasses. She hated talking with someone whose eyes she couldn't see. "Yes, Lance told me. But he didn't give much detail. How did Faulkner escape?" She thought she'd better act interested and ask all the questions that someone who was curious and worried would.

"You know prisons. They'd never admit that they did something wrong, but rumor has it he was on a work detail cleaning the barrow pits near the freeway. Got in a scuffle with an officer, who shot him. Faulkner managed to knock out the guard and steal his gun before disappearing."

This story confirmed what Faulkner had already told her. "Was the officer badly hurt?"

"Just his pride. Guess he was new, and Faulkner took advantage of his inexperience. Glad you're all right." Sheriff Padraic took off his shades as though he wanted a better look at Jo, like he was assessing her reaction.

Jo looked straight into his all-seeing green eyes. "We're fine." She had to be very careful not to out-and-out lie. But not telling what she knew was lying. She hated being in this situation, torn between doing what her heart told her to do and what she ought to do.

He smiled, and that Irish grin of his made Jo envious of his wife. Sheriff Padraic was a lucky man; he had the white-picket fence, a loving wife at home, and six children between three and eighteen who loved him. He'd been on the force for over twenty years. He'd seen it all and then some. He rubbed his chin. "Glad all is well."

At that moment, Jo heard the door to the clinic shut, which meant Rhett had awakened and was coming down. She walked toward the sheriff's SUV, hoping he'd get the hint. "Well, don't worry about us."

Rhett and the wolf bounded down the stairs and over to them.

"Hey there!" Sheriff Padraic smiled, his love for kids evident by the kind look on his face. "Got something for you." He opened his car door and reached inside. When he straightened, he had an open package of red licorice. He glanced at Jo. "Don't mind if he has one, do you?"

She shook her head.

"Thanks," Rhett said and eagerly pulled a stick out of the package. "Can I eat it now? We've had lunch."

"Sure." Jo knew the game the sheriff was playing. He liked to win people over with kindness to get them to tell him what he wanted to know. But in this case, Jo was glad because if Rhett was eating, he wouldn't be as likely to say something about Faulkner.

The wolf sniffed at the sheriff's boots, which seemed to bother the man. Rhett bit off a piece of licorice. "Why's Uncle Denny saddling Apollo?"

Denny walked out, leading the horse by the reins. He shook the sheriff's hand. "How's it going?"

The sheriff nodded his okay and offered some licorice to Denny.

He pulled a handful out of the package, nodded a thank you, and mounted the horse. "Come on, squirt. I'll give you a ride to the top of the hill and back." He leaned over and offered a hand up to Rhett.

"Mom, can I?" Rhett pulled Jo's arm, hope brimming in his bright eyes.

She knew at any moment her son could mention Faulkner's visit. He had no idea what was going on. And for that, Jo was glad, but she was also scared. She glanced up at her brother.

Denny gave her a look that said, *Better I take him with me than leave him here with you and the sheriff.*

And he was right. "Sure. Just be back in an hour so you can do your chores."

Rhett grabbed Denny's arm and swung up behind him. "Don't worry, Mom," Rhett said. "The garbage has already been taken out."

Denny kicked the horse, and off they went. Jo was grateful she'd spoken to Denny and had him to help her. She didn't know how long she could count on her brother, but he'd be a good ally to keep Faulkner's visit a secret at least until they found out what they could about their father's death.

Watching Denny and Rhett ride away with Jacob following behind, Jo was more than anxious to get Sheriff Padraic on his way.

The sheriff offered her some licorice, but she shook her head. He tossed the package back in his vehicle. "Look, Jo, I didn't want to say anything in front of Denny and Rhett, but I can be plainspoken with you. Headquarters believes Faulkner is on a mission of revenge. He's armed and dangerous. With your wedding in a few weeks, I have every reason to believe he's coming here. I think you should go stay with Lance and Edward."

"I'll be all right. Remember Denny's here. He'll keep Faulkner away. Besides, my business is here."

The sheriff rubbed his chin. "I should assign you a surveillance team, but truth is, I don't have the men right now. There's a Harley-Davidson gathering north of town. Most of the time, I don't have a lick of trouble with that bunch, but there always seems to be a troublemaker or two in the crowd. Keeping them in line is straining my resources." He stared at her. "Denny and Faulkner never did get along, did they?"

Jo shook her head. "Nope, they never did."

"I suppose you'll be all right." Sheriff Padraic was about to get in his car but stopped. "Ex-husbands tend to carry grudges, and their targets are most generally their ex-wives. I've seen too many women murdered. Do you own a gun?"

Jo shook her head. "I don't want one around Rhett."

"I understand your concern. I have a houseful of children, but I've taught them gun safety and how to handle a weapon. When I'm not wearing my gun, I keep it in a safe. You might want to buy both. Today if possible." The warning in his eyes told Jo he was dead serious.

"I'll think about it," she said.

He got in his SUV and rolled down the window. "Lance has a lot of guns—" He paused, and Jo knew he was remembering that one of Lance's guns had killed Coulton. "I brought that up because once you marry Lance, you're going to have to teach Rhett about guns anyway." Sheriff Padraic started his vehicle.

"I know. Don't worry about us. We'll be fine," she said. As he drove off, Jo couldn't help but wonder if she really believed her last three words.

* * *

Faulkner awakened with a start. Something was wrong. Night had fallen, and the sounds of crickets and frogs surrounded him. But there was something else. What had awakened him?

He scanned the silhouettes of bushes and tall pines, searching the shadows. Had some type of predator found him? Couldn't be human, not out here in the middle of the night. Chills goose bumped his arms, and his entire body shivered uncontrollably. A headache jackhammered within his brain while weakness pinned him to the ground.

Something moved on the other side of the bushes. A bear? A hungry mountain lion? He could see nothing in the darkness.

Suddenly, a pair of glowing yellow eyes appeared.

Fear paralyzed Faulkner, but his mind screamed for him to move. Yet those eyes held him captive. The wild animal was ready to attack, and Faulkner was powerless to escape.

CHAPTER EIGHT

FAULKNER WATCHED IN HORROR AS the eyes of the animal steadily moved toward him. Finally, his will to survive sprang to life. He grabbed the revolver and aimed between the yellow eyes creeping closer and closer, ready to attack. Faulkner's index finger pressed against the trigger.

Suddenly, a boot kicked the gun from his hand. Before Faulkner knew what was happening, someone grabbed his hands and tied his wrists together behind him as if he were a calf being roped.

Faulkner tried to kick his attacker, but the predator he'd aimed his gun at doubled back and bit his leg, jerking and growling.

"Jacob!" The voice was Denny's. The wolf let go of Faulkner's leg.

Denny hefted Faulkner up and slung him over his shoulder like a heavy slab of meat.

A jagged pain surged through Faulkner's wound. He gulped for air, trying to breathe and stay conscious.

"Been looking for your sorry hide most of the day."

"Leave me," Faulkner slurred.

"Would if I could, but Jo thinks we need you to find out what happened to our father. Me, on the other hand, I'm going to use this opportunity to get even for all the hurt you caused my sister." He stopped.

Faulkner could hear a horse stomping. He tried to turn his head to have a better look, but all at once, Denny's iron arms thrust Faulkner from his shoulder onto the horse's back. Knifelike pain stabbed through Faulkner's vitals. His head bumped against the animal's side. The horse sidestepped and snorted.

"Whoa, boy." Denny tried to calm the animal. The horse broke away and reared up. Faulkner was flying through the air. He landed with a thud, hitting his head. His mind whirled with visions of Jo, Rhett in his Superman pajamas, and the cold penetrating eyes of a wolf.

And then nothing.

* * *

Jo paced in the dimly lit stable, kicking loose hay on the ground. Every once in a while she'd stop to peer out the wide doors into the night. Denny had returned with Rhett hours ago. She'd fixed them something to eat, and then Denny had gone searching again. Jo and Rhett tended to the clinic animals while they waited. By the time they'd finished, Rhett was tired and had gone straight to bed. That was more than two hours ago. Jo stared at her wristwatch, wishing she could will the hands to stop.

Eleven thirty.

Denny'd had enough time to scour the entire mountain several times.

Where was Faulkner? Jo didn't think she would ever forget the haunted look in his eyes that seemed to always be there. He'd aged in prison. The man had been through so much. His world had been tipped, tossed, and turned upside down in the last seven years. Add to that his escaping, getting shot, and losing a lot of blood from his bullet wound. Jo suspected he was also running a fever. How long had he been wounded before she'd cared for him? Infection must have set in. With him lost on the mountain, Faulkner's condition could be far worse by now. Another thought occurred to her. The scent of his wound could attract a bear. She'd heard rumors that one had been prowling around Swan Valley. That wasn't far away. A bear could roam over five miles a day. It could very well be near Fall Creek.

Pacing, Jo glanced back and saw the fringe of the gunnysacks she'd pulled off of her father's trunk. It reminded her that she needed to close the trunk and put the sacks away. Thoughts of her father came to mind. She peered into the night and again wondered what his hunch had been. What had he stumbled upon that had made him think Cassandra had been murdered? Her father and the Wymers had been friends for years.

Doc Powers had been their family doctor, and they had invited him to all of their celebrations. Perhaps her father had come across something one day when he had been at their place. That could have happened. Deciding she might as well take care of the trunk because standing there willing Denny to appear was not making it so, she started toward the rear of the stable.

She passed Argi's stall. The fawn came to the gate, wanting Jo's attention. "What's the matter? You feeling neglected?" Jo reached over and stroked between the little deer's soulful eyes then glanced into his hay-laden stall. He had plenty of food and water to last until morning.

The animal's big brown eyes expressed something akin to sympathy and concern. "I'm okay. Why don't you settle down like the cow?"

Jo nodded toward the Hereford lying on her nest of fresh straw. When Jo had done her night check, the cow's wounds had improved. In fact, tomorrow she planned to call the Beasleys to tell them they could come and get her. But could Jo risk it with Faulkner here, *if* he were here?

She couldn't think like that. Denny would find him.

Thinking of tomorrow, she knew it would be hard to put on a front and go through her daily routine. She and Lance were supposed to meet with the caterer for their wedding. Lance wanted to marry at the ranch. They had a huge deck and large patio in the back with tons of room for family and friends to dance and have a good time.

How could she go with him and act like everything was normal? Maybe she should cancel and tell Lance she was overwhelmed with work. He could take Sophie, their cook and housekeeper, to help him choose what to serve. Most of the people coming were Lance's friends and family. Sophie would know what they liked more than Jo would. Denny and Rhett were the only family Jo had.

For a second, she thought of her mother, but there was no way she was going to try to find that woman. Over the years, Jo's resentment toward her had become as deep as the gorge near Table Rock. Her mother had up and left when Jo was four and had never touched base with them again. Jo had no idea where she lived, nor did she want to know.

Returning her thoughts to tomorrow and Lance, Jo knew he'd be concerned if she didn't show up to talk with the caterer. She needed a good excuse. She didn't have a large clientele, so that was out. Not many ranchers hauled their animals up the mountain to see her. For that, she felt bad. But the choice to build her clinic on a mountaintop was hers. She liked living away from civilization. Wild animals needed tending too. She had not regretted her decision, and except for the meager cash flow, she was happy.

She earned the bulk of her living working for Wymer Rodeo. It brought in enough funds to tide her over for the winter. Denny took odd jobs here and there, so when he wasn't buying mining equipment or working with Lance, he pitched in what he could.

She heard Apollo's nicker, heard his hooves tromp up the gravel driveway to the concrete pad. The wolf appeared in the doorway first and hobbled up to her. "Hey, boy." She knelt and hugged the animal. "Did you find Faulkner?"

Denny walked in, leading Apollo, a body slung over the horse's back. "Is he dead?" Panic spilled over her.

Denny shook his head. "That would solve a lot of problems, wouldn't it? But no. I found him under some brush near the creek."

She rushed to check Faulkner. With him unconscious and hanging over the horse, she couldn't see much. "At least you found him." She dashed to her workbench. Hanging above her on the wall was a tube-framed animal stretcher made of heavy vinyl. Jo used it for animals that didn't weigh over two hundred pounds. She grabbed it off the wall and pulled open the restraint straps. "Lay him on this, and we'll take him upstairs to the spare bedroom."

Denny scowled.

"He needs a bed," she defended. "The surgery table isn't comfortable. If I have to operate, we can take him back down to the clinic."

Denny groaned, tied Apollo to the stall, then hefted Faulkner onto the stretcher.

As they passed through the clinic, Jo grabbed her medical bag. Upstairs, they passed Rhett's room. He was still sound asleep. Jo paused a moment and closed Rhett's door.

They had to set the stretcher on the floor in the spare room while Jo turned down the bed. Then she motioned toward the mattress. Denny maneuvered Faulkner up to sit on the side.

"Would you mind helping me undress him?" Jo said.

Grumbling, Denny untied Faulkner's hands. Jo held him upright while her brother roughly stripped the clothes from Faulkner's body until he had on only his underwear. Jo eased him back. With beefy hands, Denny pulled him straight in the bed. Finished, he said, "Still need to put Apollo in his stall and give him some oats. That horse was a real trooper. And I found this." He held up Faulkner's gun.

Grabbing the key ring in her pocket, she handed her brother the keys. "Please put it in the medicine cabinet and lock it."

Denny nodded.

Jo looked back at Faulkner and noticed a lump on the crown of his head that hadn't been there earlier in the day. Even through his thick tousled hair, his scalp looked like an overripened plum.

"What happened here?" She continued to study the bump.

"Fell," Denny said.

She smoothed Faulkner's hair away from the injury. "It must have been some fall to leave a mark like that. Though I'm not surprised. He was so weak when he left." She turned to look at Denny, but he'd already disappeared.

Getting back to the task at hand, Jo slowly pulled the bloody bandage from Faulkner's wound and dropped it in the wastebasket. The flesh around the stitches was raw and black and puckered. Dark, dried blood had pooled around each stitch, but the suture had held. She worried about the bleeding, but it seemed to have stopped. If it started again, she'd operate.

She quickly grabbed what she needed from her bag: sterile pads, alcohol, gauze, and tape. She dabbed at the dried blood, careful not to press too hard but enough to clean the skin. Faulkner's belly shuddered several times. She knew that even though he was unconscious, he could feel pain. She hated to pour alcohol on the wound, but she had to cleanse the site. Tipping the bottle, she drizzled some over the reddened skin and stitches.

Faulkner jerked and moaned but didn't waken. With another pad, she wiped away the excess. Untwisting the cap from the Neosporin tube, she squirted a good dose on the wound. Next, she opened a packet of sterile gauze and, with extra care, laid it over the stitches and taped down the edges.

Faulkner shuddered beneath her hand, and Jo realized he was chilled. His body was compensating for the fever by shivering. Worried about infection, she pulled a hypodermic from her bag and loaded it with a good dose of amoxicillin. Sticking the 22-gauge needle in his right deltoid, she shot the antibiotic into his muscle. Finished, she quickly pulled the blankets around him, hoping he would soon relax.

Denny poked his head in the doorway. "Apollo's bedded down. How's it going in here?"

Light from above cast shadows on Denny's dark-rimmed eyes. His lids were puffy. The scars from chicken pocks on his left cheek were visible. He had to be tired for those to show so plainly.

Jo closed her bag and rose to her feet. "Not good. I'm worried about infection. You probably saved his life, finding him when you did." She glanced back at Faulkner.

"I was afraid of that." Denny yawned.

She didn't know if he meant he was afraid about infection or that he'd saved Faulkner's life. Probably the latter. She rolled her eyes and motioned for Denny to follow her out of the room. In the hallway, she stopped. "Go to bed. I'm going to sit up a little while with Faulkner."

"You owe him nothing, you know." Denny folded his arms.

"We may owe him more than we think, especially if we discover Dad's death was no accident. We wouldn't even be looking into his death if it weren't for Faulkner. He risked a lot coming here."

"He came here to stop you from marrying Lance." Her brother's get-real gaze meant he could read between the lines.

"Maybe . . . at first, but he didn't know Dad was dead."

"Dad's death was an accident, plain and simple. The only reason I didn't tell the sheriff about Faulkner earlier today was because of you . . . and Rhett. I know you're trying to shield the kid from the fact that his father was convicted of murder. But someday you're going to have to tell him. The longer you keep Faulkner here, the sooner that day will arrive."

"I know, and I'll deal with it, but Faulkner has no one else to turn to but us." Jo stared at her brother, hoping he understood her reasoning.

He grimaced. The thought of being someone Faulkner could turn to must have rankled him . . . or was it something else that made him uncomfortable? Jo wasn't sure. She wasn't sure about a lot of things except that she needed to help Faulkner.

"I don't like leaving you alone with him." Denny rubbed his dirt-smudged chin with the back of his hand.

"He won't hurt me, if that's what you're worried about."

Denny yawned again. "Okay, but if I get up in the night and find you're still sitting here, I'll spell you."

"Thanks. I might take you up on that." She watched her brother walk down the hallway and into his room. For all her older brother's faults, Jo knew he loved her and wanted what was best for her. Once Denny fell asleep, nothing would wake him until morning, though he didn't close the door like he usually did. Maybe that was his way of watching over her.

Jo went back to the spare room. Somewhere in the closet, she had an ice bag. That would help the lump on Faulkner's head. Finding it in the back under several blankets, she fetched it and went to the kitchen to fill it with ice.

Returning, she carefully placed it on Faulkner's head and sat down in the willow rocker Denny had made for her. She covered herself with a yarn-tied quilt and settled in for a long night.

As she watched Faulkner's chest rise and fall, Jo leaned her head back and rested it on the rocker. Her thoughts drifted to Lance.

How would he react if he learned about the kiss Faulkner had given her? That would be a secret she'd take to her grave. If she and Denny could find out if their father had been murdered and if they could somehow learn who had really killed Coulton, it would make it so much easier to tell Lance about helping Faulkner. Surely, once they proved that Lance had wrongly accused Faulkner, Lance would be so filled with regret that he might even help Faulkner get reestablished in life. Things could still work out.

That was *if* the real killer could be found.

And if the killer were found and it came out that this person also killed Faulkner's mother, then Faulkner would also have peace in regards to her death.

Jo thought of her father. Could it really be possible that his death was connected to the others? And how on earth could she and Denny learn what happened on Table Rock Mountain so many years ago? There were no witnesses. Her father had been alone. If there'd been evidence on the trail, it was long gone by now. Two winters had passed. Hikers had been all over that mountain. Just what did she expect to find?

She had no idea, but she was determined to find out.

* * *

Jo awakened to a knocking noise. She thought someone was rapping on the door. But then she looked over at Faulkner's bed. Severe chills shook him so hard that the bed was bumping against the wall. She noticed that the ice bag had fallen from his head onto the floor.

Good grief! His fever must have spiked even higher. She had to get his temperature down and fast. Her father had shown her procedures for extreme cases. Jo raced to the bathroom to grab several washcloths and soak them in cold water. Wringing them out, she hurried back to Faulkner. She pulled the blankets down and placed a cold washcloth under each arm, on each wrist, and on his forehead.

What else could she do? Her father had said that in a pinch, a person could put on cold socks and that would help bring a fever down. She'd stuffed Faulkner's socks in the boots when she'd taken them off of him.

The boots were at the side of the bed. She pulled out the socks and found they were ripe. She hated to put them back on Faulkner. She hurried down the hall to the laundry room to see if Denny might have left a mismatched set in the laundry basket. Flipping on the laundry room light, she grabbed a black and a brown sock from the bin and rushed to the kitchen to put them in the freezer for a spell. She needed to switch out the compresses on Faulkner with colder ones.

She dug around in the towel cupboard in the bathroom and found a few more washcloths. She doused them with cold water, wrung them out, and went back to the spare bedroom. Jo made the switch and took the warmed ones back to the sink. She kept up the routine for a good ten minutes before retrieving the socks from the freezer.

Pulling up the blanket and sheet at the foot of the bed, she tugged the socks over Faulkner's pale feet. He moaned and tried to pull away, but she grabbed hold and completed the task then gently bundled his feet in the blankets.

Jo stared down at Faulkner. His face was pale and sweaty. With a trembling hand, she gently laid her palm on the side of his face. His eyes opened. He stared up at her like he thought she was a mirage. His brows pinched together. Tears pooled in his bloodshot eyes. He opened his mouth and said, "God sent you." Then he drifted off again.

Oh, Faulkner. Please don't die. Her heart felt trampled. Again, she switched the washcloths. Jo lost track of time as she worked, but finally, Faulkner's shivering calmed, and he lay very, very still.

Worried, she felt his neck for the main artery. A thready pulse, but at least he was still alive. She smoothed his tousled, ebony hair away from his brows. He was still warm but much better. Maybe she could give him a cool bed bath. That would help take the fever down as well.

As she turned to leave, Jo noticed a cut on his jawline, hidden by his beard. It looked bad. She needed to treat that as well. She went to the bathroom and grabbed a washcloth, towel, and bar of soap. She also picked up a pair of scissors and Denny's new razor that he hadn't even opened. He'd be upset, but if she had to use it, she'd explain . . . Well, he'd still be upset, but she wanted the razor to be sterile. If Jo was lucky, she could treat the wound just by trimming the beard.

She filled a hand basin with cool, soothing water, returned to the room, and set the small tub on the nightstand.

She slowly slid the sheets and blankets down to Faulkner's waist. A shadow of hair crossed his pectorals and ran down his sternum. She looked at his chest and the scars she'd noticed before when she'd operated on him. One appeared deeper than the others. Her hand had a mind of its own, and she reached to lightly trace the mark. His chest moved beneath her hand, rising and falling with each breath. She used to lay her head on that chest and listen to the rhythm of Faulkner's heartbeat.

She had to stop this and get to work. Jo rapidly washed Faulkner's arms and chest, careful not to get the bandage wet. She finished his bath, collected all the cold compresses in the basin, and pulled the blanket and sheet up to his shoulders. She wanted clean water to treat the cut on his face, so she returned to the bathroom, dumped the dirty water out, filled the basin with fresh water, and returned.

Settling on the edge of the bed, Jo studied Faulkner's face. Dark, shaggy hair made him look like an Irish wolfhound that hadn't been groomed for a very long time, but he was still good looking, with high, sculptured cheekbones, a long nose, and wide-spaced eyes with thick, long lashes. Laying a towel under his chin, she took the scissors from the nightstand and began to cut the hair around the wound.

The cut was about two inches long and looked deep in one spot. She wondered if she needed to put stitches in it but couldn't tell. To really see it, she was going to have to shave along his jaw. She clipped as much beard away as she could then opened the new razor, soaped up the site, and shaved around the wound the best she could. Once she got a better look, she realized the gash wasn't bad. A couple of Steri-strips would work fine.

She glanced at the rest of Faulkner's face, and her heart sank. He now had half of a shaved face. She couldn't leave him like that. Deciding to shave off the rest of his beard, she tilted his head and went to work, being as careful as her shaking hands would allow. Done with his cheeks and chin, she gazed at his mustache. It looked lopsided where she'd trimmed too much. She was going to have a lot of explaining to do when he woke up. Knowing it needed to be done, she shaved his upper lip. When she finished, Jo once again rinsed the washcloth in the water and, with circular motions, cleansed the soapy residue off him.

The job completed, she taped two Steri-strips over the cut on his jawline and looked upon her work. His skin looked soft and smooth. Her eyes trailed to his strong, square chin then to his full lips. They were badly chapped. Memories flashed of his kiss when he'd left her standing in the stable only hours ago.

Shaking it out of her thoughts, she grabbed a jar of Vaseline from the night table. After dipping her finger into the jelly, she leaned over and traced her index finger over his lips, becoming mesmerized. Suddenly, his arm wrapped around her middle as he turned on his side. He mumbled something inaudible but kept sleeping. Shaken, Jo carefully eased his arm from her.

Guilt settled upon her. She looked around, expecting to see Lance standing beside her. Silly. He was home, where he should be. But the door was open. Denny or Rhett could have seen her staring at Faulkner's lips and seen his arm wrap around her. How ridiculous was she? In a few weeks, she was supposed to marry Lance. What had come over her?

Her only excuse was exhaustion. Two nights of sitting up with Faulkner as he teetered between life and death had made her do things she ordinarily wouldn't. People did stupid things when they hadn't had enough sleep.

She looked at Faulkner. He appeared to be resting well. She pulled the covers up to his chin and tucked him in.

She decided she needed rest too. She finger-combed her hair away from her flushed cheeks and picked up the towel and hand basin. She clicked off the desk lamp and left the night-light on. As she reached for the door handle, she glanced back at Faulkner. Heaven help her, a yearning swelled within her. Was she falling in love with him again?

No! She couldn't.

Lance was her happy ever after. Life with Faulkner was filled with pain. But was the pain Faulkner's doing or someone who had manipulated and killed the only people who could help him? Jo was Faulkner's last hope—well, her and this God he thought had sent her. Maybe He had.

She looked up. "God, if You're listening, we need a plan and soon."

CHAPTER NINE

A STEADY STREAM OF LIGHT playing on Faulkner's face awakened him. Again, he was in different surroundings. He had awakened in the night to find Jo standing over his bed, watching him. He must have been near death for her to have looked so concerned. He knew she'd been scared and worried, and beneath all of that, a trace of lost love had surfaced—or maybe he had been hallucinating.

Staring at the rough, wood-beamed ceiling overhead, Faulkner wondered what Jo would think if she knew the haunting horrors of prison life he carried. They were scars on his mind that would suddenly break open and bleed into his soul, leaving him spent and limp from ugly remembrance. Like a lingering shadow, his past stalked him and seemed to suck breath from his very lungs, replacing fresh air with the stench of prison: smells of old urine absorbed in dank concrete walls, of soiled cell mattresses, and of blood—a scent so indescribable and so memorable that bile rose to his throat at the thought.

He had been more fortunate than most though. Once the warden had tasted Faulkner's cooking, he put him on KP duty much of the time, taking him away from the thugs who haunted him. Now something else haunted Faulkner: his guilty conscience. Hiding at Jo's was putting her and their son in danger.

I've got to get out of here and face Lance before the sheriff finds me.

He rose up on his elbow. The severe pain in his side had tempered to an ache. Even the dizziness that had plagued him had become a thin haze. He felt better but weak. He grabbed the side of his bed and forced himself to sit. His head throbbed, and he reached to rub it but immediately regretted it. Whatever had hit him had left one heck of a mark. His hand brushed against his cheek. No beard? He scrubbed his palm over his face. Not only was his beard gone, but his mustache as well. His fingers stopped on some type of strange tape on his jaw. A bandage?

He needed to find a mirror—but after he got dressed. Faulkner glanced around the room, looking for the clothes Jo had given him to wear. They were folded and sitting on the top of the desk. The boots were on the floor. A weakness pulled at him. And truthfully, there was some residual pain in his wound but not enough to keep him down. He was well enough to get dressed and do what he had to.

Rolling out the chair from beneath the desk, he sat. Faulkner tugged the flannel shirt on. A small bloodstain spotted the material, but that didn't stop him. He stuck his legs in the jeans, rose, and zipped them up before plopping back on the chair. It rolled a little, making him teeter for a second. Righting himself, he reached for the boots. The pair of socks he'd worn before were inside. He looked at the pair of mismatched socks on his feet. They were comfortable so he left them on, took out the previously worn ones, and jammed his feet in the boots.

Buttoning his shirt, he cautiously made his way to the bedroom door, opened it, and found a short, narrow hallway. The rosy glow of morning sun shone on the floor in the distance through what he thought could be kitchen windows. The mouthwatering smell of bread baking curled an imaginary finger, beckoning him down the hall. His stomach growled. Before leaving he had to get something to eat.

At the end of the hall was an open space where one could see the kitchen, dining room, and living room with no walls dividing the areas. He glanced into the kitchen section. No sign of Jo. Knotty-pine cabinets gleamed of polish. The countertops were clean, with barn-shaped canisters and a red toaster on top. A blue-speckled campfire coffeepot sat on the stovetop, and a pair of burnt, worn pot holders lay on the counter. The oven was on, and the timer set with only five minutes left, so the bread was still cooking. At any moment, Jo would return to take it out. If Faulkner hung around, he'd risk running into her, and his chances of leaving without causing a scene would be nixed.

He decided to keep going. Walking through the dining area, he noticed a laptop, phone, and notepad on the sidebar. He continued on and passed a small farmhouse dining table. A pink pig cookie jar sat in the middle.

Again, his stomach growled. There was a good chance the jar was filled with Jo's delicious chocolate chip cookies. Faulkner hadn't tasted them in well over seven years. He could easily grab a couple on his way out.

Lifting the pig head by the snub-nosed snout, he peered inside to find what looked like peanut butter cookies. Not chocolate chip, but they would do. He reached in and pulled out a couple. Before stepping away from the table, he took a bite. Bland, tasteless, and definitely no sugar. He spit it in his hand. This was not a cookie. Something touched his pant leg.

Faulkner very slowly glanced down. Two beady eyes peer up from a black-and-white body. He'd never been this close to a skunk in his life. What the heck was a skunk doing in the house? Did Jo know?

A small deformed paw reached out as if the creature were asking for a piece of Faulkner's cookie. He had several options. One: give the animal what it wanted. Two: take the skunk out and risk angering it. Or three: give the critter a cookie and find Jo so she could deal with it. Finding Jo would delay his leaving, but he couldn't very well sneak off and leave a skunk in her house. Faulkner warily and begrudgingly dropped a cookie to the floor. The creature immediately took the bait.

Faulkner eased away, heading for the living room, where he could see stairs that led down to the clinic. He kept a nervous eye on the skunk to make sure it didn't follow.

As he reached for the banister, a weird trembling call, like a hollow whistle, sounded beside him. Startled, he looked up. Beside the stairs, perched on an artistically arranged tripod of tree branches, was a small, practically featherless owl.

The bird looked as if it had been scalded and plucked. Big round gargoyle eyes leveled a hypnotic stare at Faulkner as the bird's head moved from side to side, almost separate from the stationary body. The owl was the ugliest, eeriest animal he had ever seen, a creature that belonged in *Tales of the Crypt*.

Stepping back, his foot landed on something that gave a piercing yowl. Faulkner jumped away as a large cat with a stumpy tail and long limbs streaked past him into the living room. The feline ran into a large pine-stump coffee table and collapsed to the floor.

Was the thing dead or alive? Faulkner couldn't leave without seeing if the creature was all right. He guardedly made his way to the cat, giving a wide berth to the owl, whose incessant screeching was as nerve jarring as prison sirens.

The cat's large padded paws covered its head.

"Hey, kitty." With the toe of his boot, Faulkner rubbed the animal's red-tinged, yellowish-brown fur.

No response.

Faulkner knew the animal was no ordinary house cat and could be from the lynx family. He should get down on the floor to check it, but the last thing he wanted was to get eye level with the thing.

Jo would never forgive him if he killed one of her critters.

Sucking in a stabilizing breath, he crouched down on all fours. He reached and stroked the feline's back. The fur was soft. Resting his hand on the animal's side, he felt it breathing.

"That there is Confucius." The voice was that of a child's.

Faulkner craned his head to look behind him. Rhett was dressed in jeans and a striped T-shirt. He wore a cowboy hat and boots. Already Lance was influencing the boy.

Faulkner sat on the coffee table.

Rhett picked up the lynx that was an armful for him. "See, Confucius is cross-eyed and because of something weird with the inside of his ears, he runs into things a lot." A loud purring started. "Did you scare him?"

Faulkner marveled at the child, talking as if it was no big deal to speak to an adult he really didn't know. "I didn't see him on the stairs and may have stepped on him a little." Faulkner remembered the skunk. "Did you know there's a skunk in the kitchen?"

Rhett laughed. "That's Daisy. Uncle Denny found her in a poacher's trap. She's Mom's pet now."

"You and your mom have very odd pets." Faulkner smiled. "For instance, what is that?" He pointed to the freakish bird that had quit squawking and was watching them.

Rhett carefully laid the cross-eyed lynx on the floor. "Spock's a screech owl. Hey, did you know if you hear a screech owl that means you're going to die? Lance told me that. He's my mom's boyfriend.

"Anyway, see, last year when the road crew put down new tar on the main road, Spock somehow flew right into their machine. Mom and I were coming home from town when we saw them taking the bird out. They were going to kill it right there, but Mom told them to let her take it. Most of Spock's feathers fell out. He was in bad shape for a long time. But Mom was able to help him."

"Maybe it would have been best for the bird if your mother had let it die. Look at him." Faulkner shook his head.

"Mom's always trying to help those who can't take care of themselves." Rhett looked up at Faulkner as if to say, *That includes you.*

Faulkner wondered how much Jo had told the kid about him. She obviously hadn't told him Faulkner had been convicted of murder, or the boy wouldn't be talking to him now. And the chances of her telling him that Faulkner was his father were slim to none. He stared at his child, who was wise beyond his years.

At that moment, they heard someone coming up the stairs. "Rhett, are you up here?" Jo rushed in, dressed in her usual attire of jeans, T-shirt, and boots. "Oh, Faulkner, you're up—and dressed, I see." Though she appeared calm, Faulkner noticed the worry that framed her face at the sight of him with her son. "Rhett, come with me." She hustled him to the kitchen.

Faulkner followed and leaned against the wall. Jo set wire cooling racks on the counter then grabbed pot holders and opened the oven door. As she retrieved the golden brown loaves, her silky hair fanned around her shoulders. Through the kitchen windows, the morning sun spotlighted lighter tones of red in her glossy hair. Once all of the pans were out, she closed the oven door and grabbed a cube of butter from the fridge.

"Faulkner didn't know about Confucius, Daisy, and Spock." Rhett's eyes focused on the bread Jo had taken out of the hot pans onto the cooling rack. "Can I have some?"

"It's too hot." Jo's gaze was torn between Faulkner and her son.

"Ah, Ma, come on. It's the best when it's hot," Rhett whined.

"That's true," Faulkner added. "Nothing beats homemade bread fresh from the oven." Especially Jo's delicious bread.

A smile tugged at the corners of her mouth. "All right." She pulled out a cutting board and, using a towel to hold the bread, cut off the heel. She slathered butter on it and gave it to Rhett. "Now go do your chores."

Rhett fled down the stairs, and Jo called after him, "Don't forget to add water to Apollo's trough."

"Ah, Ma."

"Don't give me lip, young man." Jo sounded stern, but Faulkner knew she was all bark and no bite.

Rhett disappeared from view.

With the boy gone, Jo looked at Faulkner. "I've only told Rhett that you're a guy who got hurt at the rodeo the other night. He knows you left and that Denny found you and brought you back. But that's it. And I'd like to somehow keep it that way."

Faulkner knew she was right. Still, it tore him up inside to be so close to his son and the woman he loved yet unable to really be part of their lives. "Can't say that I blame you. You're doing a good job with him." He watched her lay a towel over the cooling bread.

She gazed up. "Do you want some?"

"I'd be a fool not to." He smiled.

Jo quickly cut him a piece and one for herself as well. Buttering their slices, she said, "This morning Denny and I were going to take Rhett to Table Rock to look around, but then Lance called Denny to help at the ranch. Then I called the Beasleys to pick up their cow, and they just left." She handed Faulkner his slice.

The fact that Jo and Denny were trying to find evidence that their father may have been killed made Faulkner realize that perhaps he wasn't as alone in this battle as he had thought. He wanted to leave so Jo wouldn't be incriminated in his escape, but if she could find evidence that backed up his theory, that was a big step in the right direction and would help him in the long run.

The bread was warm and inviting. Maybe he could stay a little longer, at least until he learned what Jo could find out. The bread not only tasted like a piece of heaven but also reminded him of the past: Jo's first batch of bread after they were married, how happy she was to cut him a slice and hand it to him proudly. He rallied from that savory moment and said, "If you're worried about Rhett, I'll watch him while you go."

"No way!"

"Look, you want answers to your father's death. So do I. The sooner we know what happened, the better for everyone. I'd go with you, but I can't run the risk of someone recognizing me. You can trust me, Jo. You've saved my life twice in two days. Plus, you've given me a shave." He rubbed his chin, careful of the odd bandages.

"You noticed, huh?" She seemed to squirm.

"Hard not to."

"You had a gash on your jawline. I couldn't see it very well, so I had to shave a little. But then it looked lopsided so . . . Sorry."

"No big deal." He'd never tell her, but he felt better having the hair off his face. "I owe you more than I could ever repay. I promise not to tell Rhett I'm his father or that I've escaped prison. Please let me watch him while you're gone."

She ate her bread as she thought. "I really need to get this settled. I've risked everything having you here. I still don't know how I'm going to tell Lance about helping you."

"You can't *ever* tell him," Faulkner said. He knew Lance. He'd never forgive Jo.

"He's going to be my husband. We've sworn to each other that we'll keep no secrets between us." Jo glared at Faulkner.

He'd only kept one secret from Jo. A big one. But it really wasn't so much a secret as it was a decision he made without her. "Look, I didn't tell you that if I was convicted I'd divorce you because you would have talked me out of it. But I had to, Jo. I couldn't bear for you to be burdened with me or for our child to have the stigma of a father convicted of murder."

"That's history and has nothing to do with Lance and me." She set her half-eaten bread on the counter.

"It has everything to do with it. Because of me, you don't trust your own judgment anymore. You need to trust yourself. You know darn well you can't tell Lance you watched over me through the night."

Her eyes grew wide with surprise.

"I know you did it only to save my life, but Lance would never see it that way. You know he wouldn't." Lance was a manipulator. Faulkner'd seen it firsthand many times when he'd lived at the ranch. "I know what he's capable of doing, and it isn't pretty."

"What are you afraid he would do?" Jo stared at him as though she was having major doubts about Faulkner, not Lance.

Could Faulkner make the claim that if things didn't go Lance's way and if push came to shove, he could become dangerous? Jo would think Faulkner was crazy, that the years in prison had made him delusional. He had to build the case against Lance before making such an accusation. "At least hold off telling him until I solve who really killed Coulton." Faulkner bit at his lip and set what was left of his bread on the counter next to hers.

She eyed him. "Proving all that is going to take some time. I was supposed to meet the caterer this morning. Fortunately, Lance cancelled because of some trouble at the ranch, which is why Denny had to drop everything to go help. But honestly, how can I stand before a preacher in a couple of weeks and commit to Lance when I'm withholding the truth from him?"

"Do you think Denny will tell Lance I'm here?" Faulkner knew they were best friends.

"No. My brother is many things, but he's not stupid. He knows I'm the one who should tell Lance."

"You can't. Not now. You've got to postpone the wedding at least until after we get this solved once and for all." Though Faulkner was relieved that Jo implied she couldn't marry Lance until the truth came out, she still hadn't become completely converted to the idea.

"That's a last resort. I still have some time to get this mess straightened out." She picked up her bread and ate the rest of it. "I suppose I could go to Table Rock myself. I just don't know what I'm looking for."

Faulkner tried to help. "Something your father could have dropped, though it has been a long time. But it might help trigger something you've forgotten by going there."

"I suppose you're right. And leaving you with Rhett isn't so bad. After all, he is your son. I know I've told you once, but I have to say it again: you can't tell him you're his father. I know I need to tell him soon. He's going to start school in a month or so, and he's bound to find out, but later is better." Her forehead wrinkled with concern.

"Of course I won't tell him." Though he wished with all his heart he could tell Rhett he was his father, he had to let Jo handle this the way she thought best.

"No one should be coming to the clinic. But if someone stops by, don't answer the door. I have a message box on the porch. If it's important, they'll leave me a note. I'll call Lance's place and leave a message for Denny that I've gone to Table Rock without him."

She started for the stairs, talking as she went, making a mental checklist. "I'll take the horse with me in the trailer. The farmer who owns the property on top of the mountain sometimes blocks the old road. Plus, I'll be able to check other places if I ride on horseback from Kelly's Canyon." Jo stopped when she noticed Daisy making her way to Faulkner.

He stared down at the furry black-and-white animal. "Can't you take the skunk with you? She belongs in the wild, doesn't she?"

"No. Just don't get her riled because there's no telling what she'll do." Jo disappeared down the stairs. She called up, "Her treats are in the pig cookie jar on the table. You can give her a couple."

No wonder those cookies tasted horrible. For a moment, Faulkner thought Jo was insane to keep a skunk in the house, but as he thought about it, he realized there was no way she would unless she'd taken out its scent glands. Jo was just giving him a bad time.

Faulkner went to the pig cookie jar and fetched another cookie for Daisy. He sat at the table and broke it into pieces, giving the skunk a little at a time. All the while, his mind was on Jo.

Once again, God had been watching over him. With His help, answers would come.

CHAPTER TEN

RIDING APOLLO FROM KELLY CANYON to Table Rock, Jo found herself alone on the trail. But it *was* Monday and the middle of the day. Weekend bikers and campers had gone home. As she rode, her thoughts went to her father and his last hours alive as he'd hiked.

Of course, he'd come on a Wednesday, a doctor's usual day off. She wondered if he'd taken this trail or the one on the other side of the mountain. She wished Denny had come with her. He didn't know from where their father had fallen, but Denny had found his body, so he probably had a good idea where to at least begin the search.

Surely their father had taken this trail. The path was lined with fragrant pines and slender quaking aspens, and every once in a while, a pretty mountain meadow would come into view. Late blooming wildflowers of yellow, white, and blue were scattered in the foliage of dogwood, chokecherry, and low-growing huckleberry bushes. The huckleberry season had ended just a week or so ago. Huckleberry pie had been one of her father's favorites.

His final hike had been in the spring. He'd taken his camera with him in case he was fortunate enough to come upon the mountain's spring babies. In the past on other hikes, he'd taken pictures of mama bears with their cubs, a rare photo of a wolf with her pups, and, of course, lots of deer and an occasional moose. Jo had kept all of his photos in his trunk—the trunk she still hadn't taken care of. When she returned home, she'd close it and maybe look at her father's photos again.

The trail became steep as she neared the summit. Jo leaned forward, trying to ease Apollo's burden as the horse climbed the rocky path. Riding over the crest, she came to the top of Table Rock. On the flat surface stood farmland. In a month or so, the farmers would plant winter wheat. She rode near the edge and climbed down from Apollo.

Still holding the reins, she walked a little closer. Had her father fallen from this ledge? She gazed down on the gorge, where the Snake River wound back and forth on its way to the valley basin. Wind kissed her cheeks and tousled her hair as she tried to place herself in her dad's shoes, or rather his hiking boots.

He'd always taught her to not walk to the edge of an overhang and to always be mindful of her surroundings. No, this wouldn't be the spot where he fell. He'd probably ventured off the main trail and followed an animal path, which made sense because, of course, he had his camera. What better way to get a good shot than to follow where animals traveled?

Noticing a trail off to the side, Jo wondered, was this the path her father had taken? She tied Apollo in the shade of some trees away from the cliff. The horse should be all right. Besides, she didn't plan on taking too long. She wasn't much of a hiker, even though she'd been out countless times.

The trail was narrow and steep in places. Large rocks here and there made good footholds. Still those were few and far between. She grabbed hold of the brush along the trail, hoping the roots were deep enough to hold her weight. When the path leveled through a grove of tall pines and aspens, a red-tailed squirrel ran in front of her, stopped, looked back at her in warning, and then disappeared into the forest foliage.

"Coward," Jo called after him.

She continued walking for a while before stopping. The hike was beautiful, but she found nothing that would prove her father had been murdered. There'd probably been many people up there since his death. Someone had surely picked up something interesting and walked off with it, not even knowing what it was or that it could be evidence of a crime.

Feeling defeated, she turned around to hike back up to Apollo. She heard something or someone coming down the trail. It could be an animal, but it was probably a straggling hiker left over from the weekend. Through the trees, she caught sight of a familiar Stetson. "Lance?"

She took a few more steps then waited for him to come into view. He came around the pines smiling. "Hey! Fancy meeting you here." He feigned surprise.

Jo knew he was teasing. "Oh, like you come hiking Table Rock so often."

"When Denny and I received your message, I decided we could take a break. It's only a few miles from the ranch. Takes less than a half hour to get here on horseback. Your brother's topside with the horses. Where's Rhett?"

Of course, since Denny was with Lance, he expected her to have Rhett. "I called a babysitter."

"You never call sitters." Lance appeared perplexed.

And why shouldn't he? Jo very rarely left Rhett with anyone who wasn't family. "Yes, I do. You don't know everything about me."

Lance tipped his hat back, staring at her.

She had to change the subject and fast. "Isn't it beautiful up here?"

Lance kept his gaze on her. "Sure is." He took hold of Jo and kissed her long and hard.

Startled, she didn't know what to do. She wanted to pull away but knew she couldn't . . . shouldn't. Good grief. Lance was her fiancé. She should want to be in his arms.

But after talking with Faulkner and after last night, tending to him like she had when they'd been married, her wifely tendencies toward him had been awakened. She felt she'd gone back in time. A wellspring of guilt and confusion nearly took her breath away.

Finally, Lance pulled back and stared into her eyes. "You all right?"

"Why do you ask?" She tried to mask her tumbled feelings.

"Since the night you had to put Loco down, you've been distant. And with Faulkner on the loose—"

"I'm fine. It's just that being here . . ." She glanced around, "where Dad was before he died, I'm feeling blue." What she said was partly true.

Lance put his arm around her shoulders. "I understand. Seems this is the day to think about fathers. I have more bad news."

"What?" She didn't like the sound of that.

"Remember when I told you I thought Dad was not telling me everything that bothered him the other day when he came home drunk?"

Jo nodded.

"Well, he drank not just because of Faulkner's prison escape. He learned his cancer has returned." Lance leaned into Jo.

Shortly after Coulton and Cassandra had died, Edward Wymer had been stricken with colon cancer. Her father had told Jo that sometimes when people went through a horrible ordeal, it weakened their immune system and made them good breeding grounds for cancer cells. Her father had successfully treated Edward, but now, with her father gone, Edward probably didn't take as good care of himself as he ought to. "I'm so sorry, Lance. But he's beaten it before. He'll do it again."

"You know what might help?" Lance stopped and placed his hands on her shoulders.

"What?" She looked up at him.

"If we moved up the wedding." Sincerity showed in his eyes.

She couldn't believe it. Here she'd considered asking Lance if they could postpone the wedding, but now . . . now what was she supposed to do?

"It would really mean a lot to Dad to have you and Rhett become part of the family. He loves Rhett as much as I do, and to have him living with us at the ranch would really boost Dad's morale."

"But—" She needed time to think. Thoughts spun through her mind: Faulkner with Rhett, Faulkner pleading with her to postpone, and Faulkner gazing at her as she tried to fight his fever. Then she thought of Coulton, Cassandra, and her father, all dead before their time , and maybe by the hand of the same killer. Who could have been capable of committing such horrible crimes?

"I know what you're gonna say," Lance said as though eager to fill in the silence. "We're getting married in a couple of weeks anyway. But what if we elope? We wouldn't have to fuss with a formal wedding, which would be good with Dad being sick and all."

This conversation was growing wildly out of control. Jo couldn't handle it. "I can't talk about this here." She started up the path. "We're walking a path my father may have taken on the day he died. I came *here* to . . ." She couldn't tell him she came here to find evidence that her father may have been murdered. She'd sound crazy, which was what her entire situation was right now. Crazy.

"Why *did* you come here?" Lance climbed ahead of her, up an especially steep part of the path, and reached back to give her a hand.

Jo stared at his calloused palm. Her gaze followed to his arm, to his face, and to his eyes. "I came here to grieve. I'm so sorry to hear about your father." She reached for his outstretched hand just as he pulled it away. She shouldn't have mentioned his father when she'd spoken of grief over her own father's death. Lance probably felt that she thought his father would die as well, and that's not what she'd meant.

Feeling that she'd been insensitive to his needs, Jo grabbed hold of an outreaching dogwood bush and pulled herself up to stand next to him. "Lance, your father will beat his cancer."

"It's different this time. With Doc gone, well, Dad's giving up. I thought if we hurried and got married, it would give him something to hang on to."

He was pushing her to agree. Jo stepped away and stared down the jagged cliff. All at once, she realized this could have been where it happened, where her father had tripped. Her gaze glided down the rock face below. Was that where he'd died? Vertigo hypnotized her, pulled her, coaxed her to take another step. She felt herself tilting forward and couldn't stop.

Strong hands grabbed hold of her arms, bringing her back to the here and now. "Are you all right?" Lance stared at her, studying her face. "You looked like you were going to step off." Worry furrowed his forehead.

Shaken, Jo struggled to understand what had happened. "I don't know. I need to get away from here. I need to go home." She stepped from his hold and started up the last stretch of the climb that would take her back to Apollo.

Denny met her at the crest, holding the reins of all three horses. He took one look at her and said, "You okay, sis?"

Lance was behind her. "No, she isn't."

"I'm fine," she said a little too loudly. Her voice echoed off the cliffs below. "Fine, fine, fine." Hearing her voice made her realize her temper had gotten the best of her. She took a cleansing breath. "Really. I was feeling a little sad on the trail, was all." Once again, she stared down at the gorge below.

Lance slung his arm around her waist. "I shouldn't have pressed about getting married. We'll talk about it later." His gaze followed hers down the jagged cliffs. "It's interesting that we've been talking about Dad on practically the same spot he last saw your father."

"What? I've never heard this before." She looked at Denny to see if this was news to him too.

"You never told me anything about that." Denny glared at Lance.

"I thought I did." Lance shrugged like it wasn't a big deal.

"Well, you didn't. What gives you, your father, or the sheriff the right to keep information about our dad from us?" Denny's face flushed red. Jo was relieved that Denny was as upset as she was over the matter.

Looking at Denny, Lance said, "I thought you were with me and Dad when he told Sheriff Padraic." Lance tugged off his hat and rubbed his chin. "Oh, I know what it was. You were down in the gorge with your father and the paramedics when we discussed it. If I remember correctly, we stood in this very spot. Dad said Doc was in good spirits earlier in the day but must have forgotten an appointment because he seemed anxious to get down the trail." Lance put his hat back on.

Jo noticed that Denny seemed to calm down a little, which was good. She needed to ask Lance more questions and didn't want him to clam up because Denny was upset. "Was Edward hiking with my father?"

"Oh, no. If my father's horse or truck can't take him where he needs to go, he thinks it's not worth his time. No, he was feeling guilty that he'd left Doc instead of asking him to go home with him."

"He shouldn't feel guilty over that. Accidents happen." Jo turned away from the view, wishing she could also turn away from feelings of betrayal.

Why hadn't the sheriff or Lance mentioned that Edward had spoken to her dad?

She went to Apollo and mounted up. Denny and Lance got on their horses too.

Lance rode his bay beside her. "I'm concerned about you. Do you want me to follow you back to the horse trailer?"

"No, you and Denny have work to do. I don't want to keep you any longer than I already have. I'll be fine." She smiled at him, trying her best to reassure him that her crazy moment had passed.

Lance nudged his horse to go.

"I'll see you at home," Denny said, passing her.

Jo nodded as he rode away. She should have asked Denny more questions, like where he'd found their father and what trail he thought their dad had taken, but she wanted to be able to talk freely with her brother and not where Lance could overhear them. Besides, standing on the trail and nearly stepping off the edge a while ago, Jo felt like she knew where it had happened.

Following the trail back to Kelly Canyon, she kept wondering why no one had told Denny and her that Edward Wymer had seen their father the day he died. Someone could have easily told Denny while he was with their dad's body. But whether they told Denny or not wasn't a big deal; the fact that Edward had seen their dad at the trailhead was. This was new information.

Jo had come to Table Rock to find answers, but she was riding away with more questions than she'd had before. Obviously, she was going to have to talk with Edward Wymer about that day.

And for that matter, the sheriff as well.

CHAPTER ELEVEN

FEELING WEAK, FAULKNER SAT ON the couch in the living room, watching his son carefully feed the screech owl perched next to the railing by the stairs. The skunk had disappeared, for which Faulkner was grateful. The lynx lay on a rug in a patch of sun shining through the glass doors in the dining area. And the three-legged wolf sat watching Rhett. In one hand, the boy held out a strip of finely cut chicken for the owl. In his other hand was a container labeled "Spock" filled with more chicken strips that he'd taken from the fridge. The bird warbled, raised its pitiful, nubby wings, and pecked at the food.

"So how long do you think you'll need to feed Spock by hand?" Faulkner asked.

"Don't know." Rhett shrugged. "Forever, I guess."

"You do it very well for someone your age." He wanted to give the boy confidence.

"It's really easy. You want to try?" Rhett looked at him.

He shook his head. "I think you've got it handled. What are your other chores?"

"I help feed the small animals. Mom and Uncle Denny take care of Apollo, Mom's horse, and any big animals that have to stay at the clinic. I've been around critters all my life. Oh, and I have to do house chores too, like take the garbage down the mountain to the dumpster with Uncle Denny. I make my bed, clean my room, the usual stuff." Rhett lifted a shoulder. "What do you do when you're not hurt?"

Faulkner hadn't expected that question. He couldn't very well tell him he spent his days in prison cooking for hundreds of men or every once in a while clean trash out of the barrow pits along the freeway with a guard standing over him. He decided to talk about what his life had been like before his dramatic detour to prison. "I used to drive race cars."

Rhett's eyes grew as big as wheel wells. "My father did that too. Mom doesn't like to talk about him much. She gets all sad and stuff. He never comes around, so I figure he's dead or something."

Faulkner was devastated. He couldn't let his son think he was dead, but he'd promised Jo he wouldn't say anything. "Could be a lot of reasons why your father's not around."

Rhett shrugged. His face lit up. "Do you want to see one of his trophies?" Rhett snapped the lid shut on the owl's food and returned it to the fridge, the wolf shadowing him the whole way. The boy pulled a stool over to the sink and washed his hands. "Ma says after handling animal food I have to wash up." He grabbed a hand towel from the oven door, wiped his hands, and jumped down. "You gotta come to my room to see his trophy."

Faulkner eased up from the couch.

"It's the neatest, biggest trophy in the whole wide world. It's not really my dad's. It's his father's. He won the Winston Cup. But if my dad had lived, he would have won one even bigger and better." Rhett was nearly bouncing off the walls as they headed down the hallway. The three-legged wolf followed behind him, ever watchful of her cub.

Faulkner was deeply touched that Jo had kept the trophy. After his conviction and after his mother had died, Jo must have gone through their things, keeping what she thought would have been of value to her son. But she also knew how much the cup meant to Faulkner. Rhett opened the door to his room. Faulkner leaned against the threshold.

Rhett's room was a typical little boy's: a small desk with a PlayStation and TV on top, a chair beside it, shelves with toys and books, a toy box brimming with model cars and stuffed animals, a dresser, and a twin bed with a nightstand beside it. However, on a shelf above his bed was the Winston Cup trophy. The shiny golden cup brought memories of Faulkner's dad to life: how he smelled of gasoline, how he smiled with a tilt of his head, and how his low bass-sounding laugh always made Faulkner happy. Tears gathered in his eyes. He brushed them away without Rhett noticing.

A bitter memory replaced the ones he'd just been thinking of. When he had arrived at the Wymer ranch after his mother married Edward, he'd had no intention of spending much time there. He had been nineteen, and some of his father's backers were already grooming Faulkner to become a driver. He kept an apartment in Vegas to be near the speedway, but in the off months, he stayed with his mother.

He missed her. One day, Lance saw the Winston Cup in Faulkner's room and made a comment that he hoped Faulkner was a better driver than his dad. Faulkner hauled off and decked him. A fist fight ensued. Coulton broke them apart, and when Faulkner's mother learned about the incident, she asked Lance what he'd said. He lied and told her he only meant that Faulkner needed to be careful.

Lance was a great manipulator and a liar. Probably had been most of his life. Though, to be fair, perhaps it wasn't his fault. What little brother could stand always having his father compare him to his perfect older brother all the time? Faulkner could tell that in Edward's eyes, Lance was always lacking in some way or another.

"Says 'Dangerous Dan' right here." Rhett was standing on his bed, pointing at the inscription. The wolf lay down on a huge pet bed in the corner.

"That's awesome." Faulkner needed to sit down. He pulled the chair from the desk and eased to the seat. He noticed a small black rock next to the TV. He picked it up. "Cool stone."

Rhett's face beamed. "Uncle Denny and I found it in the cave behind Fall Creek Falls yesterday. I'm going to add it to my collection."

"There's a cave there?" Faulkner had heard rumors of one years ago but had never checked into it.

"Oh yeah. Nowdays you have to use a boat to get to it, and most folks don't even know it's there behind the waterfalls. Uncle Denny knew about it because there used to be a trail leading to it. But the trail got washed away by the river. Uncle Denny keeps a canoe hidden in the willows so we can go there anytime. We found an old coat that somebody must have left there a while ago because it was all dusty and dirty. I think it's a pirate's, and there's probably buried treasure somewhere in that cave."

"Sounds like a neat place." Faulkner could well imagine it would be fascinating to a young boy.

"When we go, I like to pretend Captain Hook lives there." Rhett paused a moment. "Uncle Denny doesn't really like to play. He's always collecting watercress, picking gooseberries, or panning for gold, but when he's finished, we go exploring." Rhett's eyes became wide. "There's bats in that cave."

Even the mention of bats made Faulkner uneasy. Long ago when he and his mom lived in Nevada, a bat had gotten caught in their screen door. Faulkner had been fifteen at the time. His mother screamed in terror, so he'd manned up and taken care of it while his mom disappeared into the house. Faulkner had told her he got the bat off with no problem and it flew away, but what really happened was the bat had died on the door. Just died right there.

Faulkner hadn't thought of that for a very long time. It wasn't a pleasant memory, and he'd always blamed himself even though the bat's death wasn't really his fault. He realized the thing must have been mortally injured when it had landed on the door.

Rhett jumped off his bed. "Are you hungry? 'Cause Mom said I could fix us some PB and J sandwiches with her bread if we wanted."

"PB and J sounds great." Faulkner stood up, but before following Rhett and the wolf down the hall to the kitchen, he glanced at Dangerous Dan's trophy, wishing with all his heart that his life and his father's had been different.

* * *

When Jo returned home from her trip to Table Rock, she found Faulkner asleep on the couch. For some reason, Jacob slept on the floor next to him, which seemed odd. The wolf usually followed Rhett. Her son was in his room playing his PlayStation. All was well, though she wondered if Rhett and Jacob had been the ones babysitting Faulkner instead of the other way around.

She tended to her animals and completed some paperwork. By then, Denny had returned. He'd gone straight to his room. Jo wanted to know what her brother thought about Edward Wymer seeing their father on the trail the day he died. This new information was like a sliver in her hand, and every time she touched the spot, it hurt, but she'd have to wait.

Jo cooked hamburgers for a late dinner. As they ate, Faulkner and Denny said nothing, but they didn't need to. Rhett was going on about his rock collection, feeding Spock, and the new game on his PS3. He didn't seem to notice that the adults were silent. Faulkner excused himself early and disappeared to the spare room.

As Denny cleared their plates, Jo took Rhett to bed. When her son settled under his covers, he looked up at the Winston Cup on the shelf. "I showed Faulkner the trophy."

"You did?" Jo couldn't help but wonder what they'd talked about. Worry quickly followed.

"Yeah. He liked it. Did you know he used to race cars too?" Rhett yawned.

"I think I remember him saying something about that." Jo was a little relieved. If Faulkner had told Rhett he was his father, her son would have led with that topic, not race cars.

"But I think seeing the trophy made him sad. I wonder why he doesn't race anymore." Rhett closed his eyes with sleep chasing his words.

"I'm sure he has his reasons." She could tell he'd fallen asleep by the change in his breathing. Her little man had had a busy day. And he didn't even know how special it really had been to have his father with him. Turning off the overhead light in Rhett's room but leaving on the night-light, Jo noticed the wolf wasn't on his bed in the corner. She quietly closed the bedroom door.

As she passed down the hallway, she glanced in Faulkner's room and saw he wasn't there. Her brother's room was empty as well. Maybe Denny was playing host and keeping Faulkner company. Yet, knowing how her brother felt toward Faulkner, she knew that wasn't likely. Finding neither of them in the living room, she checked the front deck and found Faulkner resting on one of the lounge chairs, but no Denny.

"So while I was with Rhett, Denny abandoned you?" She plopped down on the other lounge chair next to him and noticed that Jacob lay beside Faulkner on the deck. Was the wolf watching over him?

"I think it was a mutual parting of ways." Faulkner smiled at her. His eyes had dark circles around them and were droopy. But the rest of his coloring was good. His hand drifted down and stroked the wolf. Faulkner may feign a dislike for animals, but he really did care.

"Where's Denny now?" She scanned the mountain meadow below her cabin on the other side of the trees that lined the dirt road to her home. She loved this view from her deck. Many mornings and evenings she could watch moose or deer grazing. Tonight, however, the meadow looked quiet, peaceful. The sun was beginning to set. Brilliant pink-and-gold colored clouds fanned across the evening sky. Jo could never sell this place. Not only was her clinic here, but she'd also helped build it. She'd hang on to it no matter what.

"Said he had to see a man about something, and off he went." Faulkner leaned his head back. "I know my being here makes him uncomfortable."

"He believes you killed his good friend. The only reason he hasn't called the sheriff is I told him about your suspicion that someone killed Dad, plus his loyalty to me and his concern for Rhett. Denny promised to wait until we found more answers before he called. Besides, he owes me big-time. He'll have to deal. I need to tell you what happened today at Table Rock." Jo proceeded to explain that she'd found out Edward had seen her father before he fell, that Edward's cancer had returned, and that Lance wanted to elope. While she spoke, Faulkner's tired face became wrinkled with deep lines across his forehead and at the sides of his eyes.

"What did you tell him?" Faulkner stroked his brow.

"I left it up in the air." Jo rested her elbows on the arms of her patio chair.

"Do you love him, Jo?" His gaze met hers.

"I wouldn't marry him unless I did." She met his look.

"A simple yes or no will do. Do you love him?" He seemed determined to have a direct answer.

"In my own way, yes. But not like I loved you." There. He'd asked for honesty, and she was going to give it to him. "I don't think I could ever love someone like I did you when we were married."

Faulkner's face gentled. "I wish I could do things over. If only I hadn't gone to help Mom that night when she called."

"A good son goes to help his mother when she needs him." Jo hoped Rhett would do the same for her. "Long ago you told me what happened that horrid night, but maybe if you went over it again, something might come to you."

"I've gone over every detail for the last seven years. I have a hard time believing that one more go-through is going to help, but it won't hurt either." His tongue wet his lips, and he closed his eyes. He scrubbed his hand over his face. "When I arrived, she was on the front porch, claiming Chugger Gibson had been lighting firecrackers."

"I hate that part of the rodeo, when clowns set those off. Makes the animals hard to calm down." Jo had tried many times to talk them into using some other diversion, but they felt the crowds liked the loud bangs.

Faulkner continued with the story. "Chugger claimed he wasn't. I knew Mom was just drunk and probably saw fireworks on TV that confused her. Mom also thought Chugger knew when Edward would be home but refused to tell her. Chugger kept saying he didn't know and that after buying what stock they needed at the cattle auction, Edward had him load up the animals and sent him home. I sort of felt sorry for Chugger. He'd obviously had a long, hard day, was tired, and, through no fault of his own, found himself caught between his boss and wife.

"I got Mom to go in the house. As I took her to her room, she told me Edward was having an affair with some woman named Connie. I knew that wasn't true and told her Edward loved her."

"What did she say to that?" Jo couldn't help but feel bad for Faulkner's mother.

"As I recall, she didn't answer, just kept sipping her martini." Faulkner's voice trailed off.

Curious about who else had been at the ranch, Jo asked, "So where were Coulton and Lance? She'd called because they'd been teasing her earlier; they must have been there somewhere."

"Mom always felt those two hated her, but I asked where they were and was sorry that I had. Bringing them up was like throwing gas on an engine fire. She started crying, telling me they were horrible to her, that they hated her, and that they were always thinking of ways to keep her and Edward apart. I honestly don't know if they'd ever been there that night before I arrived."

"Your poor mom." And on top of believing her stepsons hated her, his mother also thought her husband was cheating.

Faulkner shrugged. "I knew she'd feel better after she got some rest. I talked her into going to bed, but she wouldn't settle down and wanted one of her pills. I found them in her medicine chest in the bathroom, but there was only one left. She told me she had an appointment with your father the next day and would get more.

"I gave her the pill. After that, she wanted me to read to her. When I was little and after my father had died and it was just Mom and me, she used to have me read out loud to help my reading skills. As time went by, it became more of a bonding thing for us. So I read until she fell asleep."

When Jo and Faulkner were married, he'd read to her too. Some of her fondest memories of their time together were hearing his strong, male voice as he read a new book to her.

"I decided I was going to stay and have a talk with Edward to find out what was going on. After a while, I grew tired of my mother's book and decided to get another one from the den. The light was out when I entered, but I kicked something on the floor. When I turned on the light, I found a revolver on the carpet."

"That should have been your first clue that something was wrong." Jo couldn't imagine a gun not being kept under lock and key.

Faulkner took a deep breath and sighed. "Well, I was worried that in my mother's drunken state, she'd dropped it there. So I picked it up to put it away. As I walked around the desk to the gun case, I found Coulton lying facedown on the floor in a puddle of blood.

"I set the gun on the desk and pulled him over in hopes of reviving him. Right away, I could see he was dead. I reached for the phone to call for help, but the gun was in my way so I picked it up to move it and was struck over the head. Lance had come in without me realizing it and thought I was hurting Coulton. And the rest is history." Faulkner grew quiet. A thin trace of perspiration showed on his face in the fading light of the sunset. His hand once again stroked the wolf.

Jo cleared her throat. "Faulkner, I hate to even say this, but Coulton was probably dead when you arrived. Maybe instead of hearing firecrackers going off, your mother heard the gun."

"Well, that's better than what I first thought," Faulkner said as though thinking out loud.

Jo stared at him. "Did you think your mother killed Coulton?" She braced herself for his reaction because she knew how much he loved his mother.

"That's exactly what I thought, especially when she didn't come to see me after I was arrested."

"Why didn't you tell me?" Jo was crushed that at the time he hadn't trusted her enough to share his innermost feelings.

"Many reasons. But mainly, I didn't want anyone, even you, to think that she could have killed her stepson or that I thought she had." He leaned back in the lounge chair once again. Remembrance had exhausted him. "Besides, what would you have done with such information?"

"Well, I would have told your attorney for one thing." Jo looped a strand of loose hair behind her ear.

"That's what I thought you would do, and I didn't want him to know." Faulkner took a breath and let it out. "I hoped Sheriff Padraic could find evidence that someone else had done it. He was questioning Mom, and I really thought if she'd killed Coulton, she would have confessed. And then . . ."

"She died." Jo filled in the blank.

"Yeah. She must have kept that appointment with your dad because it was pills and alcohol that killed her." Faulkner was gazing up at the darkening night sky.

Jo didn't want to say it, but she had to. "Don't you think she still could have killed Coulton and then killed herself?"

"No." Faulkner's voice was adamant. "If she'd killed him, she would have confessed. My mother may have been weak in many areas, but she would never have let me go to prison for a crime she'd committed. Never. Someone killed her. I thought I was the only one who thought so until your father came to see me."

"Dad was pretty upset when Coulton died. And I think he blamed himself for Cassandra's death." Jo's father had been so tired and worried. "Not long after your mother died, he told me he'd prescribed the sleeping pills for her. At that time, he blamed you for her death. Said that if you hadn't killed Coulton, your mother would still be alive. Lance finding you with the gun was pretty damning evidence."

"You've always believed I didn't do it." Faulkner stared at her, gratitude framing his tired eyes, which were even more droopy than before.

"For a while after the divorce and even after Dad believed you did it, I wondered. But underneath, I knew you didn't. And according to you, my father had a change of heart." Her mind flashed to that afternoon when she'd stood on the ridge of Table Rock and had that weird feeling come over her. "I think you're right. Someone killed my father. And I'm beginning to think Edward Wymer might know who it was."

"The Wymers know a lot more than they're telling. So you're not going to elope, right?" Faulkner bit at his bottom lip.

Jo put her hands over her face. "My life and my emotions are so screwed up right now, I don't know what to think." Putting her hands on her lap, she gazed at him. "I honestly can't move forward with anything until this has been solved. I won't put my son in danger. Tomorrow morning I'll go over and tell Lance our marriage is on hold for the time being. He's not going to like it, and I hate to add to his burden with his father's cancer and all."

"You sure you have to go over there?" Worry creased Faulkner's brow.

"Yes, I need to tell him face-to-face. And I really do want to visit with Edward. I'll see how he's feeling and ask him about the day my father died."

"You might want to talk with Edward before you tell Lance the wedding has been put on hold. When Lance hears something he doesn't like . . ." Faulkner seemed to be remembering something. "He tends to become very upset. In fact, promise me you'll take Denny with you when you talk to him. He won't do anything with your brother there."

Jo laughed. "Lance would never hurt me. He loves me."

Faulkner nodded. "He probably does, but some people still manage to hurt those they love the most."

Jo didn't have a reply as she looked at the man who had broken her heart. They sat in silence for a while, deep in thought. She wondered about what she would say to Lance and to Edward.

At that moment, she heard an automobile coming up her dirt road. "It's probably Denny." Jo strained to see through the trees.

Sheriff Padraic's SUV was followed by another patrol car.

"They know I'm here." Faulkner must have seen what she did as well. He shot to his feet and darted inside. The wolf followed after him.

"It will take them a little while to reach the house," Jo said, keeping up with him. "You've got to hide. But not here. Since Sheriff Padraic has brought other officers, he probably plans to search the place."

"They'd need a warrant," Faulkner said.

"If I don't let them, it will look like I'm guilty, and they'll just come back." Jo started for the clinic stairs. "There's a back door in the clinic that's ground level. You can leave that way. You need to hide in the forest. Wait until you know they're gone before returning."

Jo could hear Faulkner following her down to the clinic and to the back door. Spying the flashlight she kept on the entryway table, she grabbed it. "You'll need this."

He gave her a quick kiss on the cheek, squeezed her hand, and took off. Jacob went with him, and Jo was glad. The wolf would watch over him like he did Rhett.

Jo felt her cheek where the moisture from his lips still dampened her skin as she watched him disappear into the forest. *Please keep him safe*, she thought.

Taking a deep breath, she decided to go down to meet Sheriff Padraic and his men. Jo didn't know if she could face them without appearing guilty. Thank goodness Rhett was still asleep and Denny wasn't home.

With a confidence she didn't feel, Jo made her way to the stable level and opened the garage door.

CHAPTER TWELVE

As FAULKNER AND THE WOLF raced through the pines and aspens behind Jo's house, he glanced back and saw the darting beam of a flashlight.

Great! They must know I'm here.

His feet pounded the ground. Each step jarred the wound in his side, but he couldn't stop. His breathing grew labored, his vision blurry. Still, he had to keep going. If Sheriff Padraic caught him at Jo's, there would be serious consequences.

Taking a chance, he looked back again. The light seemed to follow his path. Sucking in long drags of air, he didn't know what to do. Jacob brushed up against him as if coaxing him to keep going. Faulkner grabbed hold of the wolf's collar and followed, tripping and stumbling over rocks and tree roots. He wished he could turn on the flashlight Jo had given him, but they'd see him for sure. He was going to have to trust the animal to guide him away.

They passed sharp-needled pines and clinging brush. Faulkner had to find a place to hide, a place he could catch his breath and think: under the shelter of trees or in a cave. He wasn't picky. His freedom was collapsing. He needed to face Lance and Edward before getting captured, yet he was still weak. Faulkner had wanted to appear strong and confident when the final confrontation happened, but was running out of time.

All at once, the ground dipped low to a stream. He glanced behind him to see if the cops still followed.

Whoever it was seemed closer.

Faulkner quickly looked back at the water. In the moonlight, he saw the white streambed through the water and realized Jacob had brought him to the same place Denny had found him the other night. So that meant the road to Jo's wasn't far away because that's where he'd seen the sheriff's SUV and Lance's truck. Faulkner wished he could merely follow the road down the mountain, but that would make capturing him too easy for whoever was chasing him.

Leaning over, he said to the wolf, "Now what?" Jacob licked his cheek and took off, disappearing in the brush. *Great!* Just when he needed the wolf the most, the animal up and left him. Faulkner stared at the creek. He could follow it. He charged along the grassy creek bank but abruptly came to a stop. Thick scrub brush blocked the path.

With no other option, Faulkner knew he had to get in the water. He slid down into the creek. The water wasn't cold like he thought it would be. Of course, when he'd tried to drink it before, it had been warm. A hot spring fed into Fall Creek. Grateful for this small blessing, he splashed down the creek bed, slipping and sliding on mossy rocks and mud, which jarred his wound, rekindling his pain.

Still, he pressed on the best he could. The water became deeper and deeper, climbing to his upper thighs. Frogs and crickets were in strong voice in the marshlike eddies. Something slithered past him. It had to be a snake.

The current grew stronger, swifter. Faulkner was tempted to stop, but he couldn't. He had to keep moving. Ahead, something dark covered the stream. Since he was down in the creek, he pulled the flashlight from beneath his waistband and chanced clicking it on. The light showed on a bridge. And there wasn't enough head room for him to float under. He would have to climb out and risk someone seeing him as he crossed the road.

Clicking off the light and securing it in his waistband once again, he grabbed ahold of a bush. Thorns bit into his palms. Cursing under his breath, he tried shaking away the pain.

Undeterred, he moved downstream a little and reached for another bush. Faulkner pulled himself up onto the bank.

Racing through tall, thick grasses, he pushed several plants aside as he came to the road. Immediately, the skin on his hands burned like he'd touched fire. He must have tromped through a patch of stinging nettle. *Great. The good times just keep coming.*

Ignoring the burning pain the best he could, Faulkner looked both ways on the road, watching for headlights but seeing only darkness. He looked behind him. The flashlight beam of his chaser seemed to have gained ground.

He hurried across the road and slid down the bank into the water on the other side. He quickly stuck his hands in the creek and reached until he felt mud. He smeared it on his hands, and the stinging pain calmed. He pressed on.

A rumbling noise came from ahead. The Snake River had to be close. Fall Creek fed into it. Faulkner didn't want to end up in the river because that water was cold, swift, and deadly. But with whoever was chasing him close on his heels and the road nearby, he had to follow the creek a little farther.

The current became stronger and stronger, the rumbling louder and louder.

What the . . . ? He cautiously kept going. The air grew misty. Washing the mud from his hands, he pulled the flashlight from his waistband, shining it forward. The fast moving waters abruptly ended in a few feet. This creek didn't just feed into the river—it dropped.

That's right. Fall Creek Falls. Now what? As much as Faulkner hated to admit it, he was going to have to retrace his steps, try to avoid whoever was searching for him, and head up the mountain. Tired and discouraged, he turned about, but his foot slipped.

The flashlight flew out of his hand, and he fell chin deep into the creek. The swift-moving waters pulled and tugged him along. Panicked, he tried to gain his footing, but his boots slid over slippery moss and creek-bed rocks. The relentless current pulled him closer and closer to the edge of the falls. Faulkner frantically clawed at the mud and grass of the creek bank until he grabbed hold. Drawing his knee up to climb out, he rammed it into a large rock. Taken off balance, he dropped once again into the water.

He frantically grabbed at rocks and moss, desperate to stop. But the current beat at him, pushing him along. The deafening sound of the waterfall roared in his ears.

And then he was thrust into the air . . . falling . . . with nothing to grab . . . nothing to stop the inevitable . . . until he plunged into the cold, unforgiving waters of the Snake.

* * *

The headlights of Sheriff Padraic's SUV and the other patrol car played over Jo as she stepped out to greet them. Shielding her eyes from the glare, she walked up to the sheriff's vehicle. He opened the door and climbed out.

"Hey, Sheriff. What can I do for you?" Jo tried her best to act normal.

"Two things, actually." He seemed to watch her every move. "I received another call from the warden of the correctional prison in Boise. Says a prisoner who worked in the kitchen with Faulkner told him that he thought Faulkner would try and get in touch with you." He watched another trooper get out of the other car.

Jo concentrated on what the sheriff was saying. "I don't understand. Why would he think that?"

"I'm getting there." He cleared his throat. "I guess in one of their conversations, Faulkner mentioned you, and the prisoner believes Faulkner still loves you. So the warden thinks Faulkner will definitely come here." Again, Sheriff Padraic's gaze stayed intently on Jo.

Jo was taken aback to realize it was a pleasant surprise to hear that someone else believed Faulkner still loved her. Jo didn't know how to react, so she placed her faith in her instincts. "Nice of the man to call with his concern, but he's wrong about Faulkner. He divorced me."

"Well, I put myself in Faulkner's shoes, and if I were separated from my ex-wife and just found out she was getting married to my stepbrother, who claimed I'd killed his brother, well, I wouldn't waste any time finding said stepbrother. But then I thought, if I had somehow found my ex-wife and met my son for the first time, I think she might cover for me." The sheriff's look left little doubt that he was thinking of his visit yesterday and what they'd discussed, how he'd tried to talk her into staying with Lance and Jo had insisted that she was fine.

He drew a deep breath. "I thought it best I come out and have a talk with you. Maybe check the place over. Don't mind, do you?"

Jo was shaken that Sheriff Padraic's summation was so close to what had happened and knew what she said and did next were crucial. "Of course, I don't mind. I must say I'm impressed with your vivid imagination."

He motioned for the officer who had joined them to go ahead and search Jo's place.

"Just be careful and don't wake my son," Jo called after him. She'd put Faulkner's prison uniform in the garbage. She hoped Denny and Rhett had taken the garbage to the community dumpster down by the turnoff and that Sheriff Padraic hadn't thought to go through the trash there before coming here. But she couldn't worry about what he might or might not have done yet.

"Hear that?" Sheriff Padraic asked the officer.

He nodded and proceeded to search the garage and stable area.

"You said there were two reasons you were here. What's the other one?" Jo braced herself for his answer.

Sheriff Padraic smiled. "Lance called. He demanded I place a safety detail at your place. And he told me that you've moved up the wedding."

"What?" Jo was more than a little annoyed. Lance always seemed to overreach and ignore what she wanted.

"Calm down." The sheriff put his arm around her shoulders. "He's just worried about you."

"But I told him I'm okay." She was going to have a serious talk with Lance as soon as she possibly could. "I suppose he told you about Edward's cancer too."

He nodded. "Darn shame. I think having you and Rhett move in with them will help. Edward has lost so much. Having people around who care is bound to make him feel better."

The officer had finished searching the garage and stable area and was going up to her clinic. Jo knew there was nothing there for him to find. Then she thought of Faulkner's gun. She'd asked Denny to put it in the medicine cabinet, which needed a key. She hoped they wouldn't ask to look there because even though they didn't have a search warrant, if she didn't let them, it would look like she was trying to hide something.

Trying to take her mind off the weapon, Jo decided to put the brakes on the idea that she and Lance were upping their wedding date. "I didn't agree to get married sooner. And as for Rhett and me moving into the Wymer ranch . . . my work is here."

"But haven't you and Lance discussed relocating your clinic?" Sheriff Padraic seemed puzzled.

"Not yet. But wherever we live, I plan to keep my clinic here. And while I'm worried about Edward, I also have my son to think about. I haven't told him Faulkner is his father and was convicted of killing Lance's brother."

The sheriff grimaced. "He's going to find out."

"I know, and I'll tell him. I just need the right time and place. It's such a complicated issue and a lot for a child to comprehend. And besides that, I want Rhett to get to know Edward. He's going to become his grandfather. And in a strange way, he's already Rhett's step-grandfather . . ." Jo rubbed her worried brow. "And I don't know if it's a good thing for Rhett to see how sick Edward will become from cancer treatments."

Sheriff Padraic nodded. "It will be tough, but kids are resilient. About the history of Faulkner and the Wymers, you can tell Rhett who his father is without putting him in the middle of that quagmire. Rhett seeing Edward fight cancer might be a good thing. And if Edward dies, well, dying is part of life. The sooner a kid understands that, the better."

Jo couldn't believe the sheriff's attitude since he was a family man. "If you had a choice, would you expose your young son to all those emotions?" Jo hoped this would make him rethink.

"I would. It's important to show them the good and the bad. Like I said, it's part of life." He walked into the stable. Apollo stuck his head over the top rail of his stall. The sheriff stroked the horse's forehead.

"Rhett was only four when my father died, so he already knows death is part of life. I think that's enough." Deciding to change the subject, Jo said, "I'm upset that Lance is telling people we upped the wedding date. And then to have you put a safety detail at my place, criminey sakes."

Sheriff Padraic rubbed his neck. "It's not like he's telling everyone in town. We're good friends. He's worried about you. Cut the guy a break. After all that's happened and with your being Branson Faulkner's ex-wife, it only stands to reason that he's worried about you."

Jo stepped away from him. "I can take care of myself." She began to wonder about the sheriff and Lance's friendship. They'd known each other for years. He had helped with the investigation of Coulton's and Cassandra's deaths. And he'd also investigated her father's accident. He knew details about all three deaths. Had he wondered if they were connected? And what did he think of Faulkner? "I know you arrested Faulkner, but did you really think he did it?"

He stepped back. "Didn't see that coming." He shrugged. "I go by facts. The fact remains that Lance caught Faulkner holding the gun."

"But that doesn't mean he pulled the trigger. Did you check him for gun residue?" Jo couldn't remember hearing that he had.

Sheriff Padraic rolled his eyes. "That again. There were many reasons he didn't have residue on him. This was all covered at the trial."

Worried that she was pushing too much and that the sheriff might become suspicious, Jo decided not to go on the offensive but to be more subtle. "You're probably right. That was such a horrible time. It's all a blur. And to have Cassandra die just two days after Coulton. A double tragedy for Edward . . . for all of us."

The sheriff gave a deep sigh. "Life dealt Edward a crappy hand. But I think it gave him a little comfort when I told him his wife's death was accidental. Cassandra had consumed a lot of alcohol. And when the lab work came back that she had drugs in her system . . ." He stopped as though he thought he'd said too much but added, "The woman was distraught over her son. Cassandra accidentally overdosed, plain and simple."

"Seems we've had a lot of accidental deaths." Jo hugged her arms to her body. She didn't want to bring up her father, hoping the sheriff would realize what she meant. His eyes slanted with sympathy, but he didn't say anything. Obviously, she was going to have to nudge the conversation on. "You know, my dad hiked the trail to Table Rock hundreds of times. I still don't understand how he fell. Do you think . . ." She paused, trying to appear naïve and yet thoughtful. "Well, what if his death wasn't an accident?"

Sheriff Padraic pulled off his hat and drove his fingers through his thick, turflike hair. "Jo, accidents can happen to anyone at any time. Have you talked to Lance about this?"

"With the rodeo circuit and now his dad's illness, he has enough to deal with. Please don't tell him either. There's no sense in worrying him." Jo had hoped the sheriff would tell her a little more about how he'd investigated her father's death, but she was worried that she'd gone too far. At least she'd planted a question in his mind.

He nodded. "I'll keep it to myself."

The officer who had been searching the house returned. About the same time, another tall, burly officer walked up the driveway, flashlight in hand and Jacob by his side. "Thought I was onto something but turned out to be this hobbling wolf. Has a collar so I figured he belonged to you."

Jo patted her leg, and Jacob came to her. She glanced up at Sheriff Padraic.

He shrugged. "As a precaution, I had him checking the grounds around the clinic. Wanted to make sure Faulkner wasn't hiding somewhere, stalking you." He acted like it was a common, everyday thing and that he didn't suspect her of doing something wrong.

The officer who had checked inside said, "The place is secure."

"Good." Sheriff Padraic looked out at the patrol car parked next to his SUV. "You can leave your car parked where it is tonight, but tomorrow, tell the men who replace you to park where they're not conspicuous while they keep surveillance."

The officers went to their patrol car.

"Seriously," Jo said. "You already told me your force is stretched thin. You don't have enough men to keep two of them here with me twenty-four/seven. I'll be fine."

"So you bought that gun I advised you to get?" He stared at her.

"Not yet, but I've been busy." Was that ever the truth! Jo was dog tired. "I plan to get one the next time I'm in town."

"As a precaution until you do, I'm leaving a couple of deputies here."

Jo had to stop him. "Look, it's not like Rhett and I are alone." She stroked the wolf. "I have Jacob here, and Denny lives with us. My brother'll see that we're protected."

"Maybe. But if Faulkner sees a patrol car parked here, he'll be less likely to bother you. Besides—" He leaned near her. "You've got me thinking about Cassandra and your father. I don't want any *accidents* happening to you."

Jo didn't know what to think. Was he genuinely concerned? Or was there a hidden threat in his words? Sheriff Padraic sounded sincere, but there was something in the way he'd said it that made her wonder. She'd known the sheriff for years. He was a good, honest cop.

Yet as Jo watched him walk away and get into his SUV, she wondered.

CHAPTER THIRTEEN

THE BONE-CHILLING, SMOTHERING WATERS OF the Snake overcame Faulkner as he plunged deep into the river. He couldn't breathe, couldn't see, and couldn't hear because his ears quickly filled with water. He didn't know which direction to go or if he was up or down or right or left. He was in a vast, dark underworld.

Faulkner's foot collided with a rock, and he suddenly knew he was at the bottom of the riverbed. He pushed himself up, seeking life-giving air. Breaking the surface, he sputtered and gasped. Frantic, he treaded water as he tried to gain his bearings. He'd landed in an eddy of the river, the main current farther out. He dog paddled to shore and grabbed hold of a large, porous rock. It took all of his strength to pull his body out of the river.

He was numb all over, even his wound. The night's chill air breathed over him, and he shivered uncontrollably. Though Faulkner knew he was lucky to be alive, he was wet and miserable. He could sit there all night and wallow in his misfortune, or he could find a trail out of here.

Forcing his legs to do his bidding, he rose to his feet and faced the hill. The climb to the top was insurmountable covered with brush and looming trees cast in dark shadows. What was hiding there waiting for him? He couldn't imagine. But he had to try to climb out because he couldn't very well retrace falling down the waterfall.

As he walked, the numbness shielding his wound faded and his side throbbed. His boots sloshed as he slipped in a rut, knocking him to the ground, jolting his stitches. Needles of pain pricked through his wound. Feeling defeated, Faulkner curled his legs to him and sat in the bushes, listening to the river, the crickets, and the frogs. He tried to peer through the inky darkness to find a trail but couldn't make one out. Rhett had said the trail had been washed away by the river. There was no way out of there.

His scanned the large rocks and the waterfall. Could he somehow climb through the water and up the rocks? There appeared to be a ledge of some kind. But the water would knock him off. Defeated, with nearly every muscle in his body exhausted, Faulkner was at the end of his rope, hanging on to a very frayed and worn knot. *Please, God. I'm grateful I'm not dead, but I need some guidance.*

Shivering from the cold, his eyes drew to the sparkling moonlight on the river. If he weren't freezing and didn't feel like roadkill, and if he weren't running from the law and worried about Jo and Rhett, he might find the scene . . . pretty.

An old song came to mind about the moon and a river wider than a mile. Had the writer found himself in a similar circumstance?

Doubtful.

And the song had been about romance. Faulkner's story was many things, but romantic was not one of them. His story was more like a horror novel. Or a tale of revenge. No, not really revenge. Faulkner's story was about justice and finding the truth. And about appreciating the small miracles that happened along the way.

A week ago, he had been sitting in his Boise prison cell. Never in his wildest dreams did he think when he escaped that he'd end up sitting here on the west bank of the Snake River, cold and wet and wondering how he was going to get out of this situation. Strange as it seemed, this scene beat anything he'd laid eyes on in years, besides seeing Jo and his son, of course. His thoughts remained on Jo. He knew she had been warring within herself over Lance and him. When Jo married Faulkner, she'd loved him, but that love had taken a severe beating. He didn't know if she had enough left in her for it to bloom again, though she'd given him hope, telling him she would never love anyone like she loved him.

Yet she had feelings for Lance. But that was because she didn't know who he really was. Faulkner knew him all too well. He had firsthand experience.

There was that time Lance had scooped up all the little kittens he could catch on the ranch and stuffed them in a pillowcase, tied it shut, and tossed it in the river. He'd said it was what folks did in the country to control the cat population. Faulkner had argued that he could take the cats in to be neutered and spayed, but Lance had laughed at the idea, which made Faulkner angry. Later he learned that one lucky kitten had gotten away and someone had given it to Jo. Faulkner didn't care for animals, but he didn't go around killing them.

Some believed kids who killed animals could very well grow up to kill humans too. Deep in the back of his mind, Faulkner wondered if Lance was the one who killed Coulton. Though he always returned to the same question . . . why would he? Being a manipulative, dishonest cat killer didn't mean Lance would kill his own brother, but on Faulkner's list of suspects, Lance was at the top. Still, who were the other possibilities?

Jo's theory of a stranger breaking in and killing Coulton was highly unlikely. And when she'd brought up the question of his mom being guilty, it had brought Faulkner's great fear to the forefront in his mind. But he'd already crossed his mother off his list. There were others: Edward, but he wasn't home at the time of Coulton's death; Chugger Gibson had been there and had been arguing with Faulkner's mother and seemed mighty anxious to get away. He was definitely a candidate.

But still, Faulkner felt Lance had done it. The "why" nagged at him. Greed, power, jealousy. Cain had killed Abel, so history proved that someone with flawed thinking and who lived a life being dishonest could have it in him to kill his brother. Faulkner knew he had to find the reason because Coulton's death somehow spiraled into Faulkner's mother's death and Doc's.

The key was Lance. Faulkner had to confront him and somehow make him talk. An impossible feat, but sitting in prison, waiting for the truth to come out on its own hadn't worked. Faulkner had to do something, or it would be too late for the people he loved.

Faulkner had told Jo only hours ago how Lance had found Faulkner standing over Coulton with the gun in his hands. He shuddered at the memory and picked up a loose rock.

He thought of the rock he'd held in Rhett's room. He marveled at the thought of his son. The little things about the boy left Faulkner in awe: the kind way he fed the owl and talked about the critter, the sound of Rhett's youthful voice, his small hands gently stroking the wolf that seemed to always be by his side. The love Faulkner'd felt for his son in only a matter of days amazed him. And what a total surprise it had been to find that Rhett had Faulkner's father's trophy on a shelf in his room. More amazing than that was the look in Rhett's eyes as he'd gazed at the trophy. How truly grateful Faulkner was that he'd been able to spend the afternoon with his son. He'd cherish that memory until he went to his grave.

If he were to die right here sitting on this rock next to the river on this night, he'd die a happy man. Except he didn't want the shadow of his being labeled a convicted killer to one day haunt his boy. Rhett may believe his father was dead, but there would be a time in his life when he would learn the truth. If it was the last thing Faulkner ever did, he was determined to clear his name.

So he couldn't die tonight sitting here on the riverbank.

No, he had to fight.

A shiver made his teeth rattle. He just hadn't known fighting would be so dad-blamed cold. He threw the rock in his hand at the waterfall, expecting to hear it thud or splash, but nothing. It was as if the falls had swallowed the rock. Then he remembered Rhett telling him about a cave behind the water. And Rhett had said something about an old dirty coat being there too. Dirty or not, it had to be warm. Faulkner stared through the darkness at the falling water. It didn't look like a cave was behind there. He thought of *The Last of the Mohicans* and the scene where the main character and the woman he loved were in a cave behind a waterfall. The man told her to stay alive and he would find her. Then he jumped into the falls and disappeared.

Well, Faulkner had the jumping-into-the-waterfall part down. Too bad he couldn't remember what the character did after that. But it didn't matter because at the end of the movie, the guy found his woman, and they were together. Faulkner prayed Jo would stay alive and somehow they would find a way out of the mess they were in.

He struggled to his feet and began to climb.

* * *

Jo burned another pancake. All the chokecherry syrup in the world wouldn't cover the charred taste. She tossed the remains into the garbage. If she kept burning pancakes, it would take her forever to finish by the time Rhett got up and Denny returned from the doing clinic chores. Cooking was dangerous and a lost cause when she was worried.

Jo's excuse for burning breakfast was a very long night of cat naps while listening to every sound and thinking it was Faulkner returning. But he never did. Jo prayed that if he did return, he'd see the police and leave.

Earlier, around six, Jo had taken coffee out to the officers. They'd been cramped up in that car all night and probably needed someone to say "good morning" and hand them a cup of warm caffeine. They were kind and gracious and thanked her for her trouble. She'd offered them breakfast, but they'd refused, saying they'd be leaving soon. She'd reiterated that they didn't need to be there at all. They'd said nothing. So she'd gone inside to start this sorry excuse of a breakfast.

Denny must have slipped out to do chores while Jo was in the bathroom. She hadn't seen him as yet to tell him what had happened last night while he was gone. She added more pancake mix to the bowl and whisked it with a splash of milk.

"Mom, where's Faulkner?" Rhett came into the kitchen with an amazing case of pillow hair. He rubbed his sleepy eyes. He wore his Wranglers and a T-shirt but was barefooted. Jacob was with him, the wolf's tongue lolling from his mouth.

Avoiding the subject a little while longer, she said, "You need to put water in Jacob's bowl. He's completely out." Jo had spent most of the night wondering how she was going to explain Faulkner's absence to Rhett and how she was going to ask him not to talk about Faulkner to anyone except Denny and her.

"Okay, okay, okay." Rhett grumpily pulled a chair to the sink, collected the wolf's water bowl, and filled it.

Jo poured more pancakes on the griddle. She watched as her son carefully placed the brimming bowl of water on the counter, jumped down from the chair, and then eased the bowl off, setting it in its usual spot on the floor at the end of the counter near the garbage. The lynx's and skunk's bowls were at the other end. Jacob had a tendency to eat their food if given the chance, and the farther away they were, the better. The critters were curled up in their beds next to the fireplace. The wolf lapped up the fresh water.

Rhett stood beside Jo, waiting for her reply. Jo took the cooked pancakes from the griddle and poured more before answering. "Faulkner is a drifter. He had to leave, and I don't know if he'll ever come back." She flipped the pancakes just as Denny came up from the clinic.

"Who you talking about?" Denny plopped down on his chair. Jo had already set the breakfast table.

Rhett started to sit when Jo stopped him. "Both you guys"—she looked at Denny as well—"need to wash up before eating."

They moaned in unison.

"Good grief, you know better. I'm forever washing my hands." She stared at the pan, not really seeing pancakes but thinking of Faulkner, wondering what he would eat this morning and where on earth he was. She knew he was determined to head over to the Wymers'. As soon as she could, she'd drive there and have a talk with Lance. She needed to set him straight about the wedding. She also wanted to check on Edward. Jo took the golden brown pancakes off the griddle and stacked them on a plate.

With their hands washed, Denny and Rhett returned to the table just as Jo shut off the burner and carried the food to them.

"Okay, so now are you going to tell me who you were talking about when I came in?" Denny poured not only chokecherry syrup on the stack he'd piled in front of him but also maple syrup.

Rhett answered for Jo. "Faulkner. He's a drifter, and he left." He took a long drink of orange juice.

Denny stared at Jo with the you-need-to-tell-me-what's-going-on look but said, "Makes sense with the cops out front."

Rhett jumped off his chair and ran to the window to have a look. Jo shot Denny a thanks-for-nothing glare.

He shrugged and then, as though feeling sorry for speaking before he'd thought, said, "Hey, squirt, why don't we go on another adventure today?"

This brought Rhett back to the table. "Sure, but why are the policemen here?"

"They're looking for someone and stopped for a while. It's no big deal." Jo busied herself eating, even though she was so upset that food tasted bland and when she swallowed it landed in her stomach like a horseshoe.

Rhett seemed satisfied with her answer, though, as she lifted a couple of pancakes onto his plate. He grabbed the maple syrup and poured it on. "Mom, you want to come with us on our adventure today?"

"Can't, honey. I have to run over to Lance's this morning." She looked at Denny because this was the first he'd heard of her plans as well.

He nodded like he thought she should.

"I want to go with you. I didn't get to see Lance yesterday." Rhett's face scowled with disappointment.

"Not today. Besides, Uncle Denny needs your help here."

"Sure do. After our chores, why don't we go back to the cave? Huh?" Denny smiled at him.

Rhett shrugged. "I guess. I told Faulkner all about it. Too bad he's not here to go with us."

Jo and Denny looked at each other, and immediately, Jo knew her brother was thinking the same thing she was. Faulkner could have gone there to hide. How he'd reached the cave without a boat was in question. And it would have been dark. Still, she thought his being there was a definite possibility.

"Well, we'll go back today to see what we can find." Denny seemed to be trying to keep Rhett's mind off of Faulkner.

But Jo needed to cover her bases. "Rhett."

He looked at his mom as he ate another forkful of pancake.

"If anyone, even Lance, should ask you if Faulkner has been here, have them talk to me." She put her fork down. This was harder than she thought. "See, Faulkner, well, he's—"

"He's playing a game, and we're part of it." Denny interrupted her. He must have sensed that she was about to tell her son Faulkner was his father. "He's playing hide-and-seek. We play that all the time, remember? We played it a month or so ago."

Rhett nodded. "But I found Mom right away out by the willow in the meadow."

"Faulkner's hide-and-seek is a little different than the game we played." Denny had finished eating and stood. "When you get your socks and boots on, come down to the clinic, and we'll plan our day." Denny gave Jo a nod that said she owed him big-time for this.

Perhaps he was right.

* * *

As Jo pulled into the barnyard at the Wymer ranch, she didn't see Lance's truck. That was a good sign because that meant he was checking on the stock and that Faulkner hadn't been there yet. At least that's what she hoped. Actually, her deepest hope was Faulkner would be at the cave.

She pulled up to the barn and noticed the hole in the door that had been there since she was a teen. It brought back memories of the first time she'd met Faulkner.

When Edward had married Cassandra, he'd invited Jo's family over to have dinner and meet his wife and stepson. Faulkner had been a no-show, which Jo knew had greatly upset Edward. Cassandra calmed him down and made some excuse as to why her son wasn't there. She was gracious and put everyone at ease. Jo didn't really care about the stepson anyway. She was there to see Coulton.

They had dated through high school, and now that Jo was in college and Coulton was taking on more and more responsibilities at the ranch, their relationship was heading down a more serious path. Jo's high school crush was about to blossom into full-blown love.

After dinner, Coulton took her outside, down past the small stream behind their house to the firewood shed, and gave her a quick kiss and told her he had a present for her. From a cardboard box stored where no one could see, he pulled out a white, long-haired kitten he said he'd saved for Jo from the last of the litter. He knew she loved animals. After snuggling with the kitty, Jo set it down for a second and gave Coulton the kiss she thought he really wanted. When they finished, Jo realized the kitten had run off.

Coulton told her it couldn't have wandered far. Jo was worried about it falling in the stream. They split up to search. Spying the little feline as it slipped through the hole in the barn door, Jo raced to catch it. When she entered the barn, she found the kitten on the hood of a red car with a huge number five painted on it. As Jo grabbed the kitten, Faulkner rolled out on his creeper from underneath the automobile.

Grease smudged his cheeks and covered his hands as he growled, "What the devil do you want?" He leaped to his feet and then saw the kitten. A surprised smile gentled his face as he talked to the cat. "You're lucky you weren't rounded up with the others." Then he seemed to realize Jo had heard him, and his face pinched with disgust. "Keep that thing off of my car."

"This is a living, breathing creature, not a *thing*. Unlike your *car!*" Jo was puzzled that one moment he could be soft and tender to the kitten but the next could be all prickly to Jo. Hugging the soft ball of fluff, Jo added, "Her little paws hardly left so much as a paw print on your *precious* hunk of metal."

"Hunk of metal! This 'hunk of metal' is a Chevy Impala with a hemi engine and leg pipes," Faulkner spat out. He grabbed a soiled cloth to wipe his hands and glared down on Jo. The kitten yowled and leaped from her arms onto Faulkner. He grumbled as he took hold of the little one, but despite his bluster, he gently stroked the feline's tiny head. "You know," he glanced up at Jo, "all an animal does is bite, scratch, or relieve itself on you." He chuckled, and in that moment of seeing Faulkner's true loving nature behind his tough-guy act, something happened.

Kismet?

Magic?

Love at first sight?

She didn't know. But Jo's world stopped, her heart drummed against her ribs, and she knew she'd never be the same again. Coulton, Lance, her brother, and her father all slipped her mind. Faulkner had felt it too because a trace of a knowing smile replaced his stormy scowl.

That had been the beginning.

The beginning of the end.

Jo rubbed her eyes, trying to wipe the memory from her mind. She slowly got out of her father's old truck and closed the creaking door. Gazing up at the gabled white house, she wondered if Faulkner could be in there. She had to get inside and find out what was going on.

"Ah, the person who can make a bleak day sunny." The voice came from behind.

Jo whirled around to find Edward walking up to her. He reminded her of the late Ernest Borgnine in his senior years, with that twinkle in his tired eyes. Edward looked especially tired today, though he seemed glad to see her. It was obvious Faulkner wasn't there, and Jo was grateful Edward was alone. She dreaded that she was going to have to disappoint Edward and had hoped to speak to Lance before she told anyone the wedding needed to be postponed, but maybe it would be best this way, after all; telling Edward first was what Faulkner had suggested she do.

Like a loving father, Edward slung his arm around her shoulders. "Come up and keep your future father-in-law company until Lance gets back. He shouldn't be long."

Jo leaned into him. "Sure. You're the man I wanted to see anyway."

CHAPTER FOURTEEN

THE CHEERFUL SOUND OF BIRD chatter and the sun's rays shining through the falls awakened Faulkner, the sun displaying fractured light with prisms of red, yellow, and blue in the mists. The moment only lasted a second, but Faulkner felt the Lord had given him a gift to lighten his spirits.

Stiff as a crowbar, he pulled himself to a sitting position. The old coat he'd found, thanks to Rhett, fell to his side. He glanced down into the darkness of the cave and heard squeaking and scurrying. Probably river rats or bats or . . . pirates. He smiled, thinking of Rhett.

Faulkner's clothes were still damp in the creases. Forcing his fingers to function, he unbuttoned his shirt and looked at his side. In the thin light of morning, he could see that the dressing over his wound was partially scrunched, the tape barely hanging on. He pulled it off and set it beside him. Though his skin around the wound was still red, the stitches held, and he thought despite his tumble in the waterfall and swimming for his life the night before, it looked better. His stomach growled, which was a good sign because it meant he was alive. The bad thing though was that he had no idea how he was going to find something to eat.

He leaned against the cave wall and tilted his head back to rest. His arms and legs ached. He wasn't moving. Closing his eyes, he listened. The birds continued to sing. It had been so long since he'd heard birdsongs. He didn't realize how much he'd missed it. Their chirps and melodic warbling lulled him back to sleep.

* * *

"I'm going to beat you, Uncle Denny." The voice brought Faulkner awake with a start. He heard footsteps coming up the path. His hand felt beside him for the walking stick he'd found last night on his climb to the cave, but it was gone. He must have knocked it away in his sleep. All at once, Rhett raced into the cave with flashlight in hand and the three-legged wolf by his side. Rhett flashed a beam of light around the walls, pausing on Faulkner.

"Faulkner? I found you!" Rhett shined the light in his face.

Faulkner covered his eyes. "Want to turn that in a different direction?"

"Sorry." Rhett pointed the beam off the cave wall and stroked the wolf. "This is a good place to hide if you're playing hide-and-seek."

Denny entered the cave—flashlight in hand as well—winded and trying to catch his breath. Between sputters, he said, "Rhett, you're not to take off like that."

"But look who I found." Rhett point the beam of his flashlight on Faulkner again. "Do we hide now and Faulkner has to find us?"

Denny shook his head. "He's playing a different kind of hide-and-seek." He gazed at Faulkner and nodded. "I wondered if we'd find you here, especially after Rhett said he told you about this place. You look awful." He stared at Faulkner like he'd sprouted another head or something.

"Happens when you go headlong over a waterfall." Faulkner started to get up, but Denny stopped him.

"Just rest there. I packed a big lunch, but we can have it now. We'd be happy to share it. Food should do you some good. Rhett, be a sport, and go back to the canoe to fetch it."

Rhett took off with Jacob. Faulkner watched the wolf as he guided Rhett down the path, much like he'd guided Faulkner the night before. He thought about how the animal had left him once they'd come to the creek, as if the wolf knew Faulkner would follow it and would be all right. No . . . that couldn't be. Then again . . .

Denny cleared his throat. "Went over the falls, huh? That had to be some landing. Wish I could have been here to see it."

"It was dark. You wouldn't have seen much." Faulkner felt uneasy with Denny. He always had, though at the moment, Denny seemed friendly enough. Faulkner would still be cautious.

"Sheriff Padraic has put a safety detail at Jo's, so it's best you stay put. And I won't tell anyone where you are just as long as you don't hurt my sister or Rhett—and when I prove my father's death was an accident, you turn yourself in. Got it?"

Faulkner nodded, though he had an addendum to Denny's demands. Faulkner was never going back to prison. He was innocent, and he planned to prove it or die trying.

* * *

Jo followed Edward into the house through the back door to the kitchen. Edward told her Sophie, his maid and cook, had gone to town and that Jo should make herself at home, and then he excused himself and headed toward the restroom.

Ever since the first time Jo had come here, she'd admired this enormous kitchen with a huge island in the center and stainless-steel sinks. Growing up cooking for her father and brother, she appreciated a kitchen with lots of room. Lance's mother had been a great cook, or so Jo had heard. She'd been killed in a car accident driving to Idaho Falls on slick roads when her children were young. Jo had never met her. She supposed that Lance and Denny having their mothers both gone from their lives was what had drawn them together as friends.

Because her mother had left when Jo was only five, she had grown up learning to cook out of necessity, but when she wasn't worried or stressed, she actually enjoyed it. She could never remember her mother cooking. Taren Powers had left nothing of a legacy behind except a letter for her husband. Jo didn't even like thinking of the woman.

"Sorry it took so long." Edward rushed back into the kitchen, guiding Jo away from bitter memories to a cheery breakfast nook. "Lance told me you're moving up the wedding. Can't tell you how much that means to me."

Jo didn't know how she was going to tell Edward that Lance had mis-spoken. She hoped somehow the words would come to her.

"So he told you about my cancer coming back?" Edward didn't wait for her answer. "Big shock, and then I heard Faulkner sprang loose from prison. Bad news comes in threes, so more's on the way."

Jo hated to be the third bit of bad news, but maybe she could frame it so it wasn't. "About the wedding—"

Edward jumped right on the word. "Yes, the wedding. Might be best out there by the stream. I think where the footbridge is would be a spot you might like the preacher to stand. There's plenty of lawn for guest chairs. Thinking of your wedding helps me not think of my own troubles.

"I'll pay for it all. I know you're still strapped paying off Denny's debts and building your own place. By the way, what are you going to do with your clinic?" Edward rose. "Would you like some coffee, tea . . . even a little brandy helps kick-start the day?"

Jo knew he was nervous. "Nothing for me, thank you," she managed to get out.

He went to the chrome-plated coffeepot and poured himself a cup. "I think we can pull off getting ready for the wedding by Monday. How about a sunrise service with the sun peaking over Mount Baldy?"

"Edward, please, come sit down." Jo was going to have to burst his bubble.

As though he suddenly recognized her somber mood, he returned to the nook. "You're worried about Faulkner, aren't you?"

"Not really." Jo looked at the older man sitting across from her. He had been sincere in his joy and now in his concern. She didn't want him to worry, but he needed to know the truth. "About the wedding, I have Rhett to think about."

Edward nodded. "He's such a great kid. He's going to fit in at the ranch much better than his father ever did, that's for sure. From the day I brought Cassandra and her son home, that kid was the stray who never joined the fold. I should have seen the bad blood between him and my boys. Might still have Coulton if I had." For a moment, Edward seemed pulled into a distant memory. He looked up, saw Jo, and smiled. "You know, Faulkner stole you away from my eldest, but at least Lance has won you back where you belong. Always thought you should be part of my family."

"That may be, but not for a while." Jo hoped this would lead to breaking the news gently.

He tilted his head, waiting for her to go on.

"With your illness, I think it would be best to postpone the wedding instead of move it up."

Edward's brows bunched together.

"You're going to have radiation and chemo treatments, which will be very taxing on your system. You'll need a lot of rest. Rhett doesn't understand that when someone is ill he needs to be quiet. And with him starting school this year, he's bound to bring home colds or flu germs. With your treatments, you can't afford to get sick." She reached over and rubbed Edward's arm.

"I'll be fine. I can wear a mask if he's ill, and I'll stay in my room. Don't you see, having someone living here full of life . . . after all we've been through . . . well, it would help more than hinder." Edward searched her face as though looking for a sign that she was giving in.

But she couldn't. "I'll bring Rhett over to visit plenty of times, but believe me, when we leave, you'll be glad we're going to my place so you can have peace and quiet." Jo smiled, hoping Edward would see the wisdom in her decision.

"Seems your mind is made up for now. Why don't I make us some lunch, and we can talk it over more." Edward started to rise.

Jo could tell he was growing tired. "No, you sit still. I'll make it. You want soup or sandwiches or both?" She went to the fridge. Opening the door, she waited for his reply.

Edward ignored her request to stay seated and got up anyway. He opened a cupboard. "I'm not an invalid yet, you know. Let's splurge and do both. I'll make the soup."

All through making lunch and eating it, Edward enumerated on the positives of having the wedding before he started his treatments. And Jo countered with concerns over his treatments and Rhett's being a handful. She even threw in Denny, which was a wildcard that went nowhere because Edward said Denny was over here more than he was at her place.

When lunch was over and as they did the dishes, Jo decided to ask him about the day he saw her father on Table Rock. "I didn't know that you saw my dad the day he died."

Edward grew solemn and nodded. "He loved that trail. Still blame myself for not asking him to come home with me for lunch. If I wouldn't have left him alone, he might still be here today."

"Did you notice anything unusual?" Jo rinsed suds off a plate and set it on the towel for Edward to wipe.

"Not really. He was happy that you and Rhett were back home and that you were starting your practice as a vet. Come to think of it, he seemed a little upset about something but didn't want to talk. Oh, how I miss your father." The topic seemed to zap the rest of Edward's energy. Jo could tell the cancer was dragging him down. She told him to go take a nap and she'd finish up. He gave her a hug, told her thank you and to let herself out, and then he left her alone in the kitchen.

Jo felt bad that she was raining all over Edward's desire for Lance to marry her. Why was he so determined for them to wed? Maybe Edward didn't want Lance to be alone after he died. Or maybe Edward wanted an heir to the ranch. She really didn't think he wanted the ranch to go to Rhett, being as he was Faulkner's child. She'd bet the old man was hopeful that she'd get pregnant right away.

The house was unusually quiet. Sophie hadn't returned yet. Faulkner had told Jo he'd found Coulton dead in the den, and the thought piqued her curiosity. Edward wouldn't mind if she looked around. Good grief, he wanted her to marry his son as soon as possible, and that would mean this house would become her home. And the kitchen . . . She gazed at the granite countertops and polished wooden cabinets, all things she'd pined for but couldn't afford.

Leaving the kitchen, she walked through the family room, where stuffed animal heads hung on the walls, trophies of Lance's and Edward's hunting abilities. A large white-rock fireplace filled an entire wall. A leather couch and chair were positioned so people could watch the fire or the plasma TV on the adjacent wall.

The den was at the front of the house, next to the door. *Hmm, makes easy access for the murderer to escape.*

The door to the den was closed. She twisted the knob and pushed it open. When she was young, she'd only glimpsed inside this room and had never ventured over the threshold. There was never a reason. Since her engagement to Lance, when they spent time with Edward, Jo avoided the room because it was a place that had changed her life.

A haunting aura guarded the den, forbidding her to venture forward. Strange how imagination and painful memories could stop a person.

She stepped in. The den was definitely "man" territory, decorated in dark browns and depressing blacks. Glancing at the floor, she wondered if it was there that Faulkner had found the gun. He said he'd kicked it before he could turn on the light, so it probably was the place.

A large ornate desk sat in front of an impressive gun cabinet filled with rifles and shotguns. So when Faulkner had found the gun, of course he would have walked over to the desk to put it back.

Jo followed the path she imagined he'd taken. Behind the desk and between it and the cabinet was where he'd found Coulton. She stared down where the body could have been. The carpet had been replaced with new, but this had to be where the body had lain.

She had a difficult time imagining Coulton dead. Alive, he'd been very good looking. He'd had one of those smiles and a wink that made a girl feel all mushy inside. He was his father's son and a cowboy at heart.

Who could have wanted him dead? She couldn't think of anyone who didn't like him. He was popular in high school, was even prom king when she was queen. And after he'd graduated, he'd become the heir apparent of the ranch. The community respected him. Jo would have married Coulton if it hadn't been for Faulkner.

And there was another thing to consider. Coulton and Faulkner had gotten along fairly well. They weren't bosom buddies, but of the two brothers,

Coulton had tried to make Faulkner feel welcomed to their family and went out of his way to include him for a while. Then something had happened between them. And he hadn't been very happy that Faulkner had stolen his girl, but even after that, Coulton had had no malicious intent toward Faulkner. She and Faulkner had been married for two years before Coulton had died. And in that time, he was always nice to Faulkner when he saw them together.

Just what had happened?

The jury had answered the question by pinning the murder on Faulkner, but it hadn't made sense to Jo then, and it sure didn't now.

"What are you doing in here?"

Jo looked up and found Lance standing in the doorway, a mad glower in his eyes and a sneer on his face.

CHAPTER FIFTEEN

FAULKNER WAS GRATEFUL FOR THE lunch Denny had shared with him: roast beef sandwiches, chips, cookies, and soda. When he asked where Jo was, Denny told him she'd received a call about an animal and had to take care of it.

After eating, they sat on the rocks outside the cave, where they had a good view of the waterfall and river, though Faulkner stayed in the shadows of the trees in case boats drifted by. Rhett searched for rocks to throw into the river.

Watching Rhett and Jacob, Faulkner asked Denny, "What's the story with the animal?"

"I actually found him up near my gold mine. His leg had been shot up. Where there's one wolf, there are usually others, so I let him be. Thought he'd die. When I got home and told Jo, she couldn't rest until I took her back up to the mine. Didn't think the animal would let her near him, but she has a way with wild beasts." Denny took a drink of his pop, wiped his mouth, and stared at Faulkner like he was the latest wild beast she'd helped.

"Did she amputate his leg right there?" Faulkner wanted to keep Denny's mind on the animal and not on him.

"Nah. She sedated him, and we loaded him up in the truck and hauled him to the clinic. She hated taking off his leg, but it was so mangled she had little choice. As the wolf recovered, he tamed right down and got used to us. Kind of took to Rhett like he was a pup or something." Denny grabbed a cookie from the sack. Before eating it, he said, "Something about you has changed."

"Seven years in prison will do that." Faulkner didn't care for Denny inspecting him, but he didn't want to make a scene and draw Rhett's attention. If he heard them talking about prison, that would only make him curious, which would not be good. Besides, the boy was having fun, throwing bigger and bigger rocks into the water, watching the splash with each grow larger and larger.

"No, this is underneath all that. It's like you're desperate, yet there's a peace about you. Can't figure it out." Denny finished off his cookie, all the while staring at Faulkner.

"Could be that I found something to believe in beyond people." Faulkner hadn't planned to tell Denny about his conversion, but that seemed to be where this conversation was headed.

"And what is that?" Denny brushed cookie crumbs off himself.

"God."

Denny did a double take. "Really?"

"Yes." Faulkner was not going to defend his belief. Not to Denny. Not to anyone. He had found God, and he knew that whatever happened to him would be according to His will and guidance. God was the only reason Faulkner had found Jo and had survived falling over the waterfall. He knew it, and it didn't matter if Denny or anyone else believed him.

"Well, if God helps you get through the day, I guess that's a good thing." Denny stared at him. "Jo said our dad came to see you before he died. She said you think someone killed him because of that visit." The tone in Denny's voice made Faulkner wary.

"He did, and I do." He stared at Denny, never taking his gaze from him.

"I'm the one who found my father dead in that ravine. It would take a coldhearted person to do that to someone." Denny grew silent as he peered at the ground. Faulkner empathized with him. He'd lost his own father, but he hadn't seen him after the crash. He couldn't imagine how tough that had been on Denny.

"The only reason I haven't called Sheriff Padraic about you is I'm going to prove that you're lying about my father visiting you." He rubbed his chin. "Dad was a good judge of character. He always knew I wouldn't amount to much, but Jo, he had plans for her. Nearly did him in to give her to you in marriage."

This was news to Faulkner. He knew Doc hadn't been especially happy about their getting married, but he didn't think her father strongly objected either. "Your father hid his feelings very well because he always treated me kindly, that is until . . ."

"Until you killed Coulton," Denny said it matter-of-factly. "What does your God think of murder?"

"I didn't kill Coulton." Faulkner's voice rose a little too much and drew Rhett's attention. He waved and smiled at the boy, hoping he'd keep playing.

Rhett started climbing up to them.

"A judge and jury said you did." Though Denny's voice sounded firm in his own conviction of Faulkner, his eyes flickered with something . . . Could it be doubt?

Faulkner stared at Denny, hopeful to build on this thread of emotion, and said as quickly as possible, "I didn't do it. Your father believed I didn't either. Someone else killed Coulton, my mother, and your father, and I would think you would want to do everything you could to find the real killer before someone else we love ends up dead."

Rhett reached them. "Look what I found." He held a small rock up to Denny. "I think it's an agate I can add to my collection."

Denny took the pebble and turned it over and over in his hand. "Looks can be deceiving." He stared at Faulkner over Rhett's head. "We'll check it in your rock book so you have proof."

Faulkner piped up. "You don't have to prove anything to me, Rhett. If you think it's an agate, I'll believe you."

Rhett looked between Denny and Faulkner. He must have known they were talking of something other than the rock.

Denny pocketed the pebble. "It's time we headed back, Rhett." He glanced at Faulkner. "I'll bring you some supplies."

Faulkner could well imagine that with the supplies, Denny would probably bring the sheriff, but that was all right. Faulkner planned to be well on his way to the Wymer ranch by then.

* * *

Jo didn't know what to say to Lance, but she managed to improvise. "Sheriff Padraic suggested I borrow a gun from you, so I thought I'd take a look at what you have, but I've never stood here where Coulton was killed. I guess I wasn't prepared for all the emotions I'd feel."

Lance gave her a warm, consoling smile. He walked into the room, followed by Champ. The dog walked slowly but was on the mend from his surgery. Despite his stitches, he jumped up on Jo, his front paws nearly reaching her shoulders. She stroked the animal's head and helped him down. "I thought you broke him of that habit."

"I have. He's just happy to see you." Lance patted the German shepherd's head and gazed at Jo. "The last few days have been rough, haven't they? Faulkner's prison break has us all thinking of the past." Lance put his arm around her. "You know, it took me years to come in here again. Did my father as well. I can't tell you the hell we lived through during the days after Coulton's death. And with Cassandra dying . . . there were times when I thought my father would give up. That man has lost two wives and his firstborn son. He's amazing." Lance held Jo close. "I don't want to ever lose you."

Jo looked up at him, and all at once, his face became Faulkner's. She'd placed her palm on Faulkner's face at the height of his fever, and he'd opened his eyes and looked into hers. Her hand automatically raised to Lance's cheek.

He took her hand in his and kissed her knuckles, awakening her from her memory. Guilt and confusion fell upon her in one mighty swoop. She gulped but said nothing, trying to remember what Lance had been saying before she'd spaced out. Something like he didn't want to lose her.

But had he already?

Or had he ever really had her? She couldn't speak, so instead, she smiled to imply he wouldn't.

Lance lovingly rubbed Jo's arm. "We need to quit looking back and look ahead. Life is too short to dwell on the past. We need to think about what will be." He leaned his forehead to hers.

Jo stared into his eyes. "You're right, and that's why I think we need to slow things down a little."

Lance leaned back. "What do you mean?"

"The wedding. We should postpone getting married until after your father is well." There. Jo had finally told him.

"But I thought at Table Rock you'd agreed to move up the date and get married as soon as possible. What's changed?" Lance dropped his arms from around her.

Everything and nothing. But she couldn't say that. "If you remember right, I didn't agree. And it's complicated."

"It's only complicated if you make it that way. Do you love me?" Lance stared at her.

There was the question again. And for the first time, she wondered if she really did. Or if she ever had loved him like he wanted her to. She had known Lance most all of her life. He'd helped her through some rough times, but had she fooled herself into thinking the love she felt for him was enough? Did she love him like a woman loved a man she wanted to spend her life with? Did she love him enough to want to be with him every second of the day? Did she love him enough to get in his bed every night? Did she love him enough to give him everything he would expect from a wife?

She knew the answer.

No.

She didn't.

That love was Faulkner's. It always had been and always would be. Staring at Lance, she struggled for words, but they failed her.

"Maybe I'm pushing too much." Lance rubbed the back of his neck. "I'm feeling a little raw with the news of my father and with Faulkner on the loose. And this new bull I bought to replace Loco might not be as good as we'd hoped." He gazed up at her. "Jo, I didn't mean to put pressure on you."

Feeling like a heel, she said, "I just think we need to wait awhile. I talked to your father and told him Rhett and I will come over as often as he can tolerate us. But I can't add the stress of a wedding to the mix. It doesn't feel right."

"What do you mean, it doesn't feel right?" His eyes studied hers.

"Your father could be dying of cancer, the man everyone believes killed your brother is on the loose, and you're having financial woes. And I haven't told Rhett about his father, that he was convicted of killing your brother, and . . . well, all those are plenty of reasons to wait." She'd left off the most important reason, that deep inside she knew she didn't love Lance enough to marry him.

Or that she'd fallen in love with her ex-husband again.

The thought had raced through her mind and stopped all other thoughts from the enormity of it. Yes, she had fallen in love with Faulkner . . . again. She gazed at Lance. She was such a coward. He deserved to know the truth, and she would tell him, but not now.

Later.

Much later.

Much, much later.

"I suppose you're right. I guess I was being selfish by wanting you by my side twenty-four/seven." Lance's gaze went to the floor beside them, the spot where his brother had died. "I want to make sure you're safe, and I want to keep my father around as long as I can. Getting married right away seemed to solve both problems." Lance straightened his stance and looked at the gun cabinet. "You're welcome to borrow a gun if you want." He didn't wait for her reply. "Let's see. I think a .22 would have less recoil than a shotgun, but in a crisis, your aim might be off. Since you haven't really handled a gun before, you should have one with muscle."

He pulled open a drawer. Inside were several labeled boxes: Glock, Winchester, Remington. He grabbed a small box with the silhouette of a bull on it and set it on the desk. "This is a .45 revolver. It's called 'the Judge.' You can put bullets in it or shotgun shells. Has quite a kick, but if you hold it right, you'll be fine."

Jo stared at the gun. The thought of actually pointing a weapon at another human being made her ill. Yet, if she didn't take it, what would Lance think, especially after talking with the sheriff? The two of them were only trying to keep her safe, but she knew something neither of them did. She knew Faulkner wasn't dangerous. He was only trying to find the truth. And to do that, he believed he had to confront Lance and Edward. Though, if he showed up here, someone could get hurt, and knowing Faulkner's physical condition, it would very likely be him. The only way to stop that from happening was if the police were here. "Lance, you and your father are the ones who need the safety detail, not me."

Lance stared at her like she'd lost her senses. "We're very capable of defending ourselves." His eyes panned over the arsenal in the cabinet before him. "If Faulkner so much as sets foot on this land, he's as good as dead. And his death will be no accident, believe me."

"Accident?"

Lance handed Jo the Judge and a box of ammunition before closing the drawer. "I never keep a loaded gun in the cabinet. And yeah, the accident that he didn't get a death sentence. Don't you think that was an accident?"

Jo was appalled. "No. I'm the one who pleaded for his life, don't you remember?"

He slowly nodded. "You were married to him and didn't know better. But with him escaping prison, he's changed the game. And if he so much as shows his face here, I'll teach him a new set of rules. Don't worry your pretty little head about Dad and me."

The look in Lance's eyes said it all. He planned to shoot to kill and then ask questions later. She knew in Lance's mind he was defending his family. After what had happened to Coulton, she couldn't blame him. But he didn't know the entire story.

Nobody did.

Nobody but Coulton.

CHAPTER SIXTEEN

WHEN JO PULLED UP TO her house, she found Sheriff Padraic's SUV parked out front. *Great. That's all I need.*

She glanced at the box that held the gun Lance had given her. The Judge. Well, maybe after she showed the sheriff she had a gun, he'd call off his watchdogs. Lance had also loaned her a portable safe to keep the weapon in. She would put the gun in it and place them both in the back of her closet, where Rhett wouldn't find them.

She figured Sheriff Padraic was inside, talking to Denny and Rhett. Her son could easily slip and tell the sheriff about the man his mother had helped, and the gig would be up. It might be up right this very minute, for all Jo knew. Maybe the sheriff was there because he'd found Faulkner.

She pulled into the garage. Getting out, she stacked the gun and ammunition boxes on top of the safe and headed for the stairs. She noticed Apollo in the outside corral. With her hands full and the sheriff here, she made a mental note to have Denny take care of the horse. Argi, the fawn, watched Jo walk by, her big brown eyes following her every move as though worried. That was ridiculous. The animal needed to be fed was all, Jo thought. She would have to see to the deer later. At the foot of the stairs, she remembered she still hadn't closed her father's trunk. *Good grief.* She was forgetting everything. She'd see what the sheriff wanted and then take care of the trunk.

She slowly made her way up to the clinic. No one was there, so she continued on to the living quarters. Jo could hear Rhett's voice. As she reached the top step, she found the sheriff, Denny, and Rhett sitting at the kitchen table. "Uncle Denny didn't know if it was an agate or not, so we decided to bring it home and look it up." Rhett had been talking to the sheriff, but when he spied his mom, he said, "Look what I found at the river today." He held up a rock.

Jo set her burden on the dining room table and took the rock from Rhett. "Very nice. You should add it to your collection."

Denny stood. "Come on, squirt, I'll help you look it up so you can label it."

Rhett seemed anxious to take care of his new addition and hurried down the hall with Denny closely following. Before leaving, her brother gave Jo a look that said, *Watch your step.*

With them both gone, Jo sat on a chair by the sheriff. Patting the boxes on the table, she said, "Here's the gun and the safe you wanted me to have."

Sheriff Padraic eyed the bull on the box. "The Judge. That should do the trick. I'll load it for you before I leave. And make sure if you have to use it that you're close to whomever you're shooting at. This gun has a spray like a shotgun."

"So you're going to call off your watchdogs, right?"

"Tomorrow, maybe."

Jo noticed the empty coffee cups on the table. "Want a refill?"

"Nah. I came by because I needed to talk with you." The sheriff grew all businesslike.

"What's up?" She tried hard to appear obliging and cooperative.

"Carl Jenkins told me that after the rodeo the other night, he was stuck behind you leaving and thought he saw you drive away with a strange man in your truck. Know anything about that?"

Jo's instinct was to deny it, but she knew a truck from behind had honked at her. She'd thought the man was just being impatient, but it must have been Jenkins attempting to find out if she was all right. She could claim that he'd been mistaken. But she knew she couldn't. Things were getting too complicated. Jo had to be as truthful as she possibly could. She cleared her throat and looked into the sheriff's eyes. "It's true. 'Bout scared me to death."

"Mind telling me who it was?" Sheriff Padraic stared at her.

Jo expected an interrogation spotlight to shine in her eyes at any moment. "I didn't recognize him at first, but it was Faulkner." There, she'd said it. Now what? Would he arrest her? She imagined her entire world would explode. Yet, at the moment, it didn't.

"Want to fill in some of the blanks here?" The sheriff leaned back in his chair and folded his arms.

"He'd been shot, so I patched him up. He told me that two years ago my father came to visit him and that Dad believed Cassandra's death was no accidental overdose. Faulkner had no idea Dad had died. As we talked, we realized Dad's accident happened shortly after his visit with Faulkner."

Sheriff Padraic's eyes narrowed, but he didn't move, just stared at Jo.

She couldn't wait to see how he'd react to the rest, so she continued. "Faulkner believes someone killed my father. And that the same person was responsible for Coulton's and Cassandra's deaths as well."

"So Faulkner is why you brought all this up yesterday. Do you share his beliefs?" The sheriff seemed to patiently wait for her reply.

"I didn't at first. But the more I think about it, the more I wonder."

Sheriff Padraic leaned forward, placing his elbows on the table. "Listen to me. Like I told you before, I investigated every one of those deaths. And I'm checking into them again, but the fact remains that Lance caught Faulkner standing over his brother with the murder weapon in his hands."

"You keep saying that, but what if the murderer left the gun behind and Faulkner picked it up without realizing what had happened? As you said yesterday, there was no residue on him, remember?"

"Jo . . ." He tugged off his hat and set it on the table. "I could understand your believing this story seven years ago, but now? You're marrying Lance. Don't you believe your fiancé?"

"I believe he was overwrought with emotions that night. Did you really do a thorough investigation into Cassandra's death and my father's, or did you just assume?"

"Here we go again with your questioning my professionalism." The sheriff appeared insulted, and his face grew bright red.

Jo couldn't afford to make him angry. Not with so much riding on this conversation. "I'm just saying that at the time when Coulton died and then with Cassandra's death two days later, emotions were running high, and things could have been overlooked. Not on purpose, but . . ."

Sheriff Padraic took Jo's hand. "When the tox screen came back, I knew it was an open and shut case of either suicide or accidental overdose."

"But don't people who commit suicide leave a note?" Jo was glad she had the opportunity to bring this up. "My mother left a letter for my father when she left. I think if Cassandra intended suicide, she would have left a note. And did you ever think she could have been the one who killed Coulton?"

He rolled his eyes. "Of course I wondered, but there was no proof. And that's what you need to back up such a claim. There was plenty of proof that Faulkner killed him and no reason to go poking around to see if Cassandra did it. And the reason for her death was obvious."

"But what about my father?" Jo had to keep the sheriff thinking of possibilities. "He was an experienced hiker who would only go off the trail to take a picture and only where it was safe, unless someone was with him. Unless someone made him?"

The sheriff took a deep breath. Staring at her with concern in his green eyes, he said, "Don't do this."

"What? Try to find the truth?" Jo was perplexed by his attitude.

"The truth is staring you in the face. For some reason only your father would have known, he went off the trail and fell to his death. Doesn't matter how many times you look at it, that's the fact. I searched that trail and found nothing out of the ordinary. And no matter how many people I questioned around the area that day, no one had seen him. He was alone. And he fell."

"That's not true."

Sheriff Padraic stared at her.

"Lance told me his father saw Dad before he fell. And that you and Lance knew Edward had spoken to my father. Why wouldn't you tell Denny and me that? Doesn't seem very professional not to tell the deceased's children everything."

"I thought you knew. Besides, Edward didn't remember anything out of the ordinary." The sheriff drew a deep breath.

"Edward told me today that he knew something was bothering my father."

"Which only adds to the point that your father was probably preoccupied and accidentally fell. That's all." He rubbed his chin and gazed at her like he expected her to agree.

The finality of his words slapped Jo, adding to her hurt. Was the sheriff hiding something from her? He said he was looking into the cases again, but it was obvious he wanted them kept closed. Jo felt an emotional tsunami coming on, but she'd be darned if she'd let it hit her full force in front of this man. If he could be stubborn, so could she. As she regained her composure, she said, "Why are you pretending to look into the cases if you're so set against finding new information?"

"I'm not. But you have to tell me why one more time would be any different?" He waited.

"Because they were people I loved but, most importantly, because you missed something." She knew those last words would light a fire of some kind in the man.

But the reaction she expected didn't come. Sheriff Padraic grew very quiet as he studied her. "Okay, Jo. You know you've broken the law by harboring a fugitive. And you've put others in danger. For you to sit here and question my professionalism takes a lot of nerve. But I'm an understanding man, and you've been through hell and back the last few years. Look, I promise I'll be as thorough and open-minded as I possibly can if you tell me where Faulkner is right now."

* * *

Faulkner had every intention of leaving the cave. He had a feeling things were closing in on him, and he didn't have time to waste before facing off with Lance and Edward. But Denny had taken the canoe and left him stranded. He could swim down the river a little ways and climb out. If he kept out of the main current, it shouldn't be too dangerous. Though it would be best to wait until dark. He couldn't afford for anyone to see him.

Waiting for the sun to go down, Faulkner thought of the time he'd spent with his son today. That was an added bonus he hadn't counted on. Just seeing how excited the boy was to find a rock was another cherished moment. That conversation with Denny though had been strained. Who could blame Denny for his hard feelings toward him? Not only had Faulkner married his sister and busted up the plans Denny had had for her, but Denny truly believed Faulkner had killed Coulton, his good friend.

Denny had grown solemn earlier that afternoon when he'd spoken of finding his father after he fell. Grief still shadowed him. While Denny spoke of that horrible day, he'd had a faraway look in his eyes. At the time, it had appeared to be grief, but was it?

With clarity, Faulkner realized Denny may know more about his father's death than he'd led everyone to believe. The man was hiding something, and Faulkner needed to know what it was. It might help solve the mystery around not only Faulkner's mother's death but Coulton's as well. Yes, Faulkner had to risk staying here one more night to quiz Denny. He was coming back to bring supplies, but would he bring the law with him too?

Faulkner had to have a plan of escape just in case. He peered into the dank darkness of the cave. Just where did it go? Grabbing the flashlight Denny had left behind, he started down the passageway.

Cold, musty air met him. He panned the light around. Water seeped from the earthen walls. He found white calcium deposits built up in places. Some of the large stones jetting out of the walls and the ground looked porous. The farther he went, the more unstable the cave appeared. If an earthquake hit, this place would fall in. As the passage narrowed, an acidic scent grew stronger and stronger.

Faulkner's claustrophobia kicked in, but he could see that in a pinch, he could hide out back there. He retraced his steps, finally coming to the more open space where he'd been staying. He yearned to go outside, but not long after Denny and Rhett had left, a couple of fishermen had trolled by in a little dinghy. Before, when he'd been with Denny and Rhett, he'd stayed in the shadows and wasn't too worried. People were used to seeing those two. But he couldn't take the chance of someone seeing him here alone. Surely Denny would return soon.

Faulkner peered out at the trail. The same canoe Denny had used had been pulled ashore. Someone was coming. Holding his breath, he stared down the rocky path, praying that Denny was alone.

Jo's auburn hair caught in the fading sunlight. She came into view, huffing and puffing, a heavy pack strapped to her back. Forgetting his concern for cover, Faulkner went out to greet her. "Are you alone?"

"Well, it's good to see you too." She sounded defensive.

"I meant, it's great to see you." He would have given her a hug, but she looked annoyed, and the backpack was in the way, so he led her into the cave.

She tugged off her load and let it rest on the ground. Rubbing her eyes, she said, "You would not believe the afternoon I've had."

"Is everything all right?" Jo was risking a lot by taking care of him and hiding his whereabouts.

"Yes and no." Her nimble fingers unzipped the pack, and she pulled out her medical bag. "I want to check your wound and give you another shot of amoxicillin. Denny told me you went over the falls last night. Criminey sakes, Faulkner, you could have been killed."

"Wasn't like I did it on purpose." He sat down on the ledge where he'd slept. Leaning back, he pulled up his shirt, all the while staring at Jo. She was really here, helping him once again. He watched her as her sapphire eyes studied his wound and then as she squinted to see through the darkened shadows of the cave.

"So where's the dressing?" She pulled a flashlight from her pack, clicked it on, and spotlighted the reddened area.

He chuckled. "I went over the falls, remember?" Her long auburn hair hung about her shoulders. She pulled Neosporin and sterile dressing from her medical bag.

"I'm amazed, but it's really looking better. Maybe the plunge helped." She put the ointment on him, placing the dressing carefully on top. Then her fingers glided over some tape, skittering over his flesh, soft and gentle as she pressed. Her touch was warm, familiar, and reminded him of all he'd lost. Next, she pulled a syringe out of her bag. The vial was already loaded with medicine. Taking off the cap, she asked, "Where do you want it? In your arm? Or . . . ?"

Faulkner rolled up the sleeve of the flannel shirt as high as it would go. She stuck him and injected the medicine. Finished, she recapped the needle, dropped it in her medical bag, and stared at Faulkner. "Sheriff Padraic knows I took care of you."

"What?" The reality of his situation once again grabbed hold. He jerked his shirtsleeve down. "And he didn't arrest you for helping me?"

"I fully expected him to, but he didn't. Maybe he's using me as bait to catch you. Or maybe he believes us." She busied herself with the pack and pulled a blanket and small pillow from it. "He was at the house when I got back today. Told me that someone at the rodeo saw a stranger with me in my truck."

"Someone?" He had tried so hard to be careful. And in the rain, he thought for certain no one had noticed him.

"Remember, someone honked and you looked out the back window? Anyway, I think the sheriff was playing on a hunch." Jo bit her bottom lip.

He knew she could be right. Officers did that a lot. "So what did you tell him?"

"Everything." From the pack, she pulled out a plastic table cloth and smoothed it over the ledge beside him. Then she reached back in and got a neatly wrapped loaf of her homemade bread, a jar of gooseberry jam, and a thermos, placing them on the makeshift table as if she'd just told him some amusing gossip.

"Everything?" He couldn't believe it. "What do you mean, everything?"

She dug out two bowls, another thermos, and two Styrofoam cups. "I told him Dad visited you a couple of years ago before he died. That he believed Cassandra was murdered and that we now suspect he was murdered too."

Faulkner buttoned his shirt sleeve. "I bet that went over well."

"Not so much. He was pretty offended that I thought he may have overlooked something. For instance, why didn't he find a letter? If your mother committed suicide, she would have left one." She sat on the other side of the food and opened the thermos.

"What did he say to that?"

"He told me there wasn't one and that he found an empty bottle of sleeping pills by her bed and the tox screen showed drugs in her system. So he's convinced it was an accidental overdose."

"But I gave her the last pill on the night I went over to help her. If they found a lot of drugs in her system, she must have had it refilled."

Jo opened the thermos and poured Faulkner a bowl of hot beef stew. Placing a plastic spoon in it, she handed him the bowl.

Grateful for something warm to eat, he immediately took it, but before eating his first bite, he asked, "What did he say about your father's death?"

"Thinks it was an accident."

"His thinking it was one doesn't make it so." Faulkner blew on the spoonful of stew before placing it in his mouth. The taste of beef broth, carrots, peas, and potatoes played over his tongue. He hadn't realized how hungry he was until now. Swallowing, he said, "Did you discuss Coulton at all?"

"It's the same argument. You had the gun, Lance found you, end of story." Jo dished up some stew for herself and started to eat. Between swallows, she said, "I told him I still believe you are innocent."

Faulkner paused. It was one thing for Jo to tell him she believed he was innocent, quite another for her to tell the sheriff. How was it that Faulkner could be so lucky to have found Jo again and to have her still believe in him? The Lord was working miracles for Faulkner. "So that must have made his day."

"Not really. He wanted to know where you're hiding." She had quit eating.

"What did you tell him?" He didn't think the police had followed her. If they had, she wouldn't have come.

"I truthfully told him that I didn't know." She took another spoonful of stew and smiled at him. Covering her mouth, she said, "I didn't at the time. I had a hunch but wasn't certain. Denny told me you were here after the sheriff left."

"And Denny didn't tell him?"

"No. When the good sheriff was grilling me with all of his questions, Denny and Rhett were adding a rock to Rhett's collection."

Faulkner smiled, remembering the excitement Rhett had shown over the agate he'd found. "Do you think it's safe for me to stay here one more night?"

"That's why I brought you the supplies." She glanced at the blanket, pillow, and food.

"Denny said he was going to bring them to me."

"I convinced him to let me. He kept the safety detail occupied while I sneaked out the back door. I wanted to talk to you about a plan."

Faulkner stared at her, bewildered and grateful and wary. Not that she'd do anything to cause trouble, but she might not be aware. "Which is?"

"When I went over to the Wymers' this afternoon—"

"You what?" He couldn't believe she would do such a dangerous thing. "The Wymers'? You went there? By yourself? I thought you had an emergency animal thing." He drove his fingers through his hair.

"Good grief. I told you I was going there. I've been there a lot. Calm down and let me explain." She slid down from the ledge, walked over, and hopped up on the other side of Faulkner, sitting next to him like she thought her presence would calm him down. He had to admit, it helped. She may have visited the Wymers many times, but that was before he'd escaped, that was before more attention had been placed on what had actually happened on that ranch.

She gazed into his eyes. "I had to tell Edward and Lance that instead of moving up the wedding, we needed to postpone it."

"I'll bet that made them happy." He set his bowl of stew down and gave her his full attention.

"No, it did not. They were both very disappointed. But I told Edward that Rhett and I would visit him most every day as he fought the cancer. And Lance . . ." She paused.

Faulkner waited, worried about what she would say next.

"He was a bit upset, but he'll be okay. He showed me the guns he had in the cabinet."

"You went into the den?" A chill flitted through Faulkner as though a ghost had crossed over him.

"That's where Lance found me."

"In the den?"

"Yeah, when I arrived, Lance wasn't there. Just Edward and me. After he went to lie down, I decided to go in the den. All this time and I haven't been in there." She grew silent.

"And Lance found you. That's where you told him you were postponing the wedding. What did you say?" The irony and parallel of the situation in conjunction with when Lance had found Faulkner in the same den nearly overwhelmed Faulkner.

"I told him we needed to wait until things settled down. He was okay with it. I also told him Sheriff Padraic had been after me to get a gun and that's why I was in the den. Lance showed me the weapons. I'm amazed that after all that has happened, they still have guns in that house."

"Guns don't kill. People do." Faulkner had always believed that and even more so after what he'd been through.

"That's another argument for another day. Lance implied that if he sees you, he's going to shoot to kill. Faulkner, I can't lose you again." She glanced down at her hands. "I want you to know . . . I have no intention of marrying Lance. Not now. Not later. Not ever."

He lifted her chin. Their eyes caught and held. He wanted to tell her how much he loved her. He could see in her gaze that she loved him. All the years of being separated, all the trauma of the trial, and all the hurt from the divorce melted into the mists of the waterfall beside them.

A lock of Jo's hair fell across her face, threatening to break the spell. Faulkner reached up and put it behind her ear like he'd seen her do so many times before. Her cheeks flushed pink. Her lips parted like she was going to speak, but she remained silent. Her eyes glistened and lit with passion.

It was a passion Faulkner remembered and yearned for once again. He cupped her face between his hands and drew his lips down to hers. Though he'd kissed her before in her garage, it had been different. That was a kiss good-bye. Now he wanted her to want him as she had when they'd been married and before he'd ruined their lives. Her lips played against his. She tasted of life, of hope, and of a possible future.

Her hands glided up his arms and around his neck, pulling him to her. This was what he'd wanted all along. This was Jo, his wife and his lover. Faulkner longed to be with her as he once had, but he knew he couldn't go through with his desires. He clasped her hand and drew her to him, whispering in her ear, "We can't do this."

"Why?" she asked breathlessly.

"I made a covenant with God that I would do nothing to hurt you if I could just see you again. And He's delivered His side of the bargain. I have to do the same."

"Faulkner, right now what would hurt me would be . . ." Her eyes searched his, pleading.

"But we're not married. It would be wrong." He couldn't believe he was turning away from the woman he'd known he was supposed to be with since the first time he'd laid eyes on her. He'd lost the privilege of acting like her husband. And he'd made the big mistake of giving her away with the divorce.

"While you're engaged to Lance, we can't. As far as the world knows, you're supposed to marry him. Until you break up and until we're legally married, we can't be together. It wouldn't be right."

"Not right?" Jo reared back.

"Look, God guided me to you. He's done so much for me. I need to do everything I possibly can so He'll continue to help me. We're going to need His help to find the real killer."

"And you think that being with the woman you love, the woman you were once married to, is going to make God upset?" Jo scoffed.

"He is merciful, but I don't think I'd be able to forgive myself for crossing the line." He stroked her cheek and clasped her hand in his.

Jo took a deep breath and smiled. "I can't believe the change that has come over you. I have to say in all honesty, I'm impressed." She sighed.

He chuckled. "You mentioned you had a plan?

"Yes, tomorrow morning, I'm going to visit Edward, and while I'm there, I'm going to do some snooping around."

"Well, you're not going without me." Faulkner didn't care how much she protested; he'd come to a decision, and he wasn't backing down.

CHAPTER SEVENTEEN

PANIC COURSED THROUGH JO. IF Faulkner went to the Wymer ranch, there would be trouble. "I understand you want to confront Lance and Edward about what happened to your mother, but Lance . . . well, he says he'll shoot you on sight."

Faulkner sucked in a deep breath and let it out. "Which is why I may need your help. You could get me in the house, then I could question Edward about Mom's death. Being in prison for seven years has taught me how to read people. I'll be able to tell if Edward lies to me."

"And if he has no idea, then what?" Jo didn't mean to always question, but she needed to understand what was ahead of them.

"Then I'll focus on Lance. No one ever really pressed him about what he was doing on the night Coulton died." He paused a moment and took Jo's hand. "I'll be all right."

She rubbed his calloused knuckles. Staring into his eyes, she said, "I know you hate being stuck here in the cave, but why don't you let me question Edward again before you take such a risk. I know I can get him to tell me more. I'll even push him for information about the day Coulton died. We know Edward was away buying rodeo stock, but what was he doing all that time? And when did he come back? I can ask him questions without raising suspicion."

Faulkner shook his head. "They went over all of that at the trial. Everyone had alibis."

"You forget. I was at the trial too. The court only knew where everyone was at the time you showed up at the ranch because that's when they think the shooting happened. But obviously, it didn't. And even though they established a time of death, in the end, that's only an estimate because rigor mortis doesn't set in for at least three hours after someone dies."

Faulkner stared at her. "How do you know that?"

She smiled. "I'm a vet, remember? At the time of your trial, I hadn't gone to school, but since then, I've learned. And even though establishing the time of death for an animal is not as critical as for humans, it is important for ranchers."

"I wish this had come up at my trial," Faulkner said.

She leaned back against the cave wall. "While our police force is very professional, they don't have the technology you see on TV or in the movies. Their budget for fighting crime is small. And they don't have the manpower."

"I know." Faulkner relaxed against the cave wall beside Jo. "I must admit that I was pretty numb during that time, merely walking through the motions. Still, my lawyer should have done a better job."

"We can't sit here and think about what should have been done. What we need to do is think of a way to right the wrong. And that's where I come in." She peered deeply into his eyes. "Let me do this, Faulkner. Let me see what I can find out before you storm the Wymer fort and get arrested again." Jo was hopeful he would agree. No good would come of him going to the ranch.

"You make a good point. But it doesn't seem right that you're taking all of the risks while I'm stuck here. I've missed you." He reached out and caressed her cheek.

Tears came to her eyes. She put her hand over his. "I've missed you too." She leaned into him and kissed him on the lips.

Maintaining the kiss, Faulkner pulled his hand away, moved her onto his lap, and cradled her in his arms. Jo's entire body electrified and tingled. She had missed him more than he would ever know, more than she had even dreamed. For years, she'd blocked the feelings she'd had for Faulkner, had locked them away, not wanting to remember what she could never have. Now the lock had been opened, flooding her with hope and joy. She never wanted this moment to end.

Faulkner broke the kiss. "Promise me you won't go alone. Take someone with you."

"Again with the promises." Jo nuzzled under his chin and softly said, "I promise."

* * *

Jo returned home as the sun was setting. To leave Faulkner alone in the cave was one of the hardest things she'd ever done. But if leaving him there would keep him off the sheriff's radar, she was grateful to do so. Again she wondered why the good sheriff hadn't arrested her for helping Faulkner.

There was the chance that he didn't because he was a family man and knew the trauma that such a thing would cause Rhett, because her son would be without parents. He would lose the only parent he'd ever known, plus Rhett would find out about Faulkner: who he truly was and what he'd been accused of doing. This by no means meant that Sheriff Padraic was unprofessional, only that perhaps he didn't want to harm a child's life without knowing for certain that it was the right thing to do. And then again, maybe Jo was merely applying these traits to the sheriff because that's what she wanted to think.

She thought of Rhett and hoped Denny was able to put him to bed on time. It was close to nine. Her son had had a very big day, one he would long remember once he learned Faulkner was his father.

Making sure the police—who had parked in a grove of trees—didn't see her, Jo sneaked in the back way, going through the rear door of the stable. All seemed quiet as she passed the animal stalls. Argi and Apollo had been fed for the night. That was a good sign that Denny was keeping things on a normal schedule.

Climbing up the steps, she thought of Faulkner again and was glad she'd left him a flashlight, plenty of food, a blanket, and a pillow. She wished she could have taken Faulkner a clean change of clothes. She'd promised to visit him after she returned from Lance's the next day. She'd take him a change then.

Jo stopped. She'd forgotten to close her father's trunk again. Turning around, she went back down. She walked by grain sacks and the spot where Faulkner had dressed before his first attempt to leave. His parting kiss lingered there. This memory fed into the kisses at the cave, and her skin tingled. She had to quit torturing herself, but, oh, how she'd missed him.

Stepping over the gunny sacks, Jo flipped on her flashlight. The lighting was poor under the stairs, and she wanted to take a closer look at her father's papers. She carefully placed his sailor suit on the ground next to her, along with framed pictures of her mother and father when they were first married, her father's framed medical degree that had hung in his clinic, and his stethoscope. Digging farther in, she came to his camera.

It had been badly dinged from the fall. When Jo and Denny went through her father's things shortly after his funeral, Denny had thrown the camera away. But unable to part with this piece of her father's life, Jo had retrieved it without Denny's noticing. She placed the camera away from the other pile because she wanted to take it upstairs. The light from her flashlight caught the swirl and flourish of handwriting on a yellowed and wrinkled envelope. *Jonathan* was the only word on it. This was the letter her mother had left Jo's father, the letter he'd carried with him for years.

Jo had never read it, but now she wanted to know, needed to know, what that woman had said. How did she justify leaving a four-year-old daughter and a nine-year-old son? Jo lifted the envelope flap and pulled out the letter.

Dear Jon,

Please know that I will always be grateful for all you've done for me. You married me knowing I was in love with another man who refused to marry me even though I was expecting his child. I had but a few dollars to my name and nowhere to go. I shall always be grateful for the love and concern you've shown me and also for the love you've given my son. You've treated him as if he were your own. I gave you a beautiful daughter in Jo. I see the love you have for her. You're a good father. But I'm not a good mother, and I can't pretend anymore. Denny and Jo deserve a better mother, and you deserve a woman who loves you. Please just let me go.

Taren

Jo felt numb all over. She'd always hoped her mother had loved her, and when Jo was a teen, she'd spent countless hours on the Internet trying to find her but never could. Now Jo knew the truth, and it hurt. What kind of woman could turn her back on her own children? Jo couldn't fathom an answer.

She thought of Rhett and the love she held in her heart for him. There was no way on earth she'd walk out on him—unless his life depended on her leaving. But that was not the case in her mother's situation. Or was it? Jo had heard of mothers who had smothered or drowned their children. Those women had definite psychological problems. Perhaps that's what was wrong with her mother.

Maybe she had done the right thing. Jo would never know. And Denny

. . .

She'd had no idea her father wasn't Denny's father. Dad had worried over him as if he were his own flesh and blood. She wondered if Denny knew. If he didn't, this news could devastate him. Just who was Denny's biological father? What kind of jerk would refuse to support a woman carrying his child? In fact, he should have married her. Unlike people in Hollywood, country folks usually married when something like that happened. Her father was a noble man to have married her mother.

And he'd loved his wife. He had worn his wedding ring until the day he died. He was even buried with it on. He'd kept the sorrow of Taren walking out on him to himself. The love Jo had always felt for her dad compounded. Oh, how she missed him. She yearned to hug him and smell his Old Spice aftershave.

The best part of the letter—if there was a best part—was her mother confirming that her father loved his children. Jo had always felt her father's love. Children were important to him. For that matter, he'd made people his priority in life.

She folded the letter and tried to slide it back inside the envelope but couldn't. Inside was a newspaper clipping from the *LA Times*. A sticky note on it read, "This is all I could find. Sorry it isn't better news." Jo peeled the sticky note off to reveal death listings. She scanned the names and came to "Taren White died December 25, 1999." White was her mother's maiden name. That's why Jo could never find her when she tried looking on the Internet; she'd been looking for *Powers*. The date was well over twelve years ago. Obviously, her father had hired someone to track down his wife, only to find out she was dead and buried. Her father had kept his sorrow to himself. Maybe he thought it best that way. With a heavy heart, Jo put all of the papers back in the envelope and tucked it in her hip pocket. Coming to the papers she'd saved from her father's desktop, she found a sticky note listing errands to run, a desk calendar, pens and paper clips, a tape dispenser, a three-hole punch, a huge pharmaceutical book, and a picture of Jo and Rhett when Rhett was a baby.

Oh, how her father had loved his grandson.

On the day Jo had given birth, her father had been there, filling in for the husband who had divorced her and the mother who had left her. Joy had gentled his face when he'd seen the infant. He could have come in during the delivery, being a doctor and all, but he knew that would have made Jo uncomfortable.

But he was there shortly after Rhett was delivered, making sure the doctor and nurses took good care of mother and child. Jo didn't know how she would have pulled through those first days of being a new mother without her father. He took a week off of his practice and stayed with Jo and Rhett day and night once they were home. Her father had loved her enough for two parents.

She decided to clean up and started putting everything back. She picked up her dad's desk calendar, but it slipped out of her hand before she got it to the trunk. What was wrong with her? She was tired. The entire day had been one ordeal after another.

She picked up the calendar again and flipped through it. She found it had a couple of years in it.

Faulkner said her father had visited him two years before his death. Maybe . . . she started thumbing through it. Two years back, she found where he'd made the note of traveling to Boise. This was proof that Faulkner had told the truth and her dad really did visit him! She couldn't wait to show Denny. And if he still doubted, he could call the prison to confirm it. They had to keep a visitors log.

She stopped. But what had prompted her father to make such a trip?

Jo flipped through the month before his visit and found a note that said, "Ask Stewart at Goldman's about Cassandra's prescription."

That was more than a little odd. Cassandra had been dead for five years at that time. What would have made him question a prescription he'd written so many years ago?

She heard someone coming and assumed it was Denny. Sure enough, a moment later, he ducked under the stairs. "I'm glad to see you made it back. How was Faulkner?"

"He's doing better than I'd expected. I gave him another shot, so he should be doing really well by tomorrow." Jo's leg was asleep. She needed to stand up and stretch. Keeping hold of the calendar, she closed the trunk, locked it, and stood.

"What are you doing going through Dad's junk?" If it had been up to Denny, he would have thrown it all away the day after their father died. He didn't have a sentimental bone in his body.

"Had to put some things away." She wondered if she should show him the letter she'd found. If Jo were in Denny's shoes, she'd want to know the truth. With the hope that she was doing the right thing, she said, "Look what I found." She pulled out the envelope with her mother's writing on it. "The letter Mom wrote Dad when she left."

"Did you read it?" He gazed at Jo.

"Of course. Have you?"

"Dad showed it to me right after she left."

Jo was shocked. "You've known all this time that Dad wasn't your biological father?"

"Yeah. He told me it was our secret and that I'd always be his son." Tears gathered in Denny's eyes.

Jo didn't know what to say to that. Leave it to their father to try to protect his son. She rubbed Denny's arm. "Here's the thing though. Inside the envelope, there was also a newspaper clipping with a sticky note. Dad must have put it in later because the article was dated 1999. Anyway, the clipping is death notices. Mom died over twelve years ago."

Denny stepped back. "Really?"

Jo nodded.

"Wonder why he never told us. Guess it doesn't matter. She left us and never looked back." He shrugged like it was no big deal. But Jo knew their mother's leaving had hurt him as much as it had her. Maybe even more. And now she was dead.

Jo pulled the letter from her pocket and handed it to him. "You might want to take a look."

He took the envelope but didn't open it.

Then she produced the desk calendar. "I found something else." She showed him the page where her father had written about going to Boise. "Faulkner was telling the truth."

"Yeah, but it doesn't prove *what* he told Faulkner. Nor does it say anything about Cassandra." Denny gave her his no-big-deal smirk.

She flipped the calendar to the page about the prescription and showed him.

"Sooo?" Denny seemed confused.

"This has to have something to do with why Dad became suspicious about Cassandra's death. I think I'll give Stewart a call at the pharmacy to see what he remembers." Jo added that to her ever-growing list of things she needed to do tomorrow.

"What's that doing here?" Denny set their mother's letter on the grain sack next to him then picked up their father's camera. "I threw it in the trash after Dad died."

"I hung on to it for sentimental reasons. Who knows, I might be able to get it to work."

"Nah. I tried to turn it on several times. There was no life in it, but I'll take it and see what I can do." He turned the camera over in his hands, studying it. "The lens looks cracked."

"Do you think there could be evidence on it that might help us with Dad's case?"

"The sheriff looked at it when Dad died. It's just junk." He was about to toss it in the garbage.

"Well, if you think it's junk, I'll give it to Rhett. He won't care if it works or not; he'll just play with it." She reached to take it from him.

"Let me see if I can get it to work first." Denny kept hold of it.

As Jo turned to head up the stairs, she saw Denny pick up the letter again. She knew he would read it later when he was alone. Denny had always been a private person. Whenever he was hurt, he waited to cry until he was by himself. After their mother left, Jo passed Denny's bedroom many times and heard him crying. After reading the letter, she knew why he'd taken it so hard. Though those days were long gone, she knew he would sorrow alone in his room again tonight.

They both would.

CHAPTER EIGHTEEN

As soon as the pharmacy opened the next morning, Jo called.

"Goldman's Drug Store. Stewart speaking."

"Hi there, Stewart. This is Jo Powers. I have an odd question for you."

"There are no odd questions, only odd people. Shoot."

"Years ago, my father wrote a prescription for Cassandra Wymer for some sleeping pills. I believe it was the day before she died."

"And you want me to . . . ?" He waited for her to continue.

"So you remember?"

"Not really. Over the years, I've filled a lot of prescriptions for your father's patients."

"Here's the thing, Stewart. I was looking at his old desk calendar, and I came across a note he'd written to himself that said to call you to see if Cassandra had filled a prescription the day she died. It was probably for some sleeping pills."

"What's the date?"

Jo told him and then asked, "Could you check on it?"

"This is personal stuff. I can't tell just anyone what prescriptions are and aren't filled. I would have told your dad though, since he was her doctor." Stewart grew quiet.

"Cassandra was my mother-in-law, and she's dead. I don't think she'll object. Besides, you owe me one for taking care of your horse for free last year when he came down with colic. Remember?"

"Let me see what I can find." He put her on hold. She was grateful he was taking the time to help her. As she waited, Denny and Rhett came up from the stable. Seeing that she was on the phone at her desk, they continued on to the third floor. She hoped Denny would get breakfast going.

"Let's see here." Stewart was back. "The last prescription I filled for Cassandra was two months before she died. So she never filled one on the day she passed away. And now that I think about it, I remember your father calling about this. Told him the same thing. That was the last conversation I had with your dad."

"Did he seem upset that the prescription he'd written her the day before she died hadn't been filled?"

"No. Just told me thanks and asked how my family was. I don't think there was ever a time when your father called that he didn't ask how my family was. Your dad was a nice guy. Sure do miss him."

"So do I. Thanks, Stewart." Jo hung up. If Cassandra had run out of sleeping pills, how was it that she'd died of an overdose when Faulkner had given her the last pill two days before? She had to have gotten them from somewhere. Maybe she'd taken some out of the bottle that Faulkner didn't know about. That was entirely possible. Cassandra could have had a stash she'd come upon. There were a number of ways she could have had more pills.

But why call Jo's father for more if she already had some? That didn't make sense. Something was definitely out of kilter.

And her father knew it. Jo felt the answer was dangling right in front of her—but just out of her reach.

At least now she had more information to ask Edward about.

* * *

Lance called and needed Denny's help checking the fencing on the upper forty. Wanting to speak with Edward but not wanting to leave Rhett home alone, Jo decided to take him with Denny and her. As Jo drove, she said to Rhett, "Don't tell Edward or Lance about Faulkner."

Rhett peered up at her. "Why?"

Denny helped her. "He's still playing hide-and-seek from everyone, and he'd be very upset if we told."

Rhett's forehead wrinkled. He must have been trying to understand a game like that. "Can we stop and see him on our way home? He has to be lonely in the cave all by himself."

"Sure." Jo turned down the road lined with giant cottonwood trees that led to the Wymer ranch. As she parked, Lance came out of the barn, leading his saddled bay. His famous cowboy smile he used during rodeos brightened his face when he saw them. He could make friends with the orneriest cowpokes with his grin. He had country charm in the mere way he tilted his head.

Rhett nearly leaped over Denny, he was so anxious to get out of the truck to talk with Lance. When Denny opened the door, both he and Rhett almost fell out.

Jo chuckled under her breath as she climbed from the truck on the driver's side. Her son was not going to be happy when he learned she wasn't going to marry Lance. But maybe it would be all right once he learned Faulkner was his father. She didn't want to think about that tough conversation. She closed the door on the truck, along with her thoughts.

"Give me five," Lance told Rhett, holding his hand up for a friendly slap.

With youthful enthusiasm, Rhett gave him what he'd asked for and immediately said, "Can I go with you?"

Lance gave Jo a peck on the cheek as she walked up. "It's up to your mom."

Jo looked down at Rhett. "But we came to visit with Edward, remember? He would feel badly if you don't spend time with him."

Rhett nodded and kicked at a rock.

Denny took charge. "Come with me while I saddle up." Again, Jo owed her brother for helping her with Rhett. And she really did need to speak with Lance alone. As her brother and son disappeared into the barn, she glanced at Lance.

He tried to pull her to him, but she stepped back. She felt like a fraud and wanted to tell him the engagement was off, but she had to play the part of a fiancée for a little longer so she could find the truth. "Lance."

"Yes, Josephine." He playfully reached to take her hand, but she pulled away. That cowboy smile of his vanished as he realized she was serious. "What's wrong?"

"I've been thinking."

"I hate it when you do that. It never turns out well for me." Lance peered at her, his brows bunched together with concern.

She gave a nervous sigh. "I wanted to reiterate that I think we're doing the right thing by postponing our wedding until after Edward is better."

"Oh, that." Lance's mood shifted from lukewarm to cold. "I'd hoped you'd come to your senses and decided I was right." He checked the saddle on his horse.

She followed him. "Sorry."

He whirled around and grabbed her, taking her completely by surprise. He kissed her soundly on the mouth, hard, and with too much need.

When he released her, she wanted to wipe her mouth, but she knew she couldn't.

"Just because we're postponing doesn't mean I can't kiss my girl." He grabbed the saddle horn, stepped into the stirrup, and climbed onto his horse like he didn't notice anything out of the ordinary in her lack of affection.

But she knew he had noticed.

Was she doing the right thing? As soon as she could, she'd tell him their marriage was off. Even if Faulkner had to go back to prison and she'd be left alone with Rhett, that would be better than shortchanging Lance in a phony relationship with no passion, not to mention shortchanging herself. The sooner she got to the bottom of all of this, the better.

* * *

Faulkner was grateful Jo had left him some food for breakfast. He cut another slice of homemade bread and smeared gooseberry jelly on it. He hadn't tasted homemade gooseberry jelly in years. Jo used to make it every summer when the wild berries were ripe and ready. As he ate, he stored the extra food in the pack she'd left.

He thought about Jo going to the Wymers' and poking around. He felt cowardly staying in the cave while she took all the risks. She'd already done so much. But what could he do?

Pray. And he had and would continue to call upon God for guidance. Sitting here, waiting, was almost unbearable.

He thought he heard something through the rumble of the falls. Faulkner crept to the edge of the cave and peered from behind the steady wall of water. Denny and Lance were rowing to shore below the falls.

Panic washed over him. He knew Denny and Lance were best friends, and he should have expected this, but still, he felt betrayed. It could be they were coming to talk, but he didn't think so. Jo had said Lance planned to kill him. So that meant Denny had given Faulkner up. Well, he'd give them a run for their money.

Faulkner didn't abandon all hope. They hadn't seen him yet. He backed into the cave. Grabbing the pack and the flashlight, he took off into the deep cavern.

* * *

Jo and Rhett found Edward in the den, watching an old video of bull-riding championships. It seemed strange that he'd be in the room where so much tragedy had taken place, but maybe the room gave him comfort now. It was the last place Coulton had been alive. And it had been years ago. Even so, Jo felt weird. It could be she felt this way because she'd only been in the den once. Edward probably used the den every day.

"Come in, come in." He made room for Rhett to sit beside him on the big chair and a half. "This was the Bounty Falls Raging Bulls Contest, an event that took a lot of organizing, but did we ever make a name for our rodeo—and a lot of money to boot. Loco is in it." He peered up at Jo.

A pang of sorrow hit her.

On the screen was the cantankerous Brahma in his younger years, bucking and spinning. The rider fell to the ground. Frankie and another clown immediately diverted the beast's attention away from the rider by running in front of him and teasing him with colorful scarves.

"Who is that with Frankie?" Jo asked.

"Chugger. Before we made him foreman, he was a rodeo clown."

"He and Frankie have been with you for quite some time, haven't they?" she asked, hoping to learn something she didn't know about the duo. Chugger had possibly been around when Cassandra died, so there was a chance—slim, but a chance—that he knew something.

"Oh yeah. They're good men." Edward shrugged. "After the last rodeo, I gave them some time off. I think they went to Vegas."

There went Jo's opportunity to question them.

"Later in the fall, Lance is going to need their help moving the rodeo stock to winter grazing. Don't know if I'll be able to go this year." Edward was talking to Jo but watching the TV.

"Are you going somewhere?" Rhett looked at the man, concern claiming his little-boy face.

Edward hugged his arm around Rhett. "Well, I'm not feeling like myself."

"If my grandpa were alive, he'd make you feel better, but maybe Mom can help you. Just the other day she helped"—Rhett looked up at his mother. He must have realized he was about to say Faulkner's name but stopped. He continued—"a man who got hurt at the rodeo." Rhett patted Edward's arm.

Jo's heart hammered up her throat. What would she have said if Rhett had told Edward the name of that man? She had to say something and fast. "Rhett, I'm not a human doctor like Grandpa was. I only help cowboys with minor cuts and scrapes."

"But, Mom—"

"Oh, did you see that?" Jo pointed to the TV and the bull that was chasing down the clown.

Edward studied the screen. "That's little Abner. One of the rankest bulls we've ever had. Sold him to some guy in North Dakota."

With only Rhett looking at her, Jo put her finger to her lips for him to be quiet. He scowled at his mother. She gave him the don't-say-anything-more look. Her poor son. He had no idea what was going on.

Edward started coughing. Noticing a glass of water on the desk, Jo fetched it for him. As she did, she saw a file. A corner of an inside paper peeked out with Cassandra's name plainly scrawled on it. She took the water to Edward. He gulped it down and thanked her, handing the empty glass back to her. She returned to the desk. "Do you want me to tidy things up for you?" she asked.

Edward rose, leaving Rhett alone on the huge chair, and came to her. "I was going over some legal documents. What with more treatments ahead and not wanting to put things off, I decided to rewrite my will. Haven't updated it since Coulton passed."

He sat on the leather rolling chair behind the desk and opened the file. Cassandra's will was on top. "I was hoping after yours and Lance's wedding to add you and Rhett." He stared up at Jo.

"Oh, you don't have to do that." Talking about wills and inheritance made her very uncomfortable. "I noticed Cassandra's will."

"She was such a loving person." Edward picked up her papers. "I know people thought she drank too much, but she only did it because she was lonely. I shouldn't have traveled like I did back then. I should have been here for her." He stared at the will. "I told her when we married to leave her money to Faulkner since her wealth came from her first husband, Faulkner's father. So she did, with an addendum that if Faulkner should die or become incapacitated, her money would come to me."

Jo wondered if Faulkner knew anything about this.

"Seven years ago when Cassandra died and Faulkner was convicted of killing my son, my lawyer believed I was entitled to her money. But I didn't feel the same. I've left it alone. However, if something should happen to me, and after you and Lance are married, I think you should have the money. Especially since Rhett . . ." He glanced over at him. And Jo knew Edward thought the money should go to Faulkner's son, which was an honorable gesture. That Edward hadn't followed the advice of his attorney and had left the money alone made Jo think more highly of him.

Rhett was absorbed in the TV. Edward lowered his voice. "Well, you know that little guy has more of a right to that money than anybody else."

Jo leaned over and gave Edward a kiss on the cheek. "That's very thoughtful of you. I don't want you thinking about such morbid things. You need to enjoy life, think happy thoughts."

Edward pulled out a drawer and filed away the papers. "I'm being practical. I'm allowed. I'm old. Besides I have to be realistic." He stood and said loud enough for Rhett to hear. "I think it's time for hot fudge sundaes." The clock on his desk read 11:00 a.m. It was way too early for a heavy dessert, but Jo wasn't about to say anything.

Rhett jumped off the couch and sprinted over to them. His eyes grew large as he stared at the gun cabinet. He'd never been this close to so many weapons. Edward seemed to notice what caught the boy's attention. "Lance was about your age when I took him and his older brother, Coulton, target practicing. We need to schedule a time to do that." Edward glanced at Jo.

"He's only six." She couldn't believe he would offer to do such a thing without clearing it with her first.

"Maybe we'll have to wait, but not too long." Edward's expression dimmed.

"There will be plenty of time to teach him after you're all better," she said.

Edward stared at her. In his gaze, she saw the truth he felt. Edward truly did not believe he would live much longer.

CHAPTER NINETEEN

Faulkner kept his head down, hunched his shoulders, and raced through the dark, foreboding cave. Musty, cold, damp air enveloped him. He quickly passed the area he'd explored before and came to the narrow part. Pausing a moment, his eyes panned the earthen walls that seemed to weep. Nightmares of being trapped had plagued him much of his life. The fear stemmed from being strapped in his race car and knowing his father had died in a fiery crash.

Though a cave wasn't a race car, it still made his heart jackhammer against his ribs. His head felt light, as if he'd spun out on the speedway. The meager beams of the flashlight gave him hope. He grasped it tightly and forged ahead, always aware of his surroundings. The strong acidic scent he'd noticed the other day grew worse. Still, he kept going, his ears attuned to possible footsteps.

And then he heard them.

Lance and Denny were following him.

Frantic, Faulkner showed the beam around the cave. The tunnel forked. He chose to follow it to the left. If he went a little ways and turned off the light, he could watch to see which way Lance and Denny went. If they turned left, he'd be toast. But if they turned right, he could double back, leave the cave, and take their canoe. It was worth the risk.

Something furry brushed against his pant leg, nearly making him drop his flashlight. It had to be a rat.

Denny's and Lance's voices were more distinct. He saw the light from their high-powered flashlight.

"He's here. Believe me." That was Denny.

"He better be." Lance sounded put out.

They'd come to the fork in the cave.

Faulkner leaned against the cold dirt wall, wishing he could become one with it. Under his breath he prayed, "Please turn right."

But to his horror, they veered left, heading straight for him.

* * *

Sophie, Edward's live-in housekeeper, maid, and cook, wouldn't let Edward make hot fudge sundaes until they'd eaten lunch. Though she was in her late sixties, the Italian woman had flawless, youthful skin and dark, mocha-colored eyes. Silver highlights graced her long black hair, which she wore in a braid wrapped in a bun on top of her head. Her pudgy waist and flabby arms showed that she'd spent years cooking for others. For as long as Jo could remember, the woman had worked for the Wymers. They were Sophie's family. She told Edward, Jo, and Rhett to go out on the deck and have a seat while she rustled up some food for them.

Champ trailed Edward, looking for company since he still couldn't go out with Lance and Denny. Several Adirondack patio chairs stood on the deck, facing the backyard. Edward sat on one. The dog curled up on the deck beside Edward's chair. Jo sat on another, but Rhett stood beside his mother. "Can I go down to the stream?"

Jo glanced at Edward to see if it was all right.

He shrugged. "Boys will be boys."

She nodded. Rhett hopped off the deck and raced down to the picturesque brook, the perfect place for frogs and snakes and all the things a little boy loved to find.

Edward leaned his head back on his chair and watched Rhett play. "I remember when I was a kid and how excited I was to play in the ditch in back of my folks' place. Used to float it."

Though Jo wanted to walk down memory lane with Edward, she had a different agenda. "Where did you meet Cassandra?"

Edward cocked his head, looking at her. "Whatever made you ask that?"

She lifted a shoulder. "You talking about floating the ditch made me wonder how you two ever found each other. You're country, and she was . . . well, she wasn't."

He chuckled. "You're right about that. She wasn't. We met in Vegas. I took Coulton and Lance down to see the National Rodeo Finals. One night they went with some friends to see a show. I was left behind, so I went down to the casino for a friendly game of twenty-one, and who should I sit beside but this beautiful woman dressed in a little black dress, sipping a martini.

She'd earned quite a pile of chips and seemed to know what she was doing. I asked her for some tips, and before I knew it, we were fast friends. I've always thought we were soul mates.

"We stayed up until dawn, talking. I told her how my wife had died in a car accident, leaving me with two boys to raise. She told me about her husband who was killed in a race car accident. I actually saw that race when Dangerous Dan crashed. She told me Faulkner was determined to follow in his father's footsteps and spent most of his time at the Las Vegas Motor Speedway."

Jo could imagine Edward and Cassandra together. Edward the cowboy, Cassandra the city girl. "So yours was the typical love-at-first-sight story?"

"Pretty much. I knew I always wanted to be with her. Cassandra had a sense of humor and a wit I'd never seen before. I stayed in Vegas as long as I could and made many trips to see her after I came home, but pretty soon my business was in a downturn and needed my attention. Your father actually helped me see the light."

"My father?"

"Well, you know we go *way* back. I told him about Cassandra, and he asked me if I was ill or something because he didn't understand why I hadn't asked her to marry me. Surprised me because of all he'd gone through with Taren." Edward stopped and gazed at Jo as though he'd said something wrong.

She shrugged. After the emotional wave she'd ridden last night, she decided the best way to come to terms with her mother's leaving was just to face it. "While my father was devastated that my mother left him, he never said a bad word about her. And he didn't seem bitter either. He told Denny and me that she had a wandering heart and that he was grateful she gave him two beautiful children."

"Geez, I miss your father," Edward said. "He always had a way of making a bad situation good. I should have made him come home with me instead of leaving him on the trail that day. I'll always blame myself. He was upset about something though. I could tell because he didn't talk much. He always grew quiet when he was mulling over a problem. Especially when he was worried about you or Denny or one of his patients."

After her conversation with Stewart at the pharmacy, Jo knew her father had been worried about who killed Cassandra. But maybe he'd had a good idea of who had done it. "Did he mention any names?"

"No, just told me how sorry he was about Cassandra dying and Coulton. Come to think of it, he hadn't brought them up for quite a while before that day. He knew how their passing upset me."

Jo decided to push her luck to see if Edward would say anything about Coulton's death. "On the day Coulton died, who else was at the ranch?"

He stared at her long and hard. "You should remember that from the trial."

"I felt like I was walking in a haze with events spinning out of control all around me. I can't remember much." She looked at Edward, worried that she'd offended him in some way and he wasn't going to answer.

Finally, he said, "Well, you'd been through quite a shock and were pregnant and all. I had stayed in town that day. Had a meeting with the bank. See, I'd bought new stock at the cattleman's auction and wanted to make sure I had enough money to cover the check I'd written. I didn't want to go to Cassandra for another loan. It was just too humiliating. And I really didn't want to tell her more of my financial woes. Unfortunately, my banker wanted to go out and have some drinks. She had extended my loan only because she thought I was her friend."

"Was her name Connie?" Jo had remembered that Faulkner's mother believed Edward was having an affair with a woman by that name.

"As a matter of fact, yes. How did you know?" He stared at Jo.

Nervous because this was something Faulkner had told her recently, she said, "I don't know. I guess I heard it somewhere."

"Lance probably told you." Edward shrugged. "I've gone over and over that day with him."

Jo nodded.

"Well, I couldn't very well tell Connie I had to get home to my wife. That would not have set well since she was going through a very bitter divorce. I knew I was staying out too late but felt I had to. By the time I returned home, the place was crisscrossed with yellow crime-scene tape. And Padraic was here. He quietly pulled me aside, away from curious eyes, and told me my son had been murdered." Edward grew quiet as he stared off.

Jo knew this was hard for him, but she had to learn more. "What happened after that?"

"Lance was beside himself, pacing back and forth. Not only had he lost a brother he loved, but the young man that I'd forced upon him as a stepbrother had been the one who'd shot Coulton." Edward stared at the ground but kept talking. "But my son had a firm hold on reality 'cause he could have very easily killed Faulkner. Instead, when he found him standing over Coulton, he knocked him out. That's when Lance called the sheriff." Edward looked up at Jo. "He's a fine man, my Lance. He'll make you a darn good husband."

Instead of replying to that, Jo said, "And Cassandra? Where was she?"

Edward studied Jo. "She was sleeping. Faulkner had given her a pill, and she had no clue her son had taken one of my guns and killed my oldest boy." His voice quavered. His feelings obviously still ran deep over what had happened to his patched-together family.

In an effort to guide him away from the pain and think of other people at that time, Jo asked, "Were Chugger and Frankie there?"

"They were in the bunkhouse when it happened."

"And Sophie?"

"Bless that woman. Lance and Faulkner's fighting woke her out of a sound sleep. See, when she'd returned home after playing bridge with some friends, she saw Faulkner's car parked out front so she thought everything was fine and went to bed."

He chuckled. "When I brought my new wife home, things were dicey between Cassandra and Sophie. I think Sophie saw Cassandra as an intruder. Cassandra set her right and told Sophie she had nothing to worry about because Cassandra hated to cook. They seemed to get along pretty well after that."

Jo wondered what Sophie could remember about that night. "Speaking of Sophie, maybe I should see if I can give her a hand with lunch. Would you mind keeping an eye on Rhett?" She looked toward the brook. Her son had taken off his boots and socks, rolled up his jeans, and was now knee deep in the water.

"Sure. He can't find much trouble down there. Champ and I will watch him."

At the sound of his name, the dog raised his head. Edward patted him, and the German shepherd licked his hand.

Jo headed to the kitchen, hopeful that Sophie would have the answers she needed.

* * *

Panic coursed through Faulkner like boiling motor oil. Lance and Denny were a good fifty yards away. He had to put distance between them and himself, but it was pitch dark. He couldn't turn on his flashlight; they'd see him for sure. Shouldering the pack, he went deeper in. His feet slid in what he thought was thick mud. His hand glided over the cave's wet wall as he felt his way forward. The stench became unbearable. He brought his fingers to his nose. The ammonia smell of urine nearly made him gag.

What the? Rats couldn't climb that high. This moisture was coming from above. Above? And then he knew: bat urine.

Bats probably hung above his head this very second. He clenched his teeth and tried with all his might to remain calm and collected. He hadn't seen bats entering the cave behind the waterfall so that meant there had to be another opening somewhere. Faulkner stared ahead at the blackness. What could he do?

"Lance, he's not down here." That was Denny, and they were closer.

"What do you mean? Where else would he go?"

From the glow of their flashlight, Faulkner could see Denny point to the ceiling. Lance shone his flashlight up as well. "There are bats everywhere. Faulkner would give himself up before he'd come down here."

Denny would have normally been right. But Faulkner couldn't help but wonder if Denny'd seen him in the shadows and was trying to help. Doubtful, since he was the one who'd brought Lance here.

Lance turned around. "Little creatures give me the creeps. He must've gone right instead of left. But no matter. The other entrance of this cave isn't big enough for a man to squeeze through. He's going to have to come out the way he went in, and we'll be waiting."

"He could have jumped in the river when he saw us coming." Denny followed Lance. "Maybe we should ride the horses downstream a ways to see what we find."

"I'll do it," Lance said. "You stay by the cave entrance and wait for me."

Oh, but that was close. Faulkner heard something pounding and realized the sound was the pulse of his heart rushing blood to his head. A prickling crawled on the bare skin of his leg, under his pants, and was followed by twenty more. He shook his leg and stepped in slippery, slimy goo— guano—and the creepy crawlers skittering on his leg were bugs and insects that thrived on the stuff.

He had to get the heck out of here. But what was he supposed to do? Wait until Lance left and take his chances by confronting Denny? Try his luck at the other entrance? Whatever he did, he had to get away from this section of the cave and find a place where he could spy on Denny. Then he'd make up his mind whether or not to chance talking with him.

* * *

Jo walked into the kitchen to find Sophie loading a serving tray with a plate of beef sliders, a large bag of potato chips, and soda. "I came in to help, but you're about done."

Sophie shrugged. "Just doing my job." Surely this woman knew more about Cassandra's and Coulton's deaths than what had come out at Faulkner's trial.

"I'm glad we're alone." Jo hoped that would melt the layer of ice the woman seemed to harbor for Jo. In a way, Jo understood it since she'd been married to the guy convicted of killing Coulton. Sophie loved the Wymer family.

She gave Jo a surprised look and waited to see what she wanted.

"Edward and I were talking about the night Coulton died. And—"

Sophie held up her hand. "I have nothing to say to you or anyone else about that night."

Jo noticed that a red blush had started up the woman's neck. She'd seen this before when Sophie had become frustrated. "Why?"

"You of all people should know." She smoothed stray hairs away from her face.

"Again, I have to ask why. Why should I know more than anyone else?" Jo was perplexed.

Sophie placed napkins on the tray, her back to Jo.

Did she think she could walk by and not say another word? Maybe she'd calm down a little if Jo concentrated on Cassandra. "Look, Sophie, I really wanted to talk to you about Cassandra."

She whirled around, facing Jo. "I will not speak of the dead with you or anyone else."

"Now, don't go getting all feisty on me. I merely wanted to know what she did after Coulton died. That's all. At one time, she was my mother-in-law, and I never really got to know her, but I know you did. So I was just wondering . . ." Jo ran out of words and hoped Sophie would pick up the conversation where she'd left off.

Sophie stared at her, sizing her up. Jo had never really talked with the woman before. They'd said a casual hello, or Jo complimented her cooking, but they'd never had an actual conversation. This was foreign for both of them.

Sophie huffed and leaned against the counter. "The next day when Cassandra awakened and Mr. Wymer told her Faulkner had killed his son, she fell apart. She tried to call *you*, as I remember, but there was no answer."

Jo was thrown into her own awful whirlpool of the past. "I didn't know. My father insisted I stay with him after I was told what had happened. She didn't call my father's."

"Yes, she did. After trying to get you the entire day, she gave up. But I dialed for her the next day because she'd started drinking heavily again. Broke my heart to see her pour her sorrow into a bottle. She needed you." Sophie seemed to be studying Jo as much as Jo was studying her.

"The only reason I can think that my father wouldn't have put her through was he might have been concerned about me and the baby. I was pregnant. Having my husband accused of murder was a horrible shock." Jo didn't want to make excuses, but she had to defend herself. She wasn't prepared for Sophie's accusations.

"You asked me what she did. I merely told you." Sophie shrugged and prepared to pick up the tray.

"You're right. I'm sorry if I sounded defensive. What else did she do?" Jo had to stay focused.

"She drank and cried and slept." Sophie stared at Jo like Cassandra's drinking was Jo's fault.

"Didn't she try to see Faulkner?" Jo had gone to see him but hadn't run into Cassandra.

"She'd planned to see her son the next day after she sobered up. But—" Sophie's bottom lip quivered. She sniffed and turned away. Speaking into the kitchen, where no one stood and only Jo could hear, Sophie said, "The next day never came for her."

Sophie obviously cared a lot for Cassandra. Jo wanted to drop the entire subject, but the thought of Faulkner hiding out in the cave unable to go anywhere came to mind. He couldn't hide there forever. Jo knew if she didn't push, he could very likely go back to jail, or worse. "Was she alone the night she died?"

Sophie sniffed. "You have to understand that was a horrible time for everyone here. I had my hands full with Cassandra. I thought I had her settled down for the night when I left her. Mr. Wymer had retired early to his room. The house was quiet, so I went to bed. I never dreamed she would get up and take sleeping pills. She'd been so exhausted; I thought she'd be all right."

"Where was Lance during all of this?" Jo had heard about everyone except him.

"Your brother was helping Lance through his grief. They were gone somewhere."

"And Chugger and Frankie?"

"I really don't know. I think they were in the bunkhouse. I didn't keep track of them. My main concern was Mr. Wymer and Cassandra."

"You said Edward retired to his room, so Edward and Cassandra didn't share a bedroom?" Jo thought that was odd.

Sophie faced her again. "This is a big house. They always had their own rooms. It didn't mean they didn't love each other. But love is tested when someone comes home late or when someone drinks too much, and, well, I think they found it worked best for them to have their own space. But have no doubt, I know Mr. Wymer visited her room often." Her voice was a little too defensive.

Jo knew she was taking a risk, but she had to ask. "Do you know if Edward visited her the night she died?"

Sophie bit her bottom lip and seemed reluctant to answer. Finally, she looked straight at Jo and slowly nodded yes.

CHAPTER TWENTY

"Why did you bring Lance here?" Faulkner asked as he walked out of the shadows to confront Denny. He had waited a good twenty minutes after he thought Lance had left before making himself known.

"Had to. You should have seen how upset Jo was last night, going through our father's old trunk, trying to find evidence to save your sorry behind. She's grasping at every little thing, even going through Dad's calendar. She believes your story that someone else killed Cassandra. She's suffered enough. Things were getting too complicated. I couldn't take it anymore, so yeah, I told Lance and brought him here. I should have called Sheriff Padraic, but I owed Lance this." Denny sighed.

Faulkner peered past Denny, thinking he saw movement, but no one came.

"I thought it would be best for both you and Lance to meet face-to-face and have it out once and for all. He won't kill you because he wants to be the hero in this. He wants Jo to see you weak. But, Faulkner . . ." He gazed at him. "Things are tough. Jo is going to be right smack dab in the middle of all of this. And you put her there." Denny glowered at him.

"That was not my intention. You have to believe me." Faulkner didn't know why, but he wanted Denny to know he was doing all he could. "When I escaped, my only thoughts were to find your father. Things didn't turn out the way I'd hoped. But I'd bet my life that Lance knows more about Coulton's death than he's saying. *And* that he knows who killed my mother and your father."

"Here we go again." Denny rubbed the back of his neck. "My father fell. Your mother accidentally overdosed. That's it!"

"But we don't know for certain. All I do know is I did not kill Coulton!" He glared at Denny. "I've spent *seven* years of my life cooped up in prison, thinking about what happened that night. I know Lance or his father had something to do with it. I just can't prove it. And you must believe that I would never do anything to hurt Jo or Rhett. I love them."

"If you love them like you claim, then you should turn yourself in and quit hiding behind my sister and your son." Denny shot him a disgusted look and went to the cave's edge. He peered out past the waterfall like he was checking to see if Lance had returned. He came back. "For Rhett's sake, if you promise to turn yourself in, I'll help you get away."

Faulkner nodded. He knew Denny had a soft spot for Rhett.

"Lance will be back soon. And the problem is, he took the canoe to get to his horse so he could ride downstream. We've got to get you out of here, and that means you've got to exit at the other end."

"I heard Lance say the exit was too small for a man."

"Yeah, well, Rhett and I have been over, under, and around this cave. There's an exit big enough. Turn right where it forks. And you're going to have to belly crawl. But it'll take you out close to Jo's place. Fortunately, no one is home right now. You're not going to have much time. You'll need to saddle up Apollo and head over the mountain toward Grace's Lake."

Faulkner could hardly believe Denny was helping him. Maybe he hadn't given him enough credit. He nodded a thank you and headed back down into the inky blackness. But he hadn't made it more than twenty feet before Lance stepped in front of him. He must have entered the cave from the other end.

Shocked, Faulkner turned and glared at Denny.

He shrugged and chuckled. "I was just seeing if you were gullible enough to think I'd help you. See, between you and Lance, I pick Lance every time."

Before Faulkner could think what to do, Lance swung a right upper cut, catching Faulkner in the jaw and jerking his head back sharply. Lance followed that with a jab to Faulkner's wound and another blow to his cheek.

As Faulkner sank to his knees, fighting to stay conscious, he saw Lance's smiling face. All of Faulkner's hope, all of his yearning for a future with Jo and Rhett, crashed down on him.

* * *

"A husband visiting his wife's bedroom is no big deal unless something happened that you're not telling me." Jo stared at Sophie.

Sophie looked like she wished she could take back her nod. Instead of answering Jo's question, she said, "Mr. Wymer is waiting for lunch." She grabbed the tray and left.

What was Jo supposed to do? March out and demand Edward tell her what he was doing in his wife's bedroom on the night she "supposedly" killed herself? That would go over well. To bring up such a subject wouldn't be proper. A flash of Faulkner wounded and hiding in the cave came to her again.

Propriety could stuff it. Too much had been lost because questions had not been asked that should have been. Jo pushed open the door to the deck and found Rhett running up from the stream, socks and boots in hand, his chin quivering from the cold. *Crumb!* Jo couldn't ask what she needed to in front her son. Sophie set their lunch on the table beside Edward's chair. "I'll fix those hot fudge sundaes now so when you're ready, you can eat them." She quickly left, avoiding eye contact with Jo.

Tempted to follow her, Jo decided it was best to stay. Sophie had already told her a great deal. She wasn't likely to divulge any more.

Jo looked at Edward. He'd loved Cassandra. Jo could tell by the tone of his voice as he'd told her how they'd met. Perhaps somewhere along the way, that love had changed. Perhaps the Cassandra Edward had loved was the woman at the casino, and he hadn't been able to fall in love with the Cassandra on the ranch, his sons making him see her in a different light. And perhaps Edward really had been having an affair with Connie, the banker.

"Jo, take a load off and sit down." Edward handed her a sandwich.

Deep in thought, she hadn't realized she was standing there staring off at nothing. She smiled and took it. Somehow, someway, she had to broach the subject of him going to his wife's room on the night Cassandra died. Jo glanced at Rhett. He still stood shivering as he ate his half sandwich. "Honey, go in and ask Sophie for a towel."

He seemed relieved that she'd finally noticed and left to do as his mother had asked, which was a sure sign that he was freezing. With Rhett in the house, Jo had a small window of time to ask Edward.

"On the night Cassandra died, I understand—"

At that moment, she heard voices and horse hooves on the gravel drive near the house. Champ got up and trotted off the deck, heading for the front. Someone had obviously arrived.

"Dad, come see what we caught!" That was Lance, yelling.

Edward gave Jo a bewildered look. She shrugged. Both he and Jo left the deck and hurried to the front yard.

Denny and Lance sat on their horses, but a body lay draped over Lance's lap. Jo's walking slowed as her heart leapt to her throat. Gooseflesh spiderwebbed over her skin.

Faulkner!

CHAPTER TWENTY-ONE

Jo FELT HER HEART SHATTER into a million pieces. Faulkner lay so still, so very, very still. She rushed to him. With trembling hands, she felt his cheeks. He was warm to the touch, so he wasn't dead. She glanced up at Lance. He smiled down on her. "Your worries are over. We've nabbed him."

Afraid of what she'd say, she turned her back to Lance and stared up at her brother. Denny jumped down from his horse and put his arm around her. "I had to tell him. I know something you don't. Trust me," he said softly in her ear.

Trust him? Of course Jo trusted her brother, but what could he know that she didn't? It had to be something pretty big to betray not only her but Rhett and Faulkner too. Denny was her brother, her only family. Her trust in him was never in question. Somehow, Jo had to get through the next few moments without falling apart. She felt separated from the situation, like she was floating through the motions as she looked up at Lance, who sat on his horse with a proud, smug look on his face, probably the same look he'd worn when he'd killed his first elk.

"Take him in the house, where I can examine him," Jo spat out.

Denny reached to take Faulkner from Lance. All at once, Edward was beside him. He smiled at Lance as he climbed down from his bay. "I knew he was close. I'm just glad you nabbed him, son, before he hurt anyone else."

Sophie came outside. Rhett was with her. He had a towel wrapped around him. The boy's eyes widened as he stared at Faulkner in disbelief. Rhett's frightened gaze quickly found Jo. "What happened, Mom?"

She hugged him to her. "I don't know, dear, but I'll find out." She was tempted to caution her son not to say anything, but suddenly, it didn't matter anymore. Faulkner was injured, could be dying, and would surely be going back to jail. Rhett could learn the truth now or later. She'd hoped for later and that she could shield him a little longer, but she knew Rhett's bubble of innocence was about to burst. She had to do what she could to cushion the blow. "Stay close to me. I'm going to need you."

Sophie took the horses' reins and tied them to the fence while Denny, Lance, and Edward carried Faulkner to the house. As Lance passed Jo, he said, "You don't appear happy about this."

"I don't want to talk about it now." She glared at Lance, above Rhett's head, to let him know he'd better watch what he said around her son.

Skirting the men and their heavy burden, she opened the front door. They passed her and took Faulkner into the den. As they laid him on the leather couch, Lance said, "All I did was knock him out. He's fine. I'm calling the sheriff."

He left the room, leaving the door open. Sophie entered the house at the same time and followed him.

With Denny and Edward standing behind her and with Rhett by her side, Jo knelt to examine Faulkner. His jaw was swollen, as well as his right eye. Lance had worked him over pretty good. She smoothed his hair away from his forehead, took his pulse, and noted his breathing. How much more could his body stand? In the last few days, he'd been shot, operated on, lost in the forest, exposed to a dangerously high fever, thrown over a waterfall, and now this. Tears came to her eyes as she thought of all he'd suffered trying to find the truth of what had really happened to Coulton, Cassandra, and Jo's father. He'd given his all to the cause, firmly believing that with God's help, he could clear his name.

But Faulkner's efforts had been for naught. As soon as Sheriff Padraic arrived, he'd take him to prison. Nothing had been solved. Faulkner'd sacrificed so much. Where was his God now when he needed Him most?

"Is he going to be all right, Mom?" Rhett asked, his face pinched with worry. Even with all of her efforts to shield him from the ugliness of the past, the past was colliding with the present head-on. For her son and for the man she had always loved, she realized the truth had to come out, and she only had a matter of minutes to do it.

Rhett was a tough little guy; after all, he was Faulkner's child. He could handle it. Taking her son's hand, Jo said, "Honestly, I don't know if he's going to be all right. But there's something I need to tell you."

Rhett's innocent eyes stared at her. Complete trust graced his face.

Denny piped up. "Jo, don't."

She held her hand up and glared at her brother. Edward folded his arms and said nothing as he stared at her as though he'd never seen her before.

Jo knew deep in her heart she had to do this, and neither her brother nor Edward was going to stop her.

Keeping her back to them, Jo didn't know how she was going to tell Rhett what she needed to. Rhett had shown Faulkner the Winston Cup in his room; that could be a good place to start. "Rhett, do you remember showing Faulkner the trophy in your room?"

Her son nodded.

"And remember you told me Faulkner seemed sad?"

Again, Rhett nodded.

"The reason he was sad was that trophy was his father's."

"What?" Surprise, wonder, and disbelief lit her little boy's eyes. His shock morphed into awe, but Jo knew he'd still not connected the dots.

He stared at her. "But you told me it belonged to my dad's dad."

Against Jo's will, tears gathered in the corners of her eyes as she nodded. Her six-year-old son was smart for his age. Jo knew she wouldn't have to say anything more for him to come to the full realization of who Faulkner truly was.

Rhett appeared to think for only a moment before he looked back to Faulkner, studying him again like he was seeing the man before him for the first time.

Rhett whipped around to Jo. "Faulkner's my dad?"

"Yes," Jo said softly. "I'm sorry I didn't tell you before, but I wanted you to know now before he goes away again."

Rhett stared at her. His brows bunched together. "Goes away?" Rhett looked at Faulkner. "Goes away where?"

"Hey, squirt," Denny chimed in. "Why don't you and I go—"

Jo again put her hand up to stop him. "My son is staying here with his father."

Lance came into the den, appearing far too proud of himself. "Padraic is close by. He should be here any second."

Confusion and bewilderment captured Rhett's face. "Why is the sheriff coming?"

Jo took his hands. "Your father is a good man. Something happened many years ago, before you were even born, something awful, and your father was blamed. But he didn't do it." Jo glanced over at Faulkner. She knew she had to tell her son about Coulton's death, but the bare truth might be too much for his young mind to handle. Maybe she could soften it somewhat. "There's been a misunderstanding about your father."

"Misunderstanding?" Lance yelled.

Faulkner stirred. He was coming around.

Edward seemed to sense that this should be a private moment for Jo, Rhett, and Faulkner. "Come on, let's give them some space."

"Are you kidding me?" Lance glared at his father. "I'm not letting that mur"—Lance's gaze stopped on Rhett, and he paused before completing his statement—"man out of my sight, especially in this room." He went to the gun cabinet, took out his revolver and ammo, and locked the doors.

"By the looks of him, he's not going anywhere. You can stand in the hallway if you must, but let's give them some privacy." Edward's compassion surprised Jo, and yet it didn't. He'd lived through a lot of hardship in his life and recognized when people needed time to grieve. Except Jo's grief, and soon Rhett's, would not be over a death. They would grieve the loss of Faulkner in their lives. Denny, Lance, and Edward left the room. Jo knew Lance would stand near the doorway, listening.

Faulkner's eyes blinked open. Right away, he saw Rhett beside him. His eyes moved up to Jo. "Where am I?"

Rhett piped up. "At Lance's."

Faulkner immediately tried to sit up, grabbing his side. Alarm ricocheted in his eyes as he panned the room, recognizing where he was. Jo could hardly bear to tell him his quest to learn the truth about Coulton would soon end in complete failure. But she had to. "Sheriff's on his way. Until he gets here, I'm going to leave you alone with your son."

Faulkner stared at her as though he couldn't believe she'd said *your son* in front of Rhett. Through his gaze, he was asking if she'd really told Rhett who he was. She nodded.

Faulkner looked at Rhett then Jo. Confusion, relief, gratitude, and worry washed over his face. "Why, Jo? Why did you tell him?"

Rhett reached over and patted his father's shoulder. "It's all right. I know there's been a misunderstanding that's kept you away. Mom is good at clearing up misunderstandings, aren't you, Mom."

"I try." She stroked the back of Rhett's head. He was still barefooted from wading in the stream, his boots and socks long forgotten with all of the excitement. "Why don't you two talk while I go get your boots?" She smiled at Rhett and stood. Looking at Faulkner, she said, "Leave the misunderstanding to me. Tell your son about your race car."

Walking out and closing the door behind her, Jo ran into Lance.

He raised the gun up so she could see it. A wild and determined expression lined his face. "Don't worry. I won't let anything happen to Rhett."

Jo knew the time had come to set Lance straight about a number of things. A chill breathed over her, followed by a deep foreboding. But before she said anything, she had to get Lance to put down the gun. "Faulkner won't hurt him." She pulled on Lance's arm, coaxing him from the den's door.

Lance jerked away. "Won't hurt him? What's wrong with you?"

"Faulkner is his father." Jo took Lance's hand. "You've locked away the guns, Sheriff Padraic will be here any second, and Faulkner won't hurt Rhett. Come with me." She tried to nudge him along, but Lance didn't move an inch.

* * *

"So you know who I am?" Faulkner asked as he pulled himself to a sitting position. He yearned to take his son in his arms.

Rhett nodded. He stared down at his bare feet, looking afraid for a moment, then crawled on the couch beside Faulkner. "Where's your race car?"

The question surprised Faulkner, but he supposed a six-year-old wouldn't get into the where-have-you-been-all-my-life questioning that someone older would ask. "I had to sell it." All the money he'd made on the sale had gone to pay for his attorney during the murder trial.

"That's too bad. I've always wanted to ride in a race car." Rhett looked up at his father, admiration in his eyes.

Faulkner put his arm around his son. A wellspring of emotion filled his chest. Here he was, sitting beside his boy. His son! *His son* was sitting next to him on the couch asking about race cars. How many times had Faulkner dreamed of such a moment, and now that it was here, he had to make the most of it. "Rhett, I want you to know that I love you very much, and I would never, ever do anything to hurt you or make you ashamed of me."

Rhett's innocent face told Faulkner he had no idea what Faulkner was talking about, not yet anyway. But that would change. Soon.

"You're going to hear some really bad things about me. I want you to promise that you'll talk to your mom, okay?" Faulkner knew if anyone could make things right, it would be Jo. She'd know how to tell her boy the ugly truth far better the Faulkner could. How could he tell his young son that he'd been convicted of murder? The question was impossible for him to answer. All Faulkner knew was his heart was breaking at the thought of being taken away from his child and the woman he loved again.

"Coward!" Lance burst into the room. "As usual, you're dumping your garbage on Jo. You tell him what you did to my brother." He pointed the revolver at Faulkner.

"Lance, what are you doing?" Jo was behind him. "Don't point your gun toward my child! This has nothing to do with you."

"I'm aiming at Faulkner. And what do you mean, this has nothing to do with me? He killed Coulton. My brother's death has everything to do with me," Lance spat out.

Rhett fled to Jo, who scooped him up in her arms.

"I didn't kill your brother," Faulkner said. "Coulton was already dead when I came into this very room." He eased to the other end of the couch, trying to draw Lance away from Jo and Rhett. "I found the gun on the floor right there."

Faulkner pointed behind Lance, but Lance didn't take his eyes off of Faulkner. Very slowly and carefully, Faulkner stood and walked over to the desk. "I picked it up and was going to put it away in the gun cabinet, but I found Coulton already dead on the floor."

Lance kept the gun barrel directed at Faulkner. Faulkner needed him closer if he was going to get the weapon away from him.

"That's the same lie you told at the trial." Lance's index finger slid to the trigger.

"Lance, someone else could have come in here before." Jo eased Rhett down and pushed him behind her, shielding him with her body. "The den is close to the front of the house. Someone could have come and gone easily without anyone knowing."

At that moment, Denny and Edward rushed into the room, followed closely by Champ. The German shepherd growled. The hackles on his neck rose. He started barking and rushed toward Faulkner, ready to pounce.

"Lance, call off your dog," Jo demanded.

He looked at her for a second. With Lance distracted, Faulkner saw his opportunity to take the gun. Leaping at Lance, he grabbed the hand holding the weapon and punched Lance in the face.

Champ attacked Faulkner, biting his leg. Still holding Lance's gun hand, Faulkner tried to kick the animal away.

Lance kneed Faulkner in the groin.

Pain stole Faulkner's breath. He doubled over yet managed to keep hold of Lance. Faulkner had to get the weapon or die trying. He jerked Lance down as Champ rushed between them, and they landed with a thud on the floor.

The gun went off. A loud deafening bang reverberated through the house like a sonic boom. Gun smoke floated to the ceiling.

CHAPTER TWENTY-TWO

GUNFIRE ECHOED IN JO'S EARS. She held her breath as she stared at the men on the floor. Her world stopped. She seemed incapable of movement. She should go to them, check them, find out who had taken the bullet. Yet she couldn't budge. Her body was paralyzed and disconnected from her mind. Numbness prickled her skin.

What should she do? Everything had happened so fast, and now they lay in a heap before her. They could both be dead. Many times, Jo had seen a movie where two men struggled with a weapon and then it went off. The hero always rose unhurt. But that was in the movies . . . not real life.

Rhett's small hand took hold of hers, reminding her that she wasn't alone and that her son was safe. Pulling Rhett into her arms, she glanced at the others' shocked faces. Denny stood like a zombie, staring at the sight. All color had drained from Edward's wrinkled face as he stared at his son beneath Faulkner.

Sophie rushed into the room, her gaze magnetically pulled to the tumble of men on the floor.

A car pulled up in the driveway with red flashing lights. Sheriff Padraic had finally arrived, though too late to stop the tragedy.

Still performing her duties, Sophie left to let the sheriff in.

Faulkner moved first. He eased himself to his knees, sucking in long, deep drafts of air as he leaned heavily on the desk to stand. "Is everyone all right?" His eyes panned the room.

Relief poured over Jo. She wanted to go to him, put her arms around him, and kiss every inch of his face. But her joy vanished as she now worried that Lance was dead.

Edward rushed to his son and sank to his knees. "Lance," his gravelly voice eked out.

Lance pushed his father away. "I'm fine." When Lance moved, Jo saw that he was on top of Champ. The dog lay lifeless on the carpet. A small puddle of blood grew from beneath him.

Lance still held the gun as he scrambled to his feet. He kept the weapon pointed at Faulkner. "Look what you did!" he said. "Not only have you killed my brother, but now you've killed my dog too." His eyes burned with pure hatred and blame.

"Lance!" Sheriff Padraic walked into the room with Sophie close behind. "Put the weapon down."

With great reluctance, Lance lowered his revolver. His disoriented, frenzied moment had passed. The sheriff took the gun from him, clicked the safety on, shoved it beneath his gun belt, and went straight to Faulkner, slapping handcuffs on his wrists.

Faulkner gave no resistance. He stared at Jo. His humiliated look told her he was dying inside that she and their son were seeing him like this. Faulkner's shoulders slumped. He focused his attention on Rhett. The boy clung to Jo, unable to look at his father, or anyone else for that matter. Today the child had seen things he never should have.

Jo cleared her throat, intending to tell what she knew, but Faulkner's worried expression caught her attention. He shook his head, warning her to say nothing. Why? After all he'd been through, why didn't he want her to speak up? She didn't understand. Placing her faith in Faulkner, she said nothing and focused on Champ.

With the weapon safely in the sheriff's care, Jo automatically followed her veterinarian instincts and went to the animal, keeping Rhett close to her side. She knelt down by the German shepherd, stroked his head, and checked his eyes: glassy, nonresponsive. Next she monitored his breathing: shallow, barely a breath. She studied the wound. The bullet had hit the animal in the chest. Where had it traveled? She ran her hand over him. No exit wound, so the bullet was still inside. She'd have to operate. But not here. She needed to get Champ to her clinic, fast.

"Can you save him?"

Denny had left the men and had come to help.

"Maybe. We've got to get him to the clinic."

Sophie handed Jo a towel. It was like the woman could read her mind. Jo nodded thank you and wrapped cloth around the wound the best she could. Denny scooped Champ into his arms.

"Where are you taking my dog?" Lance had noticed them heading toward the door.

"I have to operate," Jo said, her patience growing thin. "You want me to try and save him, don't you?"

"Of course!" Lance fired back. "As soon as we take care of this, I'll follow."

Faulkner stared at Jo and Rhett, seemingly memorizing their faces, their every movement. He appeared relieved that she was going. She knew he didn't want his son to watch his humiliation of being questioned by the police, of seeing him with handcuffs and put in the police car. No child should have to witness that. Jo's heart tore in two. Leaving would take more courage and strength than she'd ever thought she had. She wanted to tell the sheriff that Faulkner had put his life on the line trying to get the gun away from Lance. If she did what her heart wanted her to do, the fire they were living in now would turn into an inferno because Lance's and Edward's anger would definitely combust. But Jo really wouldn't care if only her son weren't here to see it all.

Rhett'd already been through enough trauma. Jo would tell Sheriff Padraic her version of what happened, but later and away from the Wymers. Even though she yearned to stay for Faulkner, she had to leave. She was Champ's only hope for survival. She had to take comfort in the thought that the sheriff would keep Faulkner safe.

Taking Rhett's hand, she followed Denny to the truck. As her brother climbed inside with the dog and as Rhett got in and Jo fastened his seat belt, Jo realized the outcome of what had just happened could have been so much worse. Any one of them could have been killed, but they hadn't been.

Jo closed the passenger door to hurry around to the driver's side. She prayed that God would continue to watch over them and that somehow the truth would come out before it really was too late.

* * *

Faulkner watched as Jo drove away. He knew she didn't want to leave. But he was glad she'd understood his concerned look and had said nothing. He knew if she had, Lance would have made her pay for betraying him. And actually, what could Jo have said that would have helped Faulkner? Nothing, really.

Faulkner stared at Lance. Here was his chance, his opportunity to face off with the man who had haunted his waking moments and his nightmares for seven long years. And beside him stood Edward, the other person who had crushed Faulkner's world and any hope he'd had of a normal life. When Faulkner'd thought of this moment and played it out in his mind, Sheriff

Padraic had not been part of the scenario. But having him here might work out for the best.

"So do you have this handled, Padraic?" Lance asked. "I need to leave. Jo's upset . . . and my dog . . ."

"I actually have some questions I'd like some answers to, so sit down." The sheriff pointed to the leather couch. "Sophie, come join us."

The housekeeper had been standing near the door, behind the couch. Faulkner had forgotten she was even there. Lance and Edward sat down. Sophie filled the space on the other side of Edward, a look of concern for her boss creasing her brow.

Edward patted Lance's arm. "Jo's the best vet in the county. If Champ can be saved, she'll do it."

All three people on the couch looked at Faulkner. Sheriff Padraic had him sit in a large chair near the couch. The sheriff leaned against the desk, his arms folded as he stared at them as if debating what to ask and how to ask it.

Faulkner decided to help him out. "Sheriff, Doc Powers came to visit me a couple of years ago. He said he had a hunch my mother had been murdered and he planned to check into it."

"That's a lie!" Edward leaped to his feet. He was pretty spry for an old man with cancer.

Lance jumped up as well. "If anything, she died of a broken heart after you murdered my brother."

"Sit down!" The sheriff stared pointedly at them.

Father and son begrudgingly sat again, sneering at Faulkner like wolves ready to romp on him the second the sheriff wasn't watching.

Sheriff Padraic walked over to Faulkner's chair. "Jo mentioned that to me. Said she thought her father had been murdered because he'd visited you with his theory."

Lance huffed and leaned back. Obviously Jo hadn't shared this with him.

"Why would she think such a thing? I saw her father the day he died." Edward leaned back on the couch as well. "He was by himself on one of his fool hikes he took. Does she have evidence that someone else was with him?"

The sheriff gazed at Edward. "No, but she was pretty upset to learn that you'd seen him that day. I'd neglected to tell her. Tell me again, what were you doing up there, Edward? It's a good five miles from the ranch. Did you know Doc was hiking?"

Edward's eyes opened wide with sudden realization that he was now being looked at as a suspect. "Doc actually came to the house that morning. Said he wanted to check my prescriptions. Then he left. He seemed very upset but wouldn't talk about it. I knew he was hiking Table Rock, and I decided to see if he was all right. Met him at the trail. He was still agitated, so I left him there. I shouldn't have, but I did."

"Don't say anything else." Lance sat on the edge of the couch and stared at the sheriff. "You're really not going to stand here in my father's house and point a finger of blame at him, are you?"

"Just asking questions, is all." The sheriff studied Edward and Lance. "Not long after I left home this morning, my wife called and asked me to stop by the pharmacy to pick up a prescription for my youngest. Poor guy has an ear infection again. Anyway, while I was there, Stewart Goodman got a call from Jo, asking about a prescription for Cassandra."

Sheriff Padraic paused a moment, letting this piece of news settle on them. Faulkner felt a wellspring of hope.

Jo had actually been doing what she said she was going to do. And bless her heart. She may have stumbled upon some fragment that could open the case again. Faulkner knew he couldn't become too optimistic, but this tidbit was the best news he'd heard in a very long time.

The sheriff continued. "And here's the thing . . . Stewart got curious after Jo's call and did some more checking. Cassandra never picked up her pills, but Stew found out Doc prescribed the same sleeping pills for you." He looked at Edward. "You'd filled it the week before Cassandra died."

Edward looked crestfallen. His eyes darted back and forth.

"Whoa!" Lance glared at Sheriff Padraic. "What are you saying?"

The sheriff ignored Lance and kept his gaze on Edward. "I find it odd that shortly after Doc started looking into this, he died. And *you* saw him the day he fell. Needless to say, the fact that you had the same sleeping pills as Cassandra and she was out of them, but the tox screen plainly showed the meds in her system, seems a bit too convenient. Don't you think, Sophie?" Sheriff Padraic turned to her.

The housekeeper appeared shocked that the sheriff would say her name. "I . . . I guess."

The sheriff settled his attention on her for a moment longer. "Do you think Cassandra may have borrowed Edward's pills the night she died? She probably wouldn't have bothered Edward about it since he was grieving his son, but she could have asked you to get them. Did she, Sophie?"

"No. I was with her until quite late. She finally settled down and went to bed. Remember, that's what I told you seven years ago." She nervously looked between the sheriff and Edward.

"Do you know if Edward gave her his pills?" The sheriff had Sophie locked in his sights.

"I was going through hell." Edward quickly injected, deflecting the attention to him. "But as I told you before, I checked on my wife. She was sleeping when I opened her door. And I didn't waken her, nor did I give her pills. Besides, Cassandra was a real stickler for not taking another person's medication."

"He's right," Faulkner added. "She wouldn't have taken it on her own." One time when Faulkner was suffering with an impacted tooth, his mother was tempted to give him an antibiotic she'd had leftover, but instead, she'd dragged him to the dentist.

Sheriff Padraic shrugged, gazing at Faulkner. "But you had just been accused of killing her stepson. She may have been desperate."

Edward rubbed his forehead. He seemed to have aged ten years in the ten minutes they'd sat there. The elderly man stared at Faulkner. "She was beside herself with grief over what you'd done."

"*I didn't kill Coulton.*" Faulkner had had it. The time had come to state his case. "You and Lance know I didn't!"

"I saw you!" Lance yelled.

"You didn't see me shoot." Faulkner knew talking to him was useless.

"You had the gun!" Lance looked ready to leap off the couch at any second.

"And you knocked me out before I could explain." Faulkner turned from Lance to the sheriff. "You threw me in jail and wouldn't let me see anyone for twenty-four hours."

"Legally, I didn't have to. You were part of an ongoing investigation in which you were the prime suspect. Because I hadn't arrested you, I didn't have to let you call anyone." Sheriff Padraic appeared defensive for a minute. "But I did let Jo come see you after I charged you."

Faulkner remembered. Jo had been three months pregnant and suffering with morning sickness when he was first arrested. Her eyes had had dark circles under them. She was thin and pale and scared out of her wits to see her husband behind bars. Faulkner had tried to reassure her that everything would be all right. He'd tried to play down what had happened, had told her it was a big misunderstanding and that as soon as his mother could, she'd hire an attorney to help get him out.

"The day after Jo visited me, my mother died. I believed you'd find the truth." He looked accusingly at the sheriff.

"And he did." Lance chimed in. "I'm not going to sit here and listen to this sleazebag deny what everyone knows happened. He was legally convicted; now stop with all the stupid questioning and get him out of my father's house."

The sheriff didn't say a word. He motioned for Faulkner to get up.

"Don't you see, they're covering up for each other." This couldn't be it. Faulkner had waited too long to have it out with Lance and Edward.

Sheriff Padraic only nodded toward the door for Faulkner to leave.

What could he do? He had handcuffs on his wrists, and the sheriff was the man calling the shots. As he rose, Faulkner stared at his adversary. Lance was seething. And as soon as the sheriff left the ranch, he would go to Jo's.

With the new information he'd learned and in the state of mind he was in, something bad—something very bad—was going to happen.

CHAPTER TWENTY-THREE

WHILE DENNY PREPPED CHAMP, Jo got Rhett settled in his room with something to eat and his favorite DVD. Sitting next to him on his bed, she kissed and hugged him, so grateful he hadn't been hurt. Now her worry was his emotions. She wanted to talk to him about everything that had happened, but it might be a good idea to let him have downtime and do something normal, something that would signal to him that he was safe. "You know I love you."

Rhett clung to her. "Yes."

"And you know I won't let anything happen to you."

"Yes," he uttered again.

"The sheriff will take good care of your father."

"Can we go see him?" Rhett peered up at her.

Jo didn't know if taking her son to see his father in jail was a good idea or not. "I'm not sure if we can, but I'll call and find out." There. She'd been as positive as she could be given the situation.

"What about Champ?" Rhett said.

Of course her son was worried about the defenseless animal. "I need to operate on him. Uncle Denny is getting him ready. Will you be all right up here for a little bit?"

Her brave boy nodded. Her son would be all right. Still, she wanted to return to him as soon as she could.

Reluctantly, Jo left and made her way to the clinic. She tugged her scrubs on and washed her hands for surgery.

Denny, already dressed in surgical scrubs, helped tie her mask on her, after which he stood by, ready to help. What would she have done without her brother?

Once Jo began, it didn't take long to find the bullet. Her heart sank. "Oh no."

"What?" Denny looked up.

"It's lodged in his aorta."

"Can't you remove it?" Denny came to her side.

"If I do, he'll bleed out in a matter of seconds. I have to put him down." Jo hated saying it, let alone doing it. The dog had been through so much in the last week, and now this.

Denny went to the medicine cabinet. He had helped her euthanize animals beyond help many times before. He unlocked the cupboard, took out the phenobarbital sodium and hypodermic, and brought them both over to her. "This is going to kill Lance," he said as his eyes studied hers.

"I know, but it has to be done." She filled the syringe. Glancing at the animal, she couldn't help but feel sad. Jo stroked the German shepherd's head. He was a beautiful dog that had been loyal to his master right up to the end. If only Lance had backed down, none of this would have happened. Biting her lips together, Jo injected the lethal dose.

Champ took his last breath. The room fell silent. Denny checked the animal's eyes. "He's gone."

Filled with sorrow, Jo stitched the wound closed. As she worked, she tried to think how she was going to tell Lance. She'd seen a mean side of him today that she'd only had glimpses of in the past but had pushed aside. What would he do once she told him Champ was dead? After what had happened at the ranch, she didn't know how he would handle it. He certainly wasn't the man she'd thought he was.

Her thoughts turned to several nights ago when she'd operated on Faulkner and removed a bullet from him. He'd been very near dying as well. How odd life was. She'd never removed a bullet before. Not from an animal or a human, and now, within a week, she'd had to tend to two wounds. At least she'd been able to save Faulkner.

She heard the engine of a vehicle driving up to the building. Denny must have heard it too because he went to looked out the window. "It's Lance."

Jo finished and tugged off her surgical gloves and mask. "I'll tell him. Will you check on Rhett?"

Denny gave her a nod, shed his gown and mask, and hurried up the stairs.

She heard Lance's footsteps near the door. He knocked and then walked in.

Jo met him. He stared at her then peered past her at his dog, alone on the surgical table.

"How's Champ?" he said, dread framing his eyes.

Jo folded her arms and, with much sympathy, said, "He didn't make it."

Lance sucked in a deep breath. His gaze flitted back to the surgical table, where Champ lay. Tears puddled in Lance's reddened eyes.

Jo wanted to put her arms around him and grieve with him, but she couldn't. Champ's death was Lance's fault. And though she felt sorry for him, she was also angry. "Why don't you sit with him for a while. I need to check on Rhett."

Lance took off his hat and went toward his beloved pet.

As Jo started up the steps, Denny was coming down. "Rhett's fine. He was chasing the skunk down the hall."

"Thanks for checking on him." All Jo wanted to do was take Rhett in her arms and hold him tight. The ugliness of this day seemed to grow worse with each second. Hugging her son would not only comfort her but would also give her hope. "Go be with Lance."

Denny nodded.

As she reached the top step, her thoughts went back to Faulkner. He'd looked so beaten with cuffs on his wrists. He was innocent of Coulton's death. She knew it.

Jo had to call Sheriff Padraic to tell her version of what had happened today. But she'd do that after she checked on her son.

* * *

Faulkner decided to be as cooperative as he possibly could. He knew the sheriff was digging deeper into the events that led up to Cassandra's and Doc's deaths by the questions he'd asked. If he found what Faulkner suspected, the evidence would eventually lead him to take another look at Coulton's murder as well. Faulkner wanted to stay on the sheriff's good side.

He got in the backseat of the SUV and didn't say a word as the man pulled onto the Swan Valley Highway and headed toward Idaho Falls.

The road to Jo's came into view and seemed to pull at Faulkner. She would be home by now, working feverishly to save Champ's life.

Jo.

His Jo.

How he wanted to go to her. The sadness in her eyes as she'd looked at the handcuffs on his wrists was burned into his mind, but his son's expression tore his heart.

Only moments before Lance had burst into the den, Rhett had cozied up to Faulkner's side and asked about race cars. They'd had a genuine father/

son moment—something Faulkner had never thought possible. And Jo had given it to him.

And then the chaos ensued. Actually, chaos lived and breathed at the Wymer ranch. Faulkner and the people he loved most in the world had become victims of that place. If his escaping jail accomplished only one thing, that of Jo not marrying Lance, Faulkner would feel like it had been worth getting shot by the prison guard, going over the waterfall, and hiding in the cave. He couldn't bear to see Jo marry Lance and become trapped in a life sentence of doubt and deceit.

The sheriff drove on. The miles rushed by. They passed the ranger station as they headed into Conant Valley, and a powerful foreboding befell Faulkner. Fear burned in his chest. He didn't understand it at first. He'd experienced many moments of severe apprehension, but this was something more, like a voice warning him of a nightmare that was yet to happen. Suddenly, he knew what he had to do. "We have to go to Jo's."

The sheriff chuckled. "Yeah right. Get real, Faulkner."

"No, seriously. You've got to go there now!" The dire feeling became more intense as it grew within Faulkner's chest.

"I plan to check on her after I put you in jail." Sheriff Padraic peered in his review mirror, staring at him.

"You can't wait." Faulkner was desperate to make him listen. "Look, we've had our differences in the past, but I've always told you the truth, whether you've believed me or not. You must believe some of it because you're starting to investigate more."

The sheriff continued to drive, hardly blinking an eye but still listening.

Faulkner continued. "I don't know if you're a religious man or not, but I firmly believe God gives us premonitions that we need to act on."

"Is that why you escaped prison? You had a premonition?" The sheriff chuckled.

"Yes. See, when I read that Jo and Lance were getting married, I knew I had to stop it."

"Had nothing to do with the fact that you're jealous, right?" He wasn't buying it.

"I understand you're skeptical. But you have to admit that the things you've found out recently don't add up. You brought up Edward's medicine. And I know you respected Doc. He did come see me and told me he believed my mother was murdered. Shortly after that, Doc died. That's too much of a coincidence. I don't know who killed Coulton seven years ago, but I do know I didn't do it. I've spent seven years in prison for a crime I didn't commit, but I'll gladly go back if you'll please turn around and go to Jo's now."

The vehicle slowed down as the sheriff pulled to the side of the road. Once stopped, he turned in his seat and stared at Faulkner. "I'm not saying I believe you, but I'm not saying you're wrong either. I've seen too much in my days on the force not to believe in a higher power. Many times my life has been saved because I followed a premonition." He paused.

Faulkner didn't know what to expect. He knew he should say something but couldn't. He'd said all he could to convince the man.

"I pulled the surveillance crew off of Jo's place when I got Lance's call this afternoon. We've been having trouble on the other side of the county with a motorcycle rally. Dang! This could mean my badge." He turned back to the wheel. Shaking his head like he couldn't believe what he was about to do, Sheriff Padraic shifted into drive, looked both ways for cars, and turned the vehicle around, heading back to Jo's turnoff. "I'll deny it if you repeat me, but I've had a feeling that I need to go there since crossing the bridge."

The sheriff floored the gas pedal.

Relief tempered the anxiety in Faulkner's chest, but only a little. The concern that they might be too late was still overwhelming.

Faulkner kept a prayer on his lips as they drew closer to Jo's.

* * *

"Rhett, honey?" Jo needed the reassurance of hearing his voice. She stood in the dining room, waiting.

"Yeah, Ma."

Relieved, she said, "What are you doing?" Spock squawked as she passed his tripod of branches on her way to the hall. The bird was hungry. Jo went to the fridge and pulled out the container of chicken pieces.

Rhett came down the hallway carrying the skunk under one arm and her father's old camera in his other hand. "Daisy went into Uncle Denny's room, and you know how he hates to find her in there. So I went to get her and look what I found. A camera." Somehow he'd forgotten the ugliness of this day and was focused on something positive. But she knew she needed to tell him about Champ.

Jo took Daisy, gave the skunk a friendly rub on the head, and set her down. "Thanks for rescuing her. Come here." She guided her son to sit on the couch.

Rhett peered up at her. "Denny wouldn't tell me. Is Champ okay?"

"No, honey, he isn't. I couldn't save him." Setting Spock's food container on the couch beside her, she put her arm around his shoulders.

Rhett hugged her, dropping the camera to the floor. The thing had fallen from a cliff—a drop from the couch to the floor wasn't going to do any more damage. She rubbed her hand up his small back, holding him close.

He eased back and looked up at her. "Well, now he's in animal heaven with the others you couldn't save. Are we going to have a service?"

For animals no one owned that Jo was unable to save, they always had a service and laid flowers on their graves. "Lance is with him now. He'll probably do something at the ranch."

About to get up, Jo nudged the camera on the floor with her foot. She picked it up. "I found this camera in Grandpa's trunk last night. It's pretty damaged. Denny said it doesn't work but thought he'd take a look at it. Do you want to see what you can do with it?" Her son always talked about the pictures Grandpa had taken. It amazed him that his grandfather could shoot a picture of just a flower, and when it printed, the scene looked like it belonged on a poster.

Rhett shrugged.

Jo wanted to get his mind off of Champ. "Let's check to see if the memory card has anything on it." She thought surely the sheriff had checked it years ago when he'd had it. Since he'd given it back to Denny, it must be all right, but she still wanted to make sure. There may have been pictures from her father's hike that the sheriff hadn't thought were important but that she'd like to keep.

Jo spied her laptop on the sidebar near the dining table. "I'll check what's on the memory card while you feed Spock." She handed Rhett the container.

He took it from her. She set the laptop on the dining room table and clicked it on. At any moment, Denny or Lance could come up the stairs and the topic would switch to Champ. It seemed to take forever for the screen to come up and the system to run. Jo waited for the virus scan to complete, and then there were automatic updates that ran every time she turned the thing on. She'd never learned how to make it do updates at different times. That was on her list of things to do when life slowed down. The problem was, life never did slow down.

As she waited, she tried to pry the memory card slot cover open. It was dented and jammed. She retrieved a knife with a sharp tip from the utensil drawer and managed to slip the thin blade into the small crack of the cover. Giving it a good jerk, the cover popped off, breaking it. The memory card was still inside. Jo pulled it out and went back to her laptop. Finally, the message displayed that she was fully protected and all updates were done. She plugged the memory card into the slot. Immediately, the computer whirred as it worked to open the file. And, of course, the virus scanner had to check the card for viruses as well.

Good grief, this is taking forever. She bit at a hangnail that had been irritating her for the last few days. The camera's program opened in the center of the screen and asked if she wanted to open and save the files.

Jo clicked yes.

And waited again.

A number of picture-file names appeared. *Dad, you were busy that day.* There had to be at least fifty or so. The display large icon appeared in the upper right corner. She clicked it. Pictures appeared before her. She recognized the wildflowers of Table Rock, the birds, the trail, the view from high atop the mountain and the gorge below. There was a shot of Edward on his roan horse. More shots of flowers. By the looks of the ground, her father had hiked the path she'd hiked.

She'd passed the same trees, and she saw the place where she had to grab the bush to help her up, even a shot of the same area where Lance had found her. The last picture was difficult to make out. Staring, she realized it wasn't a scene but the palm of someone's hand very near the camera, blocking the view. She could only see part of a face between the fingers. This person was close. Very close.

Jo stared and stared . . . and then her blood ran cold.

A small scar showed on the face.

A small chickenpox scar.

It was Denny.

CHAPTER TWENTY-FOUR

"WHAT ARE YOU LOOKING AT, sis?" Denny's friendly voice came from behind as he reached the top of the stairs and came to stand by her.

Jo had been so involved in trying to figure out what was on the screen that she'd lost track of everything else. She stared at the picture unable to take her eyes from the truth. Her brother had told her he hadn't gone with their father that day. In fact, she'd called Denny to go look for their dad when he'd missed checking in that afternoon and was late for dinner. Jo turned slowly in her seat and gazed up at her brother.

Denny stared at the screen, blinking as he looked. Then his eyes grew wide. He suddenly pulled back.

Oblivious to what was going on, Rhett finished feeding Spock and was dragging a chair to the sink so he could put the empty container in it and wash his hands. "I found Grandpa's camera in your room, Uncle Denny. Mom said you wouldn't mind if I played with it 'cause it's broken."

Denny stood there, staring at the computer screen, not moving, not saying a word.

Jo studied her brother's guilty face, and deep inside, she knew the ugly truth but couldn't believe it was possible.

She heard Rhett turn on the water to wash his hands. She had to get him out of the room. She didn't want to send him down to Lance, who was grieving over his dog, but she had to get him out of here. If she merely sent him to his room, he'd listen at the door.

"Rhett, you need to let Jacob in. Go out the back way. I don't want you to bother Lance. He's with Champ." Her voice sounded foreign to her. She cleared her throat and added, "We've been gone all day; I'm sure the wolf's hungry and thirsty too." There, that would keep her son occupied for a while.

"Geez, Ma." Rhett hopped down from the chair and started to pull it back to the table.

"That's okay." Jo managed to smile at her son. "I'll take care of the chair. Go right now and get Jacob. And while you're at it, check on Argi too. When you're done, come in the back way, okay?"

Her little man nodded as he went out the back door, grumbling to himself. Once she knew he was safely away, she stood, faced Denny, and said, "Start talking. And don't leave *anything* out."

Denny rubbed his forehead. "It's not what you think. Dad wouldn't listen to me. He'd made his mind up. I tried to tell him it wasn't my fault, but . . ." Denny grabbed the back of a chair like he needed something tangible to ground him.

"What wasn't your fault? What are you talking about?" Jo needed specifics and, as much as she didn't want to know, details.

Denny drove his fingers through his hair. "He found out that I was with Lance on the night Cassandra died."

The fear of facing the truth grew exponentially. Jo tried to remember what she knew of her brother's activities that night. "So? Everyone knew that to help Lance grieve his brother's death, you took him to some of Coulton's favorite places." This was no big surprise to Jo, nor should it have been to her father.

"But somehow, Dad knew we didn't." Her brother rubbed his quivering chin. Jo had never seen him so visibly shaken. His hands shook, and his eyes darted around the room. "He thought I had something to do with Cassandra's death. And I didn't. I didn't touch her, Jo. You've got to believe me."

Though he'd said Jo's name, Denny didn't look like he recognized her. And Jo didn't recognize him. He'd morphed into someone else, some sniffling, sorry excuse of a person.

Denny went on. "When I tried to explain to Dad that all I did was get Edward's pills for Lance, he started really losing it. He'd backed me close to the edge of the mountain, but he didn't seem to care. It was like he was possessed or something. Dad even accused *me* of killing Coulton. But I didn't. I was there, but it was an accident. I wasn't even holding the gun."

Criminey! All the deaths *were* connected just like Faulkner suspected. She had to ask. "Who was holding the gun?"

"You have to understand, Jo. We'd been blowing off steam, doing a little weekend drinking like we always did back then. That night, after we'd had a few beers, we went back to the ranch, and there was Cassandra, martini in hand, wanting to know where Edward was. Lance started telling her stories that Edward was cheating on her. She must have been quite loaded before we got there. She drank so much she passed out. Coulton, who hadn't been drinking, felt sorry for her and carried her to her room. While he was gone, Lance found more hard liquor in the den. We had several more drinks, and then Lance started playing around with the guns. He wanted me to play high noon with him and draw like in the old West. When Coulton came in, he knew I was uncomfortable, so he told Lance he'd duel with him.

"Lance was so drunk. There's no talking to him when he's like that. All the guns in the cabinet were supposed to be unloaded. That's the rule. They drew, and Lance shot. We both sobered up pretty quick as soon as we realized what happened." Denny put his hand over his mouth.

Jo had a hard time wrapping her mind around Denny's story. She needed more information. "You knew this and said nothing? You watched *my husband* go to jail, and still, you said *nothing*?" Hot rage tore through her.

Denny cowered like a whipped dog. She knew he wouldn't answer her rhetorical questions, but he finally said, "I knew as soon as Lance thought things through that he'd tell the truth, but then Cassandra . . ."

Jo reined in her temper so she could hear the details about Cassandra's death. "What did you do to Faulkner's mother?"

Denny bit his lips together. Tears ran down his face. "Nothing. I swear. Lance asked me to get his father's sleeping pills. And I did. But I didn't know he was going to mix them with Cassandra's martinis. I didn't. I swear I didn't. And when she died, I told Lance I was going to Padraic to tell him everything. But Lance said I was as guilty as he was. My prints were on the pill bottle. He said he had to kill Cassandra because she was starting to remember that Lance and I were there when Coulton was alive. Lance told the police Coulton came home before we did, and we arrived after Faulkner and found him standing over Coulton with the gun. But Cassandra knew better. If she didn't die, we'd both go to jail."

Denny fell to his knees. "I tried to make it up to you, Jo. I spent all the money Dad gave me for college trying to earn enough so you'd never have to worry about money. But everything failed. So when Dad died, I decided that for the rest of my life, I would be there for you no matter what. In fact, Lance wanted to dump Faulkner's body in the river today, but I stopped him. Told him you'd see him as a hero if he took Faulkner in. That's the secret I wanted to tell you earlier."

While she was grateful her brother had stopped yet another murder, Jo wanted to hit Denny, hard. She wanted to pick up the table and pummel him with it. As calmly as she could, she asked, "Did you push Dad?"

Denny put his arms over his head and curled into the fetal position. "No . . . maybe. I don't know. I was so close to the edge as I was telling him, and I slipped. I reached for him. And he reached for me. And then he was gone. I didn't know what to do, Jo." Denny shuddered like a baby and cried into his hands.

"The sheriff never saw the camera, did he?"

Denny shook his head.

So many lies. And the truth was almost more than Jo could bear. But it was finally out in the open. She stared down at the heap of her brother. The impulse to kick, and kick him hard, gave way to the bitter taste of pity. Denny was the worst kind of evil. He was a coward with a damaged soul. Jo's brother had known the truth all these years and had lived a lie. And worse, he'd wanted her to marry the man who had been behind it all.

All at once, she realized Rhett hadn't returned. Panic rifled through her. If she had known Lance had been behind everything, she would never have sent Rhett out. Lance was in the clinic with Champ. But if he suspected anything, he might do something to her boy.

She immediately thought of the gun Lance had lent her. She'd put it in the safe she'd stored in the back of her closet.

Jo tore down the hallway, burst into her room, and dove into the closet. Her hands shook as she worked on the combination. It was easy: seven, seven, seven. The safe tumblers clicked. Jo wrenched open the small door and grabbed the weapon. Sheriff Padraic had loaded it for her last night when she'd showed it to him. Could she use it if she needed to? Could she really shoot another human being?

For her son, Jo would kill.

As she raced to the stairs, she noticed Denny was gone from the kitchen. Had he tried to warn Lance? Was his mind so corrupt that he would put her and her child in danger? Were Denny and Lance waiting for her to come down the stairs?

It didn't matter if they were. She had to go. Hurrying as quietly as she could, she went down the stairs, slowly opened the door, and peered around her clinic, fully expecting to find Lance and Denny waiting for her. But the clinic appeared empty.

Champ still lay on the table. And then she saw Denny's body on the floor. Had Lance killed him? Jo crept over to Denny. Blood smeared the side of his face where he'd been hit. She felt his neck for a pulse. The rhythmic beat of his heart was strong. Relieved, she left him there.

If what she suspected was true and Denny had told Lance what had just happened upstairs, Lance would be desperate. He'd killed Cassandra to cover his trail; what would stop him from killing Jo and Rhett? He could blame it on Denny. He could blame it all on her brother. But why hadn't he killed Denny when he'd had the chance?

Maybe Rhett had walked in on them before he could, and when Rhett saw his uncle unconscious on the floor, he'd probably fled down the stairs and Lance had chased him. *And after Lance kills Rhett and me, he'll put the gun in Denny's hand and pull the trigger to make it seem like a murder/ suicide.*

If Jo was right, Rhett was alone with a madman. Lance would expect Jo to fly down the stairs to save her son. And she wanted to, but she had to use her head, or her precious boy could die. She had to do something Lance wouldn't expect.

Again, the back door came to mind.

She could go out the clinic's back door and sneak down to the stable through Apollo's corral. The horse should still be out. She could hide behind the animal for cover.

And then what?

She didn't know. What she did know was she had to do this and pray God would help her. Filled with motherly determination to protect her son, Jo fled out the doorway.

* * *

They recrossed the bridge on the road to Fall Creek. Faulkner had walked that same creek bed as he'd fled Jo's only a few days before. Now here he was, riding in the back of the sheriff's SUV, headed up to her place.

"I'd sure like to know why Jo built her house way the heck up here," Sheriff Padraic said as he followed the winding dirt road. "When it rains, no one can get up here, and her phone goes out. Plus, the closest place is five miles from hers."

"Jo has always loved her privacy and prefers a walk in the forest over a day at the mall. Always has." While they were married, Jo had been outdoors whenever she could be. "Probably got it from Doc."

The sheriff nodded. "It's strange that Jo was attracted to you, with you being a race car brat."

"The first time I saw her, she was holding a kitten and defending its right to prance all over my car. I haven't been around animals much, but she . . ." Faulkner couldn't finish his statement that Jo made him appreciate life and all of God's creatures. He'd already said more than he should have.

Sheriff Padraic slowed and pulled over.

"What is it?" Faulkner asked, peering out the windshield. They were close to Jo's. The bend in the road ahead would lead them straight to her place. Through the pines, wild oak, and aspens, he could see the building.

"Here comes Jo's wolf. Seems to me, with everyone at the house, he'd be there with Rhett. The only other time I've seen him away from the house was the other night."

"When he was out with me." Faulkner finished the thought. "You're right. Jacob watches over the place."

"I've got one of those premonitions we talked about. Think it's best if we walk from here." The sheriff got out and opened the back door for Faulkner. Faulkner quickly climbed out next to Sheriff Padraic.

Jacob trotted up to Faulkner and licked his outstretched hands. The sheriff grabbed Faulkner and unlocked the cuffs. "I can see Lance's red truck through the trees." He pointed, directing Faulkner's gaze. It was there, all right, which meant Lance was in the clinic. "Makes sense he'd come to check on his dog, but after all the questions I brought up and after his reaction to them, I'm thinking he's not happy."

Faulkner agreed with everything the sheriff had said.

"Call me crazy, but I think I may need your help." Sheriff Padraic went to the trunk and opened it to reveal gun cases that probably contained rifles or shotguns. He didn't reach for them but grabbed a binocular case before closing the lid.

"You're not going to give me a gun?" Faulkner had been hopeful.

The sheriff shot him an are-you-kidding-me look. Faulkner didn't say any more. He knew better. He was just grateful the man had listened to him and had gone to Jo's. Being uncuffed was a bonus. And that the sheriff wanted Faulkner to go with him was even better. Faulkner wasn't about to press his luck by insisting on a weapon, though he felt very exposed. But that didn't matter. At least he'd be there in case something happened, and he did have two free hands.

They left the road, walking through brush with the wolf between them until they came to the trees. Sheriff Padraic motioned for Faulkner to get down and hide behind a pine while he pulled out his Steiner Police Binoculars.

"What do you see?" Faulkner asked in a hushed voice.

The sheriff handed the binoculars to him. The autofocus zoomed in, and right away Faulkner saw the open stable doors. Someone small was in there. It had to be Rhett. And a tall figure. Denny? He couldn't make out who it was. "Who's with Rhett?"

"Not sure. Let's see if we can get a little closer." Sheriff Padraic led the way.

The trees thinned out, and the sheriff and Faulkner crouched down behind a boulder near the road. The sheriff took the binoculars and checked again. "Oh crap!"

"What? What is it?"

He handed them to Faulkner. Again, Faulkner peered through the lens. This time the autofocus showed him what had been hidden in the shadows. Lance had a firm grasp on Rhett with one hand and a sure grip on his revolver in the other. The same gun that only hours ago had shot Champ and the same gun Lance had used to threaten Faulkner. "I thought you took that away from him."

"I did, but legally, I had to leave it." Sheriff Padraic unsnapped his gun holster. "There's not much cover here, but I want to get closer." He pointed to Lance's truck. "If we could get behind that, I could try to talk to him."

"Talk to him? The guy has my son and a gun. End of story."

"Look, if we rush in there now, you'll only get yourself killed and maybe Rhett too. You don't want that, do you?" He waited for Faulkner to answer.

"No. There's got to be something we can do." The torture of seeing Rhett with Lance was nearly too much for Faulkner.

"I plan to do my job. Don't make me regret having you with me." Sheriff Padraic stared into Faulkner's eyes.

"I won't."

The sheriff nodded. "Okay, then, I'm going to make my way to the truck and talk with Lance. You are going to stay here with the wolf, and if someone else drives up, you've got to stop them."

Faulkner nodded.

As Sheriff Padraic was about to make a dash for it, something caught Faulkner's attention. "Wait!" he hissed. He peered through the binoculars once again.

Jo was in the corral by the horse. She held a gun and, using the animal as a shield, was making her way to the stable.

Faulkner shoved the binoculars at the sheriff.

He looked through the lens. "Well, I told her to get a gun, but I thought she'd need the protection from you, not Lance, and not with her son in the line of fire."

Dread and regret reflected in the sheriff's eyes. "That thing shoots .45 caliber shotgun shells. If Jo fires, everyone in front of her is going to get hit."

CHAPTER TWENTY-FIVE

Jo rushed to Apollo. The horse nickered and pawed the ground. "It's okay, boy." She stroked the horse's soft neck. "Let's see what's going on." She coaxed him forward, trying to keep in step with the horse. As they rounded the corner of the stable, Jo's heart nearly stopped.

Lance held Rhett near Argi's stall and was focused on the clinic stairs in the back of the stable, most likely waiting for Jo to appear any minute. He had no idea she was coming from behind.

Please, God. Guide me, she pleaded as she and the horse entered the stable. Lance spun around.

She crouched farther down and let Apollo go on by himself, hopeful that Lance hadn't seen her.

He must have only seen the horse because he didn't come to investigate.

"You're hurting me," Rhett said to Lance.

Rhett's comment fueled Jo's determination to save him. Being petite, she was able to crawl under the stable fence.

"Don't mean to." Lance stroked the top of Rhett's head with the gun.

Rhett's eyes grew wide and brimmed with tears. "I thought you liked me."

"I do, kid." Lance smiled at him. "But that misunderstanding your mom was talking about at the ranch?"

Rhett nodded.

"I'm part of it." Lance squatted down beside Rhett, still holding tightly to his arm. "But I have a surprise for her."

"What?" Rhett's voice sounded tiny and vulnerable.

"I want both of you to come with me on a trip far, far away. You'd like that, wouldn't you?" Lance glanced at the stairs and stood up, not waiting for a reply.

Jo crept along the stall, closing the distance. Lance and Rhett were a mere twenty feet away. Should she call to him now? Or should she just shoot?

Her foot caught on the tine of the pitchfork leaning against Apollo's stall, and it crashed to the ground.

Lance grabbed Rhett in a choke hold, holding the boy to his chest and pressing the gun barrel against his temple.

"Lance," Jo called. Terror squeezed her throat.

He looked at her, saw that she held the gun he'd given her, and started to laugh. "If you shoot, Jo, you're going to kill your son too. The spray from that gun will get us both."

Now what was she supposed to do? The sheriff had warned her that if she planned to shoot, she had to be close to her target. The closer she was, the less spray. He'd also told her that whomever she hit at close range would definitely die. Her son's life was at stake.

She had to get closer. In an effort to sidetrack Lance, she asked, "Why, Lance? Why did you frame Faulkner for Coulton's death?"

"My father would never have forgiven me. Coulton was his favorite. Heck, he was everybody's favorite, even yours. Didn't matter what I did; I could never measure up to my brother, even in your eyes." Lance stared at her.

Jo didn't know what to say, but she had to keep him talking. She kept walking closer. "That's not fair."

"No, it isn't." Self-pity, jealousy, and accusation shone in his eyes. "I ran away after shooting Coulton because I couldn't face what I'd done, let alone face my father. But when I returned and found Faulkner standing over him, a plan fell into place."

Jo stumbled.

Lance seemed to realize what she was doing. "Don't make me shoot. Believe me, I will." Lance's finger was on the trigger.

Jo grew weak as she held her breath, afraid that the slightest movement would kill her son.

* * *

Faulkner held on to Jacob's collar. What was going on in there? He couldn't hide behind a rock and direct traffic. Keeping hold of the wolf, he sprinted toward the sheriff, who crouched behind Lance's truck.

The sheriff glared at Faulkner. "What the heck? Do you understand English? I said to stay behind."

Faulkner ignored his questions. "What's going on?"

Sheriff Padraic raised his gun and aimed. The barrel pointed at Lance. He was clearly in view, holding on to Rhett

As the sheriff began to squeeze the trigger, Jo moved even closer. "What the? She's going to get killed. I've got to come at this from a different angle. Is there another entrance to the stable?"

"Yes. It's around back. You're not going to have time."

"I will if you distract him." Sheriff Padraic stared at Faulkner.

The sheriff had just asked Faulkner to sacrifice himself. He would do anything for his family. "You got it."

Sheriff Padraic took off.

Faulkner inhaled deeply, gave Jacob a pat on the head, and stepped out in the open.

* * *

"Lance!" The voice came from behind. Jo quickly looked. Faulkner was walking up the drive, his hands held high. Jacob was with him. The wolf snarled, his hackles raised as he bared his teeth. Where had they come from? Faulkner was going to get killed.

Lance let go of Rhett and raised the gun, steadying the weapon with his other hand as he aimed at Faulkner. Rhett raced to Jo, flinging his arms around her waist. Faulkner was unarmed. And though he had the wolf as a backup, he needed Jo. She gave Rhett a hug and said, "Quick, hide in the trees."

Rhett was reluctant to leave her, but Jo pushed him to go. Obediently, her son took off.

"How did you get away from the sheriff?" Lance kept Faulkner in the sights of his gun.

At any moment, he could shoot.

At any moment, Faulkner could die for Jo and their son. She saw the rage in Lance's eyes. He'd always hated Faulkner, and that hate had developed into something unspeakable. He thought himself above the law. His accidentally killing his brother and then deliberately murdering his stepmother had given him a false sense of power and control.

Why hadn't Jo seen this long ago? How could she have been fooled into thinking herself in love with this man, this person she had thought would care for her and Rhett and keep them safe? How foolish she'd been. How utterly stupid.

Faulkner passed Jo, heading right for Lance, the wolf faithfully by his side. "Sheriff Padraic let me go."

Lance motioned with his gun. "That's close enough."

But Faulkner kept walking.

Faulkner was going to die. She couldn't let that happen. She raised the Judge and aimed, but before she could squeeze the trigger, gunfire rang out, reverberating through the stable.

Lance staggered back against the wall. Jo turned in the direction where the blast had come from.

On the stairs to the clinic stood Denny. In his hands was the .357 magnum Faulkner had brought with him from prison. The sheriff burst through the back door of the stable, complete terror and worry on his haggard face. He rushed to Lance and felt his neck. The sheriff looked up at Jo and shook his head.

Jo ran to Faulkner, wrapping her arms around him. He held her tight against him. All at once, Rhett's small arms came around their legs. Faulkner scooped up his son and held him. Jo's heart swelled tight within her chest. They were finally together as a family, but at what cost? She looked up to see Denny, sitting alone on the steps. And once again, her heart broke.

EPILOGUE

FAULKNER STOOD IN FRONT OF his mother's granite headstone. Etched in the rock were her name, date of birth, and date of death. In pretty scroll lettering were the words *Beloved Wife and Mother*. He wished she'd been buried near his father's grave in Nevada, but Edward had taken care of her funeral while Faulkner was in prison. The cemetery was small, nestled on a hill below a nearby canyon. Several rosehip bushes void of flowers swayed in the October breeze, and the long mountain grasses rippled.

It had been a hard couple of months since Lance died. During the investigation, Sheriff Padraic had stood by Faulkner, helped clear his name, and made certain all charges were dropped. Denny had been arrested for the part he'd played in Cassandra's death and for obstructing justice, and he was charged with manslaughter for the death of his father.

Jo, bless her merciful heart, believed her father's death was an accident and he probably died trying to save Denny from going over the edge. Her brother would be sentenced soon, and despite all that had happened, Faulkner hoped the judge would go easy on him.

Lance's death nearly did Edward in, especially when he found out Lance had murdered Cassandra and was the one who had killed Coulton. Sophie would take good care of her boss. Faulkner suspected the woman had been secretly in love with him for many years. She'd help him through his cancer treatments and might even give him a reason to live. Anyway, Faulkner hoped that's what would happen.

He wished when he was young that he'd taken the time to get to know Edward better. But Faulkner'd been jealous of the man and had blamed him for taking him away from Vegas and the speedway. And deep down, Faulkner had also resented him because he'd tried to take his father's place. Faulkner's love for his dead father had blinded him to Edward's good side. Now Faulkner knew how immature he'd been.

He heard the slamming of car doors and glanced up to see Jo and Rhett walking away from her father's old truck. Jacob followed behind them. They passed through the weather-beaten, gray gate of the fence surrounding the cemetery. Faulkner thanked God that on that rainy night so long ago, He'd guided Faulkner to Doc's truck. Jo and Rhett had been his salvation.

Faulkner was staying in a new bed-and-breakfast near Palisades, though he spent every day with Jo and Rhett. Thanks to Edward returning Faulkner's inheritance, he didn't have financial worries.

Jo smiled as she neared. "Rhett wanted to see where his grandmother was buried."

The boy came to stand beside Faulkner, reached up, and took his hand. Faulkner squeezed it.

"She would have been so proud of you," Faulkner said, looking down on his son.

Rhett smiled weakly. Through everything that had happened, he'd become uncharacteristically quiet and stayed close to either Jo or Faulkner at all times.

Faulkner knelt beside Rhett. "You know, someday you'll meet your grandma."

Rhett stared at him with disbelief. Faulkner couldn't blame him, but he wanted his son to realize that death wasn't the end. "Only her body is dead. Her spirit still lives."

Rhett seemed to think for a moment. Worry pinched his face. "So Lance's spirit still lives?"

Faulkner nodded. "But he can't hurt you." Faulkner smoothed a fringe of hair away from his child's eyes. "In fact, I'll bet Lance feels really bad about scaring you. And I think Heavenly Father is helping him."

Relief filled Rhett's eyes. "Good. He needs help."

Faulkner chuckled and hugged his son. Standing up, he took hold of Jo's arm and slung it in the crook of his. Faulkner had been waiting for the right time to bring up the subject of marriage with Jo. Near his mother's grave, with Mount Baldy in the background and Rhett beside them, the time felt right. Turning to her, he said, "You know, I think we should work on being a family again."

She looked at him quizzically. "But we're not married."

"I know." He pulled the ring box from his pocket and got down on one knee.

Rhett jumped up and down, clapping his hands.

Faulkner stared at the woman he loved, opened the box, and held it up. "Jo, will you marry me . . . again?"

Throwing her arms around his neck, she kissed him soundly. They fell to the sweet-smelling grass together.

"My mom and dad are getting married!" Rhett yelled. He jumped on top of them, all laughs and giggles.

Pure joy filled Faulkner. He rose to his feet then helped Jo to hers. Keeping one arm around Jo, he helped Rhett up too. His son clung to him, and Faulkner knew this was the heaven on earth he'd yearned for. He pulled Jo closer and kissed her once again.

Faulkner felt the nudge of the wolf's nose on the back of his pant leg. He reached down and patted the animal's head as he kissed the love of his life.

ABOUT THE AUTHOR

RAISED IN SOUTHEASTERN IDAHO, KATHI Oram Peterson has explored Swan Valley and Fall Creek Canyon. Her mother was born near the banks of the Snake River below Table Rock Mountain in Idaho. Kathi grew up walking the trails, paddling across the river, and hearing about her mother's life when she lived there. Her parents loved this area and eventually built a cabin in the mountains farther upriver above Palisades Dam. Every summer they'd pass through beautiful Swan Valley on their way to the cabin. Another area they spent a great deal of time exploring was Fall Creek. As in this novel, Kathi has floated Fall Creek, walked in a stinging nettle patch, and explored the cave behind the waterfall. She couldn't help but set this novel in that area.

After her children finished school, Kathi earned her English degree at the University of Utah. She worked for several years, writing and editing children's books for a curriculum publisher. Upon leaving the workforce, she turned her attention to writing novels. She currently resides in Salt Lake City. You can contact Kathi through her website, www.kathiorampeterson .com, and her blog, www.kathiswritingnook.com.